FOURTH SISTER

A HEARTH AND BARD TALE

M. L. FARB

CONTENTS

For Yaeko

First child, artist born
creating beauty before speech
our cherry blossom.

THE BARD

Myrtle couldn't be late, not after missing the previous week's tale. She pulled her frayed coat tighter as she struggled through the blinding snow to the mayor's house.

She'd woken long before the cook could rap her with a wooden spoon and had worked through the day. But the mayor's house was an hour's walk from the farm where she worked as a scullery maid, and even with rushing through her tasks, she still didn't finish until everyone else had left.

Her toes cramped with cold as snow slid between the gaping seams of her boots. She'd never experienced more than an inch of snow before. Did the druids call up the storm? The old cook said the druids no longer existed in Britain, but then she also said no one had seen the bard for forty years. Were the druids jealous?

Snow whipped through the dim circle of her lamplight. Wagon tracks, hoof prints, and footprints pitted the road, the roughness hidden in the white. She felt out her way, stumbling forward until squares of light danced ahead—the lamplit windows of the town. She quickened her steps, though her feet were heavy with snow and a long day's work, bowing her head against the wind until the large bright windows of the mayor's manor stood in front of her, the double doors closed.

Could she enter? She was a scullery maid, and this was the mayor's house. But her best friend had told her all about the bard and told her that everyone was welcome. She gathered her courage around her like a second coat, though it did little to stop her shivering, and knocked.

A servant opened it a crack. "You are late, lass. You're lucky the bard said to wait an hour for those stopped by the storm. Go in. She's reserved a place for you."

Myrtle glanced behind her to see who he could be speaking to. She was alone. "For me?"

"For all the children. Heaven knows why, but I'll not argue if it means I get to hear her tale. Come in and stop letting in all the snow."

Myrtle stepped through into a grand hall bigger than the whole farmhouse where she worked. A fire crackled at the far end, but she could not see it because of the people crowded on benches sitting in rows of half-circles facing the hearth.

"The entire town and the next one must be here," she whispered. "Where will I sit?"

"Come." The servant led her to the front-most half-circle of benches. "Make room," he said as if he'd said it many times already that evening. The children, wearing everything from embroidered wool to peasant rags, crowded closer on the bench.

One girl with a fur ruff stood and stomped her foot. "There's no more room. She should stand behind the benches like the servant she is. Besides, she came late."

Myrtle shrank back. The other girl was her master's daughter.

A figure stood from her place on the hearth bench, her slender form silhouetted against the bright firelight. "If you cannot make room beside you for your sister, then you have not room in your heart for the tale." Her voice was melodious and tinged with sharpness. Then she turned to Myrtle. "Come, child. There is room on the hearth. Sit by me."

Wonder bloomed through Myrtle as she settled on the stone bench beside the bard. She glanced back at her master's daughter and stuck out her tongue. She'd pay for it later, but tonight she'd have the best seat of anyone.

She turned and studied the woman next to her. The bard wore a white rabbit-trimmed cloak over a green dress. Her black curls framed the white fox mask that concealed her face. It was a strange mask with red ears, whiskers, and tracings around the eyeholes. Her brown eyes watched the villagers scramble and squeeze onto the benches, her gaze as lively as the mask was still. Though as the firelight danced off the surface of the fox face, it seemed for a moment alive and part of her, then a mask again.

A servant pushed the double doors shut after two more people straggled in. Flames danced in the deep fireplace as a final gust slipped through.

The bard stood and removed her mask. Her thick eyebrows sat in serious lines over her smooth, olive-toned face. "Gather closer. Tonight I bring you to Nihon, a place where mortals and spirits live side by side. A land of kami—powerful spirits, ancestor spirits, and spirits of every tree and river. A place of sparse poetry and gold-mended brokenness.

"A land where each name has meaning, and some more than one. Ichi, ni, san, shi—ah yes, shi, a simple counting number and also death.

"Come, see."

1

———

Ichi, ni, san, shi,
seven sisters born by sea,
go, roku, nana.

Our village sits on a cliff above the sea. Every day the sun ripples in a bright line along the ocean edge then rises, a fiery pearl, above the water where she sleeps. Once the sun slept in a cave and wouldn't come out for fear of the demon that drove her there. That was long ago, before the other kami made such a commotion with their dancing and singing that she ventured out to see why they could be happy.

I understood her fear. I'd hide from my demon if I could.

～

I pushed my hair from my face, then swung the ax into the soft log. Father always chopped the oak firewood, but I could handle the cypress. And with him often gone selling his pottery, I took the jobs that should have been my twin brother's. Father never asked it of me, but he never stopped me either.

"Shisei!" Mother's voice carried through the delicate shoji walls of our home. Her usual soft voice was sharpened with pain to a pearl-diver's knife edge.

I dropped my ax against a pile of yet-to-be-cut firewood and ran to the house, crushing early spring ferns that unfurled in the path.

"Shisei!"

The paper door rattled as I shoved it, sliding it to the side. Mother knelt at the table. A teacup lay on its side, staining the polished wood and tatami mats below. Her hands fisted on her knees and she pressed her forehead to the table. Her kimono bulged with our youngest sibling, the one to come in a month. The one we all hoped was a boy.

"Mother." I dropped next to her, grasping her shoulders, my fear echoing her sharp cries.

She shuddered under my touch, then slumped, panting. "Get the midwife. This child comes early."

Our empty house swallowed her words. My six sisters were scattered around our village. Father was traveling. I helped Mother lie down, then ran. Our house sat outside the village near the ocean cliff, and the midwife lived on the far side of the village in the shadows of a giant ginkgo tree. Too far apart.

I darted through the busy village market, dodging around a cart of fish, slipping between the blocking crowd that listened to a monk tell a kami story, and bumping into a woman toting a heavy basket and trailing children.

"Forgive me." I bowed as I steadied her and rushed on. Why did the midwife have to live on the far side? The streets cleared, and the ginkgo tree stood in the distance. I lowered my head and increased my stride.

And rammed into a solid body.

"Watch where you are going! Are you blind?" It was a man's voice, mocking and annoyed.

I stumbled back, holding my hand to my head. Daichi, the son of the noble Kazoku, stood in his fine silks and looked down his nose at me.

"Please, accept my most humble apology. I must get the midwife."

His face softened slightly. "Ah. Go then. But be more careful."

I bowed again and dashed the last distance to the small home beneath the ginkgo tree.

"Honored midwife, my mother needs you," I yelled through the door.

A woman slid the door open. Her face creased into a worried frown, each wrinkle shouting *we must hurry*. She grabbed a tall woven basket with straps along one side and handed it to me. I swung it onto my back. The midwife pattered on short legs through the village behind me, slowing as we wove through the market crowd. To hasten us, I would have carried her on my back too, but I was no man and had not a man's strength.

Mother's panting cries wove through the air like a red thread through silk. The midwife entered our home, muttering, "Too old to be bearing children. If the kami wanted to bless her with a son, they'd not have taken the first one."

Not true. The kami will bless us again.

I set the midwife's basket against the wall, then turned to gather my sisters.

Mother's words followed me. "Shisei, stay."

I knelt next to her, caressing her sweat-soaked brow. This was not how she was when my youngest sister came. Thirteen years more had weakened her body. What if she wasn't strong enough to birth my prayed-for brother?

The kitsune mask hung on our wall—the zenko that carried

our prayers to Inari. "Please, honored zenko, tell Inari I will dedicate myself as a maiden in her shrine if she will save my mother. I'm not much. But I work hard. Please."

The fox mask stared back at me, its eyes as empty as my heart.

"Hush and help me." The midwife drew out jars and cloths from the basket, then hissed. Mother's kimono bloomed red.

A neighbor must have noticed me drag the midwife through our village. One by one, my sisters entered. They bowed in reverence to the midwife and averted their eyes from the still form that lay shrouded in the corner. A boy. Whose spirit dwelt again with his brother.

Mother came out of a shuddering half-sleep and beckoned us to kneel around her. "My daughters—my seven pearls—I soon go to join my parents and sons."

No! I looked toward the kitsune mask hanging on the wall. *Honored zenko, tell Inari, I'll cut all the wood to heat her shrine for the next ten years, I'll spend each night creating haiku to honor her; just let my mother live.* I tucked the silent prayer onto a breath.

Then he strolled into the room, the four-tailed fox that had followed me like a shadow from my first memories. A white kitsune, invisible to all but me. A trickster, appearing for a day in a year or a week in a month. He was not a zenko. Or was he?

I bowed to him. "Please," I whispered, "if you are a messenger of Inari, I beg you, spare my mother's life."

His four tails hung subdued and his head bowed. He touched the still form of my baby brother then curled up next to Mother, laying his white head on her chest, shifting her blanket so his fur touched her skin. Mother's breathing eased. My breath eased with hers. I bowed again, pressing my hands together. *Please make her well again.*

Mother took my eldest sister by the hand. "Ichia, my first-loved daughter, you are married and must honor your husband, but I ask that you remember your father and sisters. Comfort them." Ichia bowed, then wrapped her arms around our two youngest sisters.

My second sister leaned close as Mother took her hand. "Nichika, your quiet wisdom and giving heart has always blessed me. Use it now to bless others, even in your grief." Nichika nodded solemnly as her lip trembled.

My third sister gripped Mother's hand as soon as she let go of Nichika's.

"Sanaho." Mother gasped a breath, then continued. "*True Step*, keep your confidence, but remember to see others outside of you." Sanaho's face hardened into determination.

I pulled back as Mother turned to me. I didn't need a last blessing, because she wouldn't die. I sent another prayer. *Help her heal.*

The white kitsune fixed his bright eyes on me and brushed one of his tails along Mother's furrowed brow.

She sighed and turned to my first younger sister. "Gomako. You brought joy after sorrow. Your quickness to learn is a delight. Be careful who you imitate." Gomako glanced at Ichia, then matched her quiet serenity.

Mother traced a tear down Rokue's cheek. "My beautiful picture. Even as a spirit I will take joy in watching you. Create beauty with your heart too." Rokue leaned into Mother's hand.

Nanai, my youngest sister, buried her face in the folds of Mother's kimono, her sobs rising into a storm that fit her unusual blue-grey eyes and name, *seven is ocean*. Mother wrapped her arms around her. "My child. I'll still be here, whispering my love. Listen for me." Nanai fell to shuddering silence in Mother's arms.

"Shisei."

I shook my head. "No, Mother. You will live."

"Shisei. You are sacred poetry. The line of beauty between the seen and unseen. Remember your worth."

~

Shi, shi, fourth and death.
Fourth sister and twin to death.
Brother born silent.

The spring flowers had faded with summer, and the summer blooms fled from autumn. I placed a branch of maple in the vase Father made. Its lacy red leaves trailed against the glossy green glaze of the vase and the speckled granite of our family shrine. Incense trailed upward, and water rippled as I poured it into a bowl. Lastly, I placed a new rice cake there for Mother and my brothers.

"Sheng," I whispered to my twin. "Please take care of Mother and our baby brother. You've been in the spirit world for eighteen years. Help them find the best bathhouses and most beautiful gardens. I'm trying to fill your place here. I'm not very good at it, but I am trying."

A shadow fell over the shrine. Father knelt next to me in a clay-stained kimono, his grey head bowed, his lips moving in prayer. Then he groaned to his feet. "Come, Shisei. The time of deep mourning is past."

I bowed so he could not see my shameful tears. "If only the kami had taken me instead of my twin brother, none of this would have happened."

He touched my chin, tilting my head up. "Shisei, they choose whom they choose."

I swallowed at the hurting truth, then spat it out with its bitterness. "It's my fault she died. Ever since Nanai was born, I prayed and gave daily offerings at Inari's shrine for a brother. The kami answered by giving me a brother, then taking both him and my mother away."

Father shook his head. "Then the fault is mine, too. I had added my daily prayers to yours."

I swallowed the rest of the truth. It was too bitter to even tell Father. *I am as Ichia calls me. I am Shi. Death follows me.*

2

———————

Sister brings new life,
welcome joy of nine-month wait.
I seek a new home.

Father and I brought in armloads of the split wood. The pile outside would tide us over until spring, and hopefully by then he would return from visiting the capitol. He'd been given an honored invitation to show his pottery to the emperor. Even winter would not excuse delay.

The first flakes of snow landed on my blue wood-bearing hands. We passed through the storm-shuttered porch and laid the wood along the kitchen wall.

Ichia wrapped checkered cloths around lacquered trays of fish, pickled plums, and nori-rolled rice.

Her husband, Yahito, looked up from checking bundles and bowed. "Honored Father, everything is ready. It is still morning, and the tide is good."

Father nodded, "Yes, we should go."

Ichia handed the wrapped trays of food to her husband. "Be safe. Bring honor. Return soon."

He laid his hands over hers and unspoken words passed between them. She lowered her soft brown eyes as color deepened in her cheeks. They'd been married a year, though she'd favored him since he first apprenticed to Father eight years before.

I gathered with my sisters on the back porch to watch Father and Yahito hoist tall woven baskets onto their backs, tuck more bundles under their arms, then walk the path to the cliff. They disappeared over the edge.

Only then did we run to the cliff to watch their hunched forms descend the narrow back-and-forth trail to the rolling surf. They boarded a long boat and took up oars with ten other men. The boat sailed out from the surf and became a dot on the ocean before disappearing into the grey blend of sea and sky.

Ichia held her hand over her eyes and squinted long after I'd lost sight of them. Then she turned back to the house. Rocks grated under her wooden sandals.

As we walked, Nanai nestled next to Ichia. "We'll have so much fun with you home again. I've missed you. The others are all so busy with their lessons and work, but you won't be. You don't have lessons or a husband to attend to."

A knowing smile spread on Ichia's face. "I'll be busier than the rest of you. I must prepare for family coming."

My other sisters pressed around her. "How soon?"

"In about five months."

"Do we know them?"

"Not yet." She laid her hand on the obi sash that wrapped around her middle.

Then I understood. "Does Yahito know?"

She shook her head. "No, Shi. He would have worried, and that could have disturbed the quality of his art for the emperor. He'll be back before the baby comes."

She became the center of squealing excitement. We entered the warmth of the kitchen and knelt around her. She studied each of us. "Father is bringing honor to our family by his art. We will use our time wisely and improve our talents while he is gone. I will perfect the home arts of the tea ceremony and beautiful meals. The work will make me strong to bear my child."

Sanaho cheered. Nichika, as the second oldest, had taken the responsibility to feed our family, and though she was wise in many things, she'd never mastered cooking. Nichika bowed a silent thanks.

Ichia touched Nichika's pressed hands. "You'll be busy as well. I've found a tutor to further your studies."

Nichika's bow deepened, and her face bloomed with quiet delight.

One by one, like an onna-bugeishi general setting her soldiers in rank, in a gentle tone but one we dared not disobey, Ichia gave out duties. Sanaho, the most agile and confident of us, would continue her study of the spear-sword naginata so she could protect our home while the men were gone. Gomako would study with the village musicians. Rokue had already developed the art of dance and would continue to do so. And for Nanai, Ichia had secured a place in the Nōgaku theater, which had only started accepting female actors two years before.

Ichia turned to me last. "Shi—"

"I will help you at home as I did for Mother and Father. I will do the brother's work."

She shook her head. "I've found you an apprenticeship with a silk maker. It's in the next village. You'll live with her family. I'll ask our neighbors to help with the tasks that we cannot do. The money Father left will pay for any additional help we need."

"Why?"

She wouldn't meet my eyes.

I knew. She feared for her baby. She was sending me away to protect her child.

~

Fire burns bright in home.
Tea steams and cakes stand ready.
Space for all but me.

I stomped, knocking the snow from between the two support pieces of my geta sandals, and slipped them off. Then I entered the house with my arms loaded with more split wood. One wall of the kitchen now hid behind the warmth-giving fuel.

I don't have to leave. Ichia is my sister, not my mother or father. This is my home. This is my family. She has her husband's home across the village. She can go there. I'll take care of my sisters. We've done well enough without her for a year, even when Father was gone.

Ichia stood waiting by the fire, holding Mother's zenko mask. "Shi, you always fed Mother's kitsune. You should take the mask."

I trembled at her irreverence. "He's not Mother's kitsune. He's our family's zenko. The one who takes messages to Inari. And I didn't feed a kitsune; I placed offerings at a zenko's shrine."

Ichia set the mask at my feet. "Then take the mask to protect you from your kitsune."

My kitsune! I stepped over the mask and thumped the load of wood on top of the stack. *He isn't mine. He just follows me.* I should have never told Ichia about him, but I was little when I first saw the four-tailed fox, and she was the only person at home, so I ran and told her. She hushed me, told me he was a yako—a trickster field fox—and to stay away from him. She changed in how she treated me after that, and I never told anyone else. Maybe if my twin Sheng were alive, I'd have told him, and we could have faced the fox together.

Ichia filled the mask's spot on the wall with a painting of a cherry tree in full blossom. I picked up the zenko mask, tracing the face that had watched over our family for as long as I could remember. How could she so carelessly replace it?

She knelt again by the fire, humming, as she embroidered a little silk kimono, just the right size for a baby. A white crane stood under a pine near a pool. She had half-finished a green turtle. Both symbols of long life. Life that neither of my brothers had had.

Who will tend our mother's and brothers' shrine? Who will give offerings to the zenko that guards our family?

Not me. Death follows me. I will go.

3

Snow-sodden sandals,
white kitsune by my side.
Path clear, future not.

Chill wind whispered over the new snow path, only marred by the star prints of bird tracks ahead and the double lines of my sandal prints behind. The tall pines of the forest kept the worst of the cold away. I carried a woven basket heavy with food even after two days of travel, and on the side hung the zenko mask. Ichia had packed enough food for a week's journey, though it was only a day's walk to the silk maker. I knew the way. I'd traveled it twice to deliver pottery for Father.

That was not the path I followed.

I knelt by a pond where a pine had kept it from freezing, and unpinned my hair. It flowed down my back in a heavy wave. It was my only beauty. My face was plain with thick eyebrows, thin lips, and square chin. A face for a boy. The face my twin might have had. Should have had.

"Sheng." I whispered my twin's name, "I have no more place with my sisters. I will live the life you should have had." I pulled my hair over my shoulder and hacked at it with my knife. As the black locks dropped into the pond, my tears added ripples. I bound my hair back into a short knot. I was no longer the fourth sister Shisei, but the boy Sheng—*birth and life*—making my first steps into a new life. I'd go from village to village until I found an apprenticeship where none knew me. I studied my reflection again with my hair pulled back. I already looked like a boy. My voice was naturally low. None would suspect.

The coldness of the ground seeped through the faded double layer of my kimono. I'd picked my plainest clothes, the ones that either boy or girl could wear, but hadn't thought of how thin they'd become with work. I'd better go before I chilled. I slid the knife back into my obi sash and pulled the basket onto my back.

A white fox face appeared in the pond by my wavering reflection. I jerked away, falling on my backside. The kitsune made rapid high-pitched sounds, as if in laughter, his four tails waving behind him. Why was he here? He hadn't shown himself since Mother's death three seasons ago.

I scowled at him. "You didn't save my mother."

He silenced and bowed his head.

What kind of kitsune spirit was he? Was he a zenko, a messenger of Inari—the kami over foxes and fertility—or was he a yako, a field fox, filled with mischief and delighting in tricking humans? He often played tricks on me, like tumbling a pile of wood I'd just stacked and knocking over a ladder and trapping me on the roof while I was mending it. On the other hand, he was white like a zenko and had comforted Mother.

But if he were a zenko, he'd be benevolent and help me. If he were a zenko, he'd have saved my mother, even against my shadow of death.

My scowl deepened. He was a yako, delighting in my misery just because I could see him. If I could choose between the kitsune or my curse, I'd choose the trickster kitsune. The kami were cruel to give me both a curse and a tormentor.

Still, he was a kitsune and I would be foolish to offend him. I smoothed my brow. "Forgive me for my words."

He batted at a strand of my cut hair, ignoring me.

Just as I'd ignore him. I hefted the basket and headed back to the path that would lead me north to villages I'd never visited.

A weight thumped against my back, knocking me to my knees. The kitsune darted ahead of me, and he carried Mother's mask.

"Come back!" I yelled, lunging to my feet and chasing him. He darted off the path and between bushes. Branches cracked as I shoved through the waist-high foliage. Snow puffed upward and stung my face.

The way opened onto a new path. The kitsune sat in the middle, licking a paw. Mother's mask lay beside him.

I froze, my panting breath loud in the snowy silence. He didn't look at me, but swapped to cleaning a new paw. I couldn't sneak up on him, and if I dashed, he'd run away again. Kitsune were proud creatures. Would he listen to pleading and false praise?

I bowed. "Most honored kitsune, I apologize for bothering you. I seem to have dropped my mother's mask, the one you so carefully picked up. I thank you for taking care of it. With your permission, I will now take the mask so it no longer burdens you."

He turned his attention to one of his tails, licking along the long white fur.

Please let that mean yes. I crept forward, keeping my head bowed and my hands pressed together in respect—step by slow step. His ears swiveled when I was two steps away. I lunged. My fingers brushed the mask as he caught it in his maw. His four tails fanned behind him and the high-pitched laughter sounded from his throat as he danced away again with Mother's mask, just out of reach.

Curse the trickster kitsune!

~

The fisher owl called through the darkening evening like a slow echo of the fox's laugh. I stumbled after the kitsune, my steps much slower than they had been that morning. He'd led me through brush and across streams, sometimes even along paths, always staying in sight and sometimes almost letting me touch the mask. Would he sleep just out of reach when I dropped with exhaustion and cold?

The path opened up into a village. The kitsune jogged down the middle of the empty streets. Candles winked behind many paper walls. As we passed the last home, I tripped and fell to my knees. My legs burned with a day of jogging, my throat rasped with each icy breath, while my stomach knotted with emptiness. The kitsune stopped and watched. I growled to cover the curses I wanted to say and pushed back to standing. He turned around again and strolled away from the village, between bare-branched trees.

I followed his glowing white form while the full darkness of night wrapped around us. My foot caught on a root and I fell to my knees again. *Curse him. He'll never let me have Mother's mask.* I huddled in the snow, wrapping my arms around myself for warmth.

A sharp bark shattered the silence.

My primal fear of dogs gave me strength to stand again. The kitsune was gone, and a circle of lantern light approached between the bare trees. I squinted, wavering on my feet as lightheadedness threatened to make me crumple.

"What has the fox dragged in?" The voice was deep and tinted with laughter. Hands grasped me under the arms. "Come, you shouldn't be out on a winter's night. I have enough food for two, and you look as though you could use it."

The kitsune sat behind him, glowing white, holding Mother's

mask. I struggled against the man's grip, trying to reach the trickster fox. But a bigger shape lunged between the fox and me, his bark sending snow showering from the trees. The fox fled, followed by the shadowy beast.

"No," I cried, trembling and struggling. The fox was gone, as was the dog.

"Careful, I'm trying to help you." The man scooped me into his arms. Teeth-clacking shivers overtook my entire body until I was sure he'd drop me. But he carried me firmly, his lantern lighting the path between bare trees and then a small hut with a rickety porch. He pushed open the door. A low fire burned in a dim room. He set me on a short bench and pulled off my sodden geta sandals and double-thick socks. He started to remove my kimono, but I clutched it tightly.

"Fine, fine," he muttered. "You can keep to your modesty, boy, but don't curse me nor the kami when you catch cold. Here, eat." He handed me a bowl of broth.

I held it shakingly to my lips. Some of it sloshed and dripped down my chin, but most of it made it into my mouth. It was rich with tofu, daikon, and nori. My tears dripped into it.

Sheng, our mother's mask is gone.

4

———————

One green eye, one brown,
nose crooked, skin illness-pocked,
whose is broken face?

I woke to the sweet-earthy scent of rice. Sunlight streamed across my face. I groaned. I'd overslept. I needed to get on my chores. I leapt from my sleeping mat and fell back. My entire body ached.

A face leaned over me.

I squawked and pulled the quilt up to my nose.

The man—he was a man, though at first I thought him a goblin—studied me with one mottled green eye and one brown. His pocked brow wrinkled in thought. Pock scars pitted his face. He couldn't have been older than my eldest sister, but life had left many marks. He wore a simple brown kimono—worn, patched, and spotted with clay. Reddish-tan fur stuck to the material and a tuft of fur nestled in with his tangle of black hair. He snorted through a crooked nose. "You're a skittish fellow."

I scooted further from him. "Who are you?"

He laughed, and his face softened. "Don't you remember last night?"

I looked around the strange room, trying to remember. It was sparse. A bench sat along one rough pine wall next to a stone fireplace, and before the fire lay three tatami mats, on one of which I knelt. A byōbu screen hid a corner for changing. Large paper windows sat in three of the walls, lighting the room with a filtered glow. One window was slid half open, letting in a stream of sunlight and cold. No low eating table; instead a tall table took up a third of the room. A shelf stood behind the table, packed with unglazed jars. And on the wall hung masks, beautiful masks.

Mother's mask! The kitsune! The chase! My shoulders bowed inward. It was gone.

"So you remember. Since you are the one who stumbled across my land, I'll return the question. Who are *you*?"

I said what I'd rehearsed many times before the kitsune stole the mask. The words slipped over my tongue as my heart wept for my loss. "I am Sheng, an orphan seeking work or apprenticeship."

His brow wrinkled again. "You've not borne that name long. It sits like a top layer of paint. But who is to say we cannot bear many names, each another layer of ourselves?" His brow smoothed, though his two-colored eyes remained tight at the corners. "Who was your family?"

I trembled. If he could see through my false name, what else would he see as I spoke untruths?

He brought my travel bundle from behind his back and set out the wrapped foods from Ichia. Everything was still wrapped with my sister's beautiful folds. "Your family prepared generously for your orphanhood before they died."

I bowed my head and closed my eyes in shame.

He set something in my lap. "This intrigues me more than the food."

Mother's zenko mask stared up at me. I clutched it to my chest.

"Ah, so you recognize it. I found it on my porch."

The kitsune must have dropped it when the dog chased him. Thank the kami that the man found it.

The man took hold of the mask. I gripped it a moment and then let go. He was my host; he'd fed me and given me a place to sleep. I swallowed my plea and waited for him to speak.

He turned the mask over, studying the back and edges as much as the front. "This is of fine workmanship. Who made it?"

In this I could speak truth. "It was my mother's. She made it before her marriage. And now it is mine, my only piece of her I have left. I am even exiled from her shrine."

"Ah." He picked up the mask and rotated it so it caught the light. "So you are not an orphan, but an exile. For you, your remaining family is no longer family." He laid the mask back in my lap. "Did your mother teach you the art of mask making?"

"No."

"A pity. She had talent, and such talent shouldn't die with a person. But maybe you carry it as well. We shall see." He took two bowls from the hearth and filled them with rice from a pot on the fire, laying on sliced fish and onions from a board to the side. He handed me one bowl. "You've answered three of my questions. You may ask three of your own."

He'd asked four, and I'd only answered two truthfully. "Forgive my great rudeness. Who are you and why have you helped me?"

He spoke around a mouth full of rice, "I prefer direct truth to polite lies, even if others call it rude." He swallowed and his words became clearer. "I am Takumi, the mask maker." He pointed to a painted sign above the table. The kanji for his name was 匠 未, *artisan, not yet*. "When I've truly learned to make masks as they please the kami, I will write my name as a full artisan. I have far to go. But this," he pointed to my kitsune mask, "this is poetry." He shoved the last of the rice into his mouth and jumped up. "Come, I must show you."

I followed him onto a sheltered porch. A thick roof lay overhead and thin lattice formed semi-walls. It did little to keep out winter. The cold slapped my face and stung my bare feet. Masks covered the rough wooded walls: proud ladies, fierce samurai, long-nosed tengu, river demons, and kitsune. Each intricate and beautiful.

Takumi clapped his hand on my shoulder. "You can see too. These are not good enough."

"They are much better than the ones worn at our Nōgaku theater."

"True. I've grown in skill in seven years of apprenticeship and five more on my own. I can see what they should be. But I am unable to bring them to that perfect balance of mortal and spirit, the balance needed to bridge the two worlds. I will spend a lifetime if needed. And you will help me."

"Me?"

"You seek an apprenticeship. I need an apprentice so I have more time to perfect my art."

Maybe here I'll find a place where my curse doesn't follow. He has no wife nor coming child to be hurt by me. And he's so ugly that he'll never marry. I bowed. "I most humbly accept."

A familiar yip sounded behind me. I spun around. The white kitsune poked his head around the corner of the porch.

I clenched my fists. Couldn't he leave me alone? Hadn't I provided enough entertainment the day before?

A howl shuddered the air. A wolf rounded the opposite side of the hut and bounded across to the kitsune, leaping. The kitsune disappeared as the wolf landed, leaving the wolf sniffing the wood and whining.

Takumi shook his head. "Ōkami, stop chasing ghosts and come meet my new apprentice."

I shrank back as the animal trotted over. Though wolf-shaped and his back as high as my hip, he wasn't a true wolf—at least not as shown in drawings. He had reddish-tan fur, softly pointed ears, and a tail that curled up on his back. Still, even if he was only a dog, dogs gave me almost as many nightmares as my mother and brothers dying.

Takumi scratched the wolf-dog between the ears. "Don't be afraid. He won't hurt you now that I've introduced you. And he fattens our meals with hares and ducks. Do you know how to cook?"

I stared at Ōkami, and a small smile threaded its way through my trembling. *The wolf-dog scared away the kitsune. May the kami bless the nightmarish beast.*

"Sheng," Takumi said, his voice edged with annoyance. "Do you know how to cook?"

"Uh—I mean yes." Though I'd never cooked animal other than fish, I'd learn as I went along. *Sheng,* I thought to my twin, *we will be apprenticed to a mask maker. I'll try to represent you well.*

5

Paper pressed in mold,
ground seashells and horse-hoof glue,
form mask for spirits.

Takumi crawled out backward from the kiln, his head and shoulders covered in ash. He carried three inverted clay faces bundled under one arm and set them on a straw matting beside six more. He'd packed twelve masks into the kiln and refused to let me carry any of them out. They were, "too delicate for an apprentice's fumbling fingers."

His dog, Ōkami, sniffed him and sneezed, then ran off to the woods, perhaps to hunt. I'd worked under Takumi for a month of winter, and we mostly lived off rice and egg, and thrice, duck that Ōkami brought home. To supplement it, I dug winter onions and daikon from a sheltered garden box.

Takumi didn't seem to notice when we had better or worse food and never complained of my cooking. Even when I smoked us from the hut when a greasy duck fell into the fire. His mind was constantly occupied with his masks. He sketched, molded clay, and ordered me about.

I crushed seashells, made glue, swept floors, and chopped wood for the kiln. It was peaceful work, and if I could truly forget my sisters, I could do the work for years and be content. *Forget my sisters.* The thought brought each of their faces before me. *What are they doing? Do they also find peace in their apprenticeships? How is Ichia's pregnancy?*

No. I shook my head. *Focus on the present. Create another haiku.* I studied the kiln as Takumi crawled back in for the last masks. Slowly the words formed.

Snow melts on grey kiln.
Inside, flames lick earthen face.
Fire hardens clay.

"Sheng-kun." Takumi's voice penetrated my thoughts. "Are you apprentice to me, or to the meditating monks?" He cradled the last three masks against his chest.

"Forgive me, sensei." I slid the door open so he could enter and set the clay masks on his workbench. Except they weren't masks. The outside of each was a rough bowl shape. The inside would have fit over my face, if he'd molded one to look like me. Instead, he'd created a samurai, a noble lady, and an old priest.

Without looking up, he ordered, "Reheat the glue until it is about thin bean-paste consistency."

I heated and stirred while he brought in the other masks, then filled every inch of the samurai face with overlapping layers of sekishu-washi paper. He rubbed the glue between his fingers, nodded, and mixed in a handful of crushed shells, then a few pinches more. When it had reached a consistency that satisfied him, he painted the glue and shell mixture over the paper.

Six more days passed as he layered paper, glue, and seashells, let them dry, sanded them, and repeated till each had seven layers.

~

The small room flickered with firelight. Takumi had gone on a walk— "to clear my mind for the next step," he'd said as he'd headed out the door with his only lamp and with Ōkami at his heels. Why a walk on a winter night?

Sheng, I laughed. *Our master may be strange, but he's an exceptional artist.*

I stood at the workbench studying the masks Takumi had made; the paper layered inside the clay. I picked up the old priest mask with its many wrinkles. How did he get the mask out of the mold without destroying the delicate lines? The dim light hid the fine details. It would be easier to see by the fire.

I glanced around the room. Takumi was still gone. I'd be careful. I stepped toward the fire.

My foot caught.

I fumbled. The mask slipped from my fingers. I caught it again as something shoved the back of my legs. The mask hit the wood floor with a crack.

"No, no, no!" A split ran along the clay mold.

A yip came from the corner. The white kitsune sat licking a paw as if he had nothing to do with tripping me.

I hefted the ruined mask, ready to throw it at him. "Curse you, trickster fox!"

He disappeared, his white glow lingering a moment longer than his body.

I cradled the mask by the fire, fingering it for more cracks. Another finer one ran crosswise from the large one. It was ruined. Takumi would end my apprenticeship, and I'd have to find another master.

Why did the kitsune trip me? Did he hate me so much? More likely he didn't care and did the same thing to others when he wasn't tormenting me.

I set the mask on the workbench and packed my few things

into the rice straw basket. I'd be ready to leave after I offered my profound apologies.

～

"Sheng-kun." A toe nudged me awake. "What's this?"

I scrambled to my feet. How could I have fallen asleep?

Takumi stood in the dark room, the circle of lamplight illuminating him and my wicker basket.

"Forgive me, sensei, I—I—" I couldn't bring myself to tell him I'd ruined one of his masks.

He scowled. "What did you break?"

I bowed my head. "Forgive me my most unpardonable fault. My foot caught as I carried the mask."

He rushed to the table with the lamp and carefully studied each mask. His shoulders stretched his kimono in taut lines, then shook.

"Sheng-kun," he laughed, "despite your clumsiness, you haven't ruined it, but only started the process that we will do today. And since you started it, you will finish it. I suppose if you are an apprentice, you should actually learn how to make masks."

"You're keeping me as an apprentice? I broke one of your masks."

"Huh," he grunted. "I did worse for my master, and he kept me around. I still need an apprentice, and you haven't ruined anything yet. Don't worry. Give you enough time and you will. We have work to do."

"Right now? In the middle of the night?" I stopped. Who was I to question my master, especially one who forgave my marring his art—even if it was the trickster kitsune's fault?

He looked around as if he'd just realized that it was still dark. "Get some sleep. Tomorrow you learn to birth a mask." He laughed, his deep voice bouncing off the walls. "Sheng—*to be born*

26

—will help a mask to be born. You are a well-named apprentice." He grabbed his quilt and sleep mat from the shelf and lay down on the tatami mat furthest from the fire with his dog curled up next to him. I grabbed my own bedding and lay as far as I could from master and dog, shaking my head. He was keeping me as an apprentice. He wasn't angry; he even laughed, making a joke of it. What a strange master.

"Sheng," I whispered. "We still have our apprenticeship, despite the trickster kitsune."

❧

"It's time to break the mold." Takumi held a small hammer and chisel next to the samurai mask.

"But why? Can't we use it again? You spent a month making these masks."

"No. The fine details will be lost if I pull it from the mold. It must be broken for the mask to be born," he said.

I clutched the noble-lady mask to my chest. "If we are careful, we could do it. Just lift and pull a little at a time. Only the old priest mold is cracked. We can save the rest to use again."

He gently pulled her from my grasp. "A mask should never be exactly the same as another. Each is its own, just as each person comes unlike another. Now watch."

My shoulders tensed as he laid the chisel against the corner of the mold and struck it with the hammer. Tap by tap, he formed cracks running vertically and across the rough bowl. Then he lifted out a piece, and a bearded chin peeked through. The samurai emerged from the broken clay—blank, white, and perfect. A spirit of the real warrior.

"Here. It is your turn." He held out the chisel and the hammer.

"No!" I backed away. "I've already marred the old priest enough."

"Sheng-kun, I forgot that an apprentice will never become a master unless he takes the first step, and then the next. I ruined many masks before I made one worth painting. You can do no worse than I did."

"I could. I have a talent for making things worse." Or at least the kitsune did. What would the fox do if I touched the mask again?

Takumi placed the chisel in my right hand. "Try. Or better yet, don't try. See if you can do better than the worst."

I placed the chisel along the narrow edge and struck. The hammer pinged and nothing happened.

"Harder, but only just."

I struck harder and clay flaked off.

"Further from the edge, and hold the chisel more vertical."

I struck again. A crack formed. Again and again. Sweaty minute by sweaty minute, I created spiderweb cracks. The chisel skipped sideways and flew from my hand. "Trickster field fox!" We both cursed as it clattered to the floor. Then he cursed with a sharper word as he picked up the chisel and the floor showed a scored mark.

"Forgive me." I bowed.

"You are still no worse than I was." He fingered the floor. "And you'll sand that out and re-polish it, just as I had to when I marred my master's floor." He handed the chisel back to me. "Now finish."

He lit the lamp before I finished the grid of lines. "It is time. Pull out the first piece."

I wiggled a piece at the edge.

"No. Pull it straight out or you'll destroy the details."

"I'm trying," I shot back, then bowed my head in shame.

"Good. Keep trying. I'll keep teaching."

I worked the first piece out. A section of skin showed, lined and wrinkled with age. An eye, crinkled with smile creases, showed next. I laughed as his face peeked out piece by piece. He was a mischievous priest. If a field fox took on the form of a priest, he would look this way.

Takumi took the mask, studying it. "He is worth painting."

His praise spread like sunrise over frozen hills.

Sheng, is it because I took on your name that I could do this?

6

Crocus blooms in snow,
sun-warmed enough to break free
from winter's prison.

Another month dripped away like snow melting from the eaves. I helped Takumi form thirteen more masks from clay mold to painted finish.

Removing the mask from the cracked mold was the start of many lessons. He no longer seemed content for me to perform the simple tasks, though fear clawed inside of me each time he ordered me to try a new skill.

Of course, he still formed each clay mold and painted each finished mask. I had no place there, nor would I ever. It was enough to learn to layer the paper inside the mold and carefully break away the clay. He brushed on pigments, laid gold leaf, shaded with charcoal, and varnished to protect each perfect color.

One morning he stopped me in the middle of chopping wood. "A pity your hair isn't longer. It's thick and straight enough to frame a lady's mask. You will not cut it until it reaches past your shoulders so we can use it."

"What if they think I'm a girl?" I dropped the ax as I considered something even worse. *What if Takumi thinks I am a girl?* Girls didn't apprentice to men, ever. If he discovered it, I'd be kicked out.

Takumi shrugged. "You can keep a hat on when you are out in the village."

I sighed in relief. Takumi saw nothing other than his masks. Unless I blurted out I was a girl, he'd never notice.

That afternoon, Takumi brought over a mask of the sun-kami he'd finished the day before. "What is her emotion?" He held the mask so it tilted downward, the shadows concealing parts of her face and darkening her brow, making it seem lower.

"She's angry."

"And now?" He tilted the mask so I looked straight at it. Her brow wasn't as shadowed and her eyes slanted down at the outer corners.

"Sorrow."

He tilted it yet again, and her face changed to a delighted open mouth. Her cheeks pushed up against the lower part of her eyes and turned them to laughter.

"How do you do this?" I touched the mask. It was solid. The kami's face hadn't changed, but with each tilting, she took on a new emotion.

Takumi set the mask on the mat beside him. "If you only saw the mask in the downward tilt, would you ever believe me if I told you she was happy?"

"I don't think so."

"You would trust your own eyes more than me?"

"I don't know if I even trust my own eyes."

He laughed, then let me hold the mask. I tilted her one way, then another. The changed emotion happened with the vertical tilt. Each shape of the face was perfectly placed to create the shadows and lines of the new emotion.

He knelt beside me and watched the changing emotions. "It is a trick, but it holds much truth. We see things from a certain angle. We know what we see. We know it is true. Then someone else sees it from another angle and knows just as surely what they saw is true. That is fine with buckets and teapots. But for people, we must see them from many sides to truly know them." He tilted the kami mask so her face beamed with joy. "Don't worry about what people think of you, Sheng-kun. They only see one side of you."

He stood and placed the mask high on the wall so unless I stood on a stool she'd always look happy, even in the evening dimming room. "I'm hungry," he said. "I'll cook while you break the mold on the tengu."

My shoulders tightened as I looked at the thick mold of the tengu. Instead of a rough bowl shape, the center stuck out, surrounding the tengu's long nose. I'd likely break the nose off when I chipped away at the clay. I bowed. "Sensei, please forgive me for speaking, but I am the apprentice. I'll cook so you can perform your work."

He scowled. "I will forgive you for speaking but not for shirking your learning."

"Please sensei. I'm not ready to break that mold without your help. I'll ruin the mask in it."

"Then you'll ruin it and learn in the process to be more careful." His look softened. "Very well. Go make something to eat, maybe something with only a little smoke flavor."

I cringed. Though he never complained of my cooking, he still teased me about the duck falling in the fire. It was hard living so far from the ocean and its foods. Duck was greasy and hare tough, nothing like octopus or oyster, and much more difficult to prepare. Still, he wasn't requiring me to break the mold.

I chopped winter onions and ruffled leaf cabbage, then beat eggs for tamago-yaki. The sheet of egg hardened on one side, and I caught the edge between my chopsticks to turn it over.

A ghostly scream shattered the air behind me.

I jumped, jerking my chopsticks. The thin sheet of egg slipped into the fire, sending up a billow of smoke. "Trickster field fox!" I spun around, wielding the empty pan. Where was that kitsune? The room was empty, or he was invisible.

Takumi groaned as he squinted his bi-colored eyes. "I asked for a meal with less smoke flavor. Get over here and finish the tengu mask. I'm cooking tonight."

If only he could hear and see the kitsune, he'd know it wasn't my fault. But then if he knew that a kitsune followed me and caused us trouble, he'd not let me stay.

I bowed my head. "Please, master. I shouldn't. I'm only a clumsy apprentice."

His answer came sharply. "Don't judge yourself from only one angle. You have many more faces than the mask."

I broke fine lines in the tengu mold while my own face wrinkled with lines of frustration. *Sheng,* I thought to my twin, *what does Takumi see in me? I know who I am—death-followed, kitsune-tormented, just trying to make a life where I don't hurt anyone or ruin anything. No trick of light will change that.*

Takumi's hand rested on my shoulder. "Come here." His voice was gentle. He pulled an ichigenkin from the wall and set it on the tatami mat. This was the first time he'd removed the instrument. Its slender plank body was as wide as from my fingertips to my wrist and longer than Takumi's arm. A single string stretched from one end to the other. He placed a bamboo tube around his left hand's middle finger and a slanted bamboo tube on his right index finger. He closed his eyes and his shoulders relaxed backward. "Sheng-kun, listen."

He placed the straight tube on the string and plucked with the slanted tube. A simple plucked note vibrated. He waited until it died away before moving his left hand higher on the string and plucking a new note. Single note by note, he let each ring, die away, and be. A melody floated, vibrating breaths of music and almost silent pauses.

I leaned into the music.

A note ended and instead of plucking a new note Takumi lifted the ichigenkin and set it in front of me. "Which note is the ichigenkin? Is it this?" He plucked a note. "Or this?" He plucked a different note.

"Both."

"Why?"

"Because... because."

He waited.

"Because it has many notes."

He touched the string. "It has only one string. It can only be one thing. Which note is it?"

"I did not listen when you showed me the sun-kami mask." I bowed my head.

He slid the two bamboo pieces into my hands. "You didn't. So you will play each night until you learn to see that the ichigenkin and the apprentice are not one note each."

"Yes, sensei." I bit my lip.

He laughed. "I don't ask you to be good, only to learn to create the many notes. I'll hide outside with my dog if you are awful."

"I will be."

"We'll see. Now begin."

Days later, Takumi stopped working in the middle of pinching out a new face in clay. "Today I'll show you the first step of any mask."

He brought over a slate where he'd sketched many faces. He drew an oval. "What is this?"

"I don't know."

"You don't know—yet. This—" he pointed to the oval— "is possibility. This is you, it is me, and each person. Who we can become."

"What will this become?" I asked.

He handed me the slate. "You decide."

"No. I can't!"

His bi-colored eyes crinkled. "My apprentice denies his learning yet again? You will have to apprentice to me for forty-nine years instead of seven to learn what you must. Just try. The worst you can do is never pick up the chalk. Any line will be better than emptiness."

I stared at the oval. What would it become? It narrowed at the bottom, almost like a muzzle. I sketched. My rough lines fell outside of the picture in my mind, landing in a sloppy, unrecognizable mess. I gripped the chalk. I couldn't do this. I had no talent. I could spread glue. I could chip away a clay mold, even from a long-nosed tengu, without breaking it. But to create? No. That was for an artist. I clenched my hand to rub out the picture.

Takumi caught my fist. "Wait." He whistled. Ōkami padded from his corner of the room. Takumi looked at his wolfish dog and then at the sketch. "It's a start. Try again, with him in front of you. Start with the simple shapes, then add shading afterwards."

I shook, having the dog so close, but Takumi motioned for me to start. I sketched until my fingers cramped with holding the chalk. A recognizable dog took shape on the slate, each line my own. Ōkami tilted his head and studied the drawing, huffed, then lay down with his head on his paws.

"My dog is done modeling. And your fingers are tired. You will practice sketching for an hour each day. Go to the market for tofu, a slate and more chalk." He handed me enough yen to buy food for a week, good food. Yen that would have to last until the theater directors came for their commissioned masks. But it would go to a slate. Still, I skipped a little as I headed to the market street. I'd have my own slate. *Sheng, I'll learn to be an artist. I'm sure you would have been an excellent one like Father. I don't think I'll be much of one, but I'll become better than I am now.*

On the way, I passed a man in the bright colors of a Nōgaku theater actor. He hailed me. "Is this the way to the mask maker?"

I pointed behind me. "Down that way and to your left. It is a five-minute walk past the last home. You'll know it when you see it."

He bowed in thanks and we parted in separate directions, though I wanted to turn and follow him. *What will Takumi say? How does he sell his masks? Will they pay what each is worth?* I ran to the market, grabbed a block of tofu and ran to the stonemason for the slate. His stall sat on the deck of his home, though he was missing at the moment. One other person stood there with her back to me, studying carved stone animals.

"Excuse my rudeness," I muttered as I slid by her and looked at a stack of thin slate.

"Shisei?"

I whirled. My youngest sister faced me. "Nanai!" I dropped my basket and flung my arms around her.

She hugged tightly back. "Oh, Shisei, I've missed you. I went to visit you at the silk-maker and you weren't there. She said you never arrived. I thought..." She stuttered to a stop. "I'm so happy I found you. You must come home."

I looked into her face. In a couple months she'd grown. She didn't look like a little girl, but now halfway to a woman. "Is Father back?"

"Father isn't back yet. He sent a letter saying that the emperor wants them to stay a year and create many beautiful vases before they leave. Which is why you must come. Ichia needs all our comfort, especially since her husband isn't there."

"What happened?"

"She lost her baby."

The wind of early spring snapped, whipping my short hair from under my hat. "A boy or girl?"

"Boy."

I didn't leave soon enough. I hugged Nanai again. "I can't come."

"Why?"

"I'm apprenticed to the mask maker. I must honor my contract."

The wind blew harder and slipped my hat from my head.

Nanai gasped. "Shisei! Who cut your hair?"

"I'm not Shisei. I'm Sheng. And I cannot come with you."

Her blue-grey eyes grew stormy, but before she spoke, the stone mason stepped onto the porch. She glanced at him and a surface calm covered the storm beneath. "If you are apprenticed to the mask maker, the one that our Nōgaku director came to meet, then I will visit you again. And you shall make my mask—Sheng."

I quickly paid for the slate and fled, gripping the basket in one hand and clutching the slate to my chest. An equally hard stone sat in my chest. I'd caused my nephew's death, just like all the boy babies in our family. I was Shi. *Ichia, I'm sorry I didn't leave sooner. I will never let my death shadow cross your home's step again.*

7

———

River runs constant,
different water flowing
through same river banks.

Spring rains pelted the roof, bringing me out of a comfortable sleep. I shivered. Takumi's hut was cold. Only a few chunks of fire-eaten oak glowed in the fire from the night before. It was Takumi's morning to build the fire. We swapped days, though I was the apprentice and should have built it every day. It was another of his stubborn kindnesses, even with all the work of commissioned masks in the last four weeks.

I rolled over. His bed roll was empty, the quilt sprawled to one side of the mat and the pillow rumpled.

He must have had some grand idea in the nighttime and gone off to get the supplies. He'd be back. I built up the fire, folded and stored the bedding, and made a hot breakfast of tofu soup and rice. He'd be soaked through when he returned, and spring rains weren't much warmer than snow.

The morning passed to the drumming of the rain. I set the work table in order, crushed more shells until they were a fine

38

powder, heated a small block of glue to be ready when he returned, and sketched out masks on my grey slate—sketching and rubbing away and sketching again. Mother's face took shape, then Ichia's, then each of my sisters. Each shared similar lines. After I sketched my youngest sister, Nanai, I sketched one more— my own. My face fit along the blurred outlines of the others. Tears clouded my vision and then dropped to smudge the sketch. *Where is Takumi?* I rubbed out the last drawing, then washed the slate clean with water.

The rice had grown cold; the soup simmered to half its depth. He'd be ravenous when he returned. I grabbed a packet of dried bonito from a top shelf. It wasn't as good as fresh fish, but it tasted like home. Takumi would appreciate it, if he wasn't too caught up in his new idea to notice.

A flash of white darted around me and snatched the packet.

"Come back!" I would not let him ruin another meal. I lunged.

He danced backwards, grinning around the bonito packet in his maw, just keeping out of my reach. His four tails fanned behind him. He'd had four hundred years to live, and all he could think of was stupid pranks.

"Oh, why can't you just go away and leave me alone?"

He tilted his head as if considering, and walked through the wall, taking the bonito with him.

"Oooo!" I'd have to go to market and get something else. I grabbed my conical hat and slid the door open.

Ōkami bounded against me, his wet paws landing on my chest.

I stumbled back with a scream, shielding my face and throat with my hands.

The wolf-dog slid to the ground, grabbed one of my sleeves in his mouth and tugged me.

Something has happened to Takumi. I forgot the kitsune and swallowed my fear of Ōkami, following the wolf-dog into the rain. *Why didn't he bark to let me know? How long has he been waiting on the porch?* He broke into a loping run. I followed. By the time we entered the forest, my breath came in ragged leaps. The rain pushed its way through the tight rice-stalk weave of my hat and soaked my hair. Ōkami turned and watched me as I leaned over, bracing a hand against a tree. Then he grabbed my sleeve and pulled me forward again.

Wet pine boughs slapped against me as I ran after him. Spring mud slipped under my feet. I fell twice. The brown of the mud matted and mixed with the brown of my kimono.

Through the rain came a chanting, mournful singing.

River runs constant,
different water flowing
through same river banks.

Always, yes always,
different water passing swift
through same firm clay banks.

But sky takes away,
pulling water into heavens,
leaving river dry.

I tumble through life,
bound by river walls of earth.
Spirits float above.

Bound by life's river
I reach for sky, for my home,
and am left bereft.

Takumi's voice cracked. He coughed and started singing again. It was the same melody he'd taught me to play on the ichigenkin.

River runs constant,
different water flowing
through same river banks.

Always, yes always,
different water passing swift
through same firm clay banks.

I followed Ōkami into a clearing. Takumi knelt in front of a small shrine made of black and green stone. He held his rice straw hat over smoking incense, a cup of sake, and a plate of delicately formed cakes.

But sky takes...

He coughed, and his shoulders shook.

Ōkami went and sat by his side, silent and still as the stone dogs guarding a temple.

Takumi didn't turn his head. His voice croaked, "Sky takes—" *cough*— "sky takes away, pulling—" His body shuddered with a string of coughs. He slumped forward. His hat fell from his hand, knocking over the cup and dousing the incense.

I ran to his side, pulling one of his arms over my shoulder. He was much bigger than I. His weight pulled down against me, stronger than I pulled up. I pushed against him, rolling him onto his back. Rain fell onto his closed eyes and into his open mouth. His breath smelled strongly of sake. He coughed, blinked, and stared into a place I couldn't see. His gaze shifted and focused on my face. "Little Sheng-kun. Do you come to join me in my grief?"

"I've come to bring you home."

He shivered and coughed. "Hai. You are right. I will go." He rolled back to his knees and stood wavering on his legs. Ōkami pressed against him and Takumi grasped his fur. I pulled his other arm over my shoulders, and we stumbled back to his home.

Once inside, Takumi huddled by the fire.

I touched his sodden kimono. "You need to get into something dry."

"Hai, hai." He unbound and pulled off the kimono, so he stood in loose cotton trousers. Pock scars bunched along his strong shoulders and back, and down his leanly muscled arms.

I fled outside while he finished. Ōkami nudged me with his cold nose. Instead of pulling away, I hesitantly rubbed his wet fur. He leaned against me, still silent.

"Sheng-kun." Takumi's rasping voice carried through the door. "Come back before you catch cold—and bring Ōkami."

Takumi knelt by the fire with his quilt wrapped tightly over dry clothes. He called Ōkami to his side. "You may speak."

Ōkami lifted his head and let out a mournful half-howl, then lay before the fire.

"Why?" I asked. "Why was he silent, and why were you in the woods?"

Takumi leaned against the wall. When he spoke, it was in a younger voice, broken at the edges as if torn from childhood. "I was born with these two-colored eyes. My father said they were demon eyes. My mother said it was a gift, and I'd be able to see things others could not. All it brought me was teasing from the village boys. If these eyes could have let me see the boy hiding behind a building, ready to rub my face in the dirt, then I could have called them a blessing. More so if I could have seen the future."

Takumi looked into a distance that wasn't contained in that room or that time. "My mother bore no more children, and she gave me all the care that would have filled ten children's lives. When I broke into a spotted fever, she cared for me, though the villagers said to cast me into the woods. My father wouldn't leave her. Both of them developed the spots, then burned with the fever. I began to heal. They did not.

"I stumbled through the village, still weak and my skin rashed, seeking help—though it was too late for my parents. The villagers drove me away with brooms and sticks."

He rubbed Ōkami, and the dog laid his head in Takumi's lap. "Anger burned in me as hot as the spotted fever. I wandered from village to village, stealing from gardens, porches, and boats. Spring passed into summer. I gained a broken nose on my thirteenth birthday, a gift from six boys who followed me from a village. They called me a *thieving wolf*. I fought like one, then limped away, ready to die like one in the woods." Coughing punctuated every few words.

"Then a mask maker took me in, tended to my injuries, and apprenticed me. He was far more patient than I am with you. It was years before my angry wounds healed, yet he put up with me."

A rumble of coughs left him gasping for breath. He wiped tearing eyes, then looked into my face, his voice older and curt. "I ramble. You asked why Ōkami was silent and why I was in the woods. Every year on the anniversary of my parents' death, I spend the day honoring them. This is the first year that the sky has cried with me. I taught Ōkami to be silent while I honor them. He would not make a sound until I told him to speak again." He shuddered through another string of coughs. "I'm going to sleep."

He lay down by the fire and slept the remainder of the day and through the night. When he woke the next morning, he grunted in reply to my questions about how he felt, let me feed him some broth, and slept more. Coughs racked his breathing. His lips tinged with blue.

He needed a doctor.

I ran into the village market. Mud sucked at my geta sandals, while rain pattered on my conical straw hat. The fishmonger stood at his usual stall, shielding the dried fish with an oil-paper umbrella. I slid to a stop in the mud in front of him and bowed, sucking in my breath. "Master fishmonger, where can I find a doctor?"

His usual scowl deepened. "Can't blame your illness on my fish."

"It's my master. He was out in the rain and developed a dangerous cough."

He sniffed and adjusted his straw hat. Rain streamed off it. "A dangerous cough from being in the rain? His strange eyes must make him weaker than a man should be."

"The doctor, please."

"Down that way and to the right. Has a garden and pond in front. Herbs everywhere. He charges plenty of yen. Certain you don't want to just get back to your master and let him sleep it off?"

I dashed away. I'd empty the sack of yen and work the extra years to pay it back if it would help Takumi.

The doctor followed me back, walking at a sedate pace. I carried on my back his woven basket of herbs.

As we entered, Ōkami lifted his head from Takumi's chest and whined. Takumi coughed, and his pock marks had almost disappeared into his blanched skin.

The doctor's shaved head wrinkled. "Remove the wolf-dog."

I tugged Ōkami away. He whined and struggled against my grasp as I shoved him out of the house. "I'm sorry, Ōkami. He's trying to help our master."

The dog sat on the porch and howled.

"Hush. Or you'll make it worse."

He silenced and stared at me.

I scratched behind his ears, though my fingers wanted to stiffen into a fist. "I'm going to help him. Stay." I slipped back into the house.

The doctor knelt with his ear against Takumi's bare chest. I softened my breathing over my rain-pattering heart. He'd help Takumi. He had to.

The doctor frowned as he knelt up. "A phlegm has settled in his lungs. He needs a drying herb to pull it out and another to rebalance his body. He's weak in spirit, too. If he had any friends in the village, I'd suggest you get them to visit. But they—the judgmental fools—think he's part demon. I see it all too often against those birth and illness-marked." He shook his head and focused his clear gaze on me. "You must do your best to lift his spirits."

He pulled out several herbs. "Give these to him in teas three times a day, until his coughing lessens, then twice a day. Keep him warm. Give him broths with these other herbs." He handed me more. "Help him rest."

I bowed my thanks, then held out the sack of yen. We didn't have much, nor would we until we sold the masks for the summer festival. "Honored doctor, this is all we have."

He counted through the yen, then picked up two of the herbs. "These are not as necessary. He will likely heal with only the others."

Takumi's breath rasped.

What did I have that I could give as payment? And how would I buy food to nourish Takumi if I gave the doctor all the yen? I looked around the room. Mother's zenko mask hung next to the sun-kami. It was my only possession of worth. I clenched my hands together and pressed them to my lips. My jaw trembled against my fists. *I can't give away Mother's mask. It's the only thing I have left of her.*

Takumi coughed, felt around blindly with one hand, and then rasped, "Ōkami? Have you abandoned me too?"

I took the kitsune mask from the wall, tracing a finger over the ears and nose. "Will you take this in payment instead?"

The doctor studied it, nodded, and handed back the herbs and the yen. As the door slid shut behind him, I fell to my knees. Ōkami whimpered on the other side of the door. Takumi coughed. *I can't just kneel here. Takumi gave me a new life. His life is worth more than the mask. Get up and get busy!*

I stumbled to my feet, let Ōkami in, and made the first tea.

Then, when he'd drunk it, I played a slow melody on the ichi-genkin—the instrument he'd required I play each evening of the last month—and sang.

River runs constant,
different water flowing
through same river banks.

I felt out the words as my fingers plucked the slow notes.

Banks grow thick with life.
Green pushes through winter's sleep.
Ferns unfurl 'neath leaves.

Last year's green crumbles,
feeding the plants we will eat:
autumn's gift to spring.

As the last note died away, the white kitsune walked into the room. His four tails hung subdued, and he bowed his head, just as he had when he visited my mother before her death.

"No. Go away," I whispered.

He approached Takumi.

Ōkami lifted his head from Takumi's chest, watching the fox, but he didn't bark.

"He will not die. Not like my mother. Go away!" I grabbed the nape of the kitsune's neck, his fur soft and warm in my grasp. He didn't resist as I lifted him.

Ōkami whined, watching me with lifted eyebrows. He stood from Takumi's side and grabbed my sleeve.

Why? Ōkami had chased the kitsune away before. Why was he stopping me now? "Ōkami, he'll hurt your master."

Ōkami whined again and pulled my sleeve hard enough that

my kimono slipped from my shoulder. The kitsune still did not struggle, but hung from my grasp. *Is he here to help? Can he help our master? Ōkami seems to want me to let the trickster fox go.*

I set the kitsune down. "I'll drive you from the house if you do anything to hurt my master."

Ōkami stepped aside, letting the kitsune lick Takumi's fevered face. Takumi sighed and his creased brow relaxed slightly. Then Ōkami stretched out on one side of Takumi while the kitsune curled up on the other side. Takumi breathed deeper.

Maybe, just maybe, the trickster fox was helping.

I tended to Takumi through days and nights of fevers, coughs and chills. On the days that Takumi grew worse, the kitsune appeared and he improved again. *Why is he helping Takumi?* I shook my head. I shouldn't question the kitsune's kindness. Foxes were capricious in whom they helped and whom they tormented. I would put up with a lifetime of his tricks if he healed Takumi. But why hadn't he healed my mother? Was my death curse in my family so strong that even he, a fox with healing magic, couldn't help?

I bathed Takumi's brow, then set out a bowl of inarizushi in the corner for the kitsune. The fox trotted over, licking his chops.

Sheng, he may be a trickster field fox, but he's benevolent to Takumi, and that is enough.

A week after the doctor's visit, Takumi woke clear-eyed. "Sheng-kun, we are behind in our work." He tried to stand, but thumped to his knees. "Bring the slate here."

I knelt at his side. A shiver of joy at hearing him sat over the fear that he'd hurt himself. "You must rest."

He scowled. "Who's the master? I will decide what I must do and when. Now bring me the slate." He coughed and scowled deeper.

I couldn't let him excite himself. I brought him the slate.

He traced the chalk over the stone, but his usual swift lines shook and the samurai face took on quivering fear. Takumi threw the chalk to the tatami mat, and it rolled, leaving a dusty white patch. "You will draw the next mask."

"I'm not good enough yet."

He snorted, then coughed. "I've seen the remnants of your erased sketches. Draw." He thought a moment. "The sun-kami."

Her? We already had one. And she was as beautiful as dawn.

Takumi placed the chalk on my open palm. "Draw."

I rubbed out the half-drawn samurai, leaving a pale, dusty coating over the dark slate. *The sun-kami? What does she look like? Serene? Powerful?* Familiar faces formed in the space. I traced, merging the lines with the remembered lines of my mother and sisters. The high brows of Nichika, the narrow nose of Sanaho, the fine cheek bones of Rokue. Each sister melded into the mask.

"Good, good," Takumi muttered beside me.

Face overlaid face. Years spread between mother and youngest daughter slipped together. I sketched, never rubbing out a line, but tracing what lay between me and the slate. One face I ignored.

I handed the finished sketch to him.

He studied it and handed it back. "No. It's not ready yet. You are missing something."

I looked through the layer of faces, to the one chalked onto slate. The lines where mine fit lay empty. *I am Sheng. Why do I care if Shisei's face goes with her sisters?* I sketched the corners of my eyes where they crinkled from squinting in the sun, thickened the eyebrows, and loosened a lock of the tightly bound hair so it wisped across the forehead.

"Stop!" He snatched the slate from me. "This is it. This will be the mask that is perfect balance. Set it on the table and don't touch it."

Then he slept. I made another meal to eat by myself while the chalked kami, sharing my family's faces and mine, watched from where it leaned against the wall.

Another two weeks pressed the last of winter's chill from the soil. Green unfurled in ferns and vines. Blushing plum blossoms scented the breeze that trailed through the opened paneled walls.

Takumi no longer coughed, and his hands grew steady. The longer days were not long enough for him. His orders were curt, his expectations exacting, and his results beautiful.

"Sheng-kun, crush the shells finer."

"The glue is too thin."

"Chop more wood for the kiln."

There were no more lessons, just work. We'd lost three weeks to his illness. We had to hurry. Except he wouldn't hurry. He spent careful time creating each mask, stretching out his day rather than damaging his art in a rushed moment. Each morning I tried to wake earlier, but he was always in the middle of a mask when I did. And when I fell to my mat long after the sunset, he stood at the worktable molding, crafting, creating.

Two things remained unchanged in the constantly shifting work area. One, the peg where my mother's zenko mask once hung, remained bare. He never asked where it had gone, but he didn't set another mask in its place beside the joyful sun-kami. Two, my sketch of the sun-kami bearing my family's faces sat at the back of the table. Takumi wouldn't touch it, nor did he form a mask from it. Instead, he used my slate for sketching.

So she—my mother and sisters—watched us.

8

Namazu thrashes,
shaking forests, shrines, and homes.
All Nihon trembles.

I clutched the edge of the oxcart as the wooden wheels bounced over the rutted, summer-dried road. The cart shifted and jolted. Father sat at the front with his back to me. He tapped the ox with a light stick and it hastened its steps. Fine pottery jostled, rice-straw padded between them. Some slipped and a plum vase clanked against a green glazed bowl.

I shoved the straw back. "Honored Father. We must slow. The pottery will break."

He tapped the ox again, and it lumbered into a trot. More straw shifted. I pushed some into place and twice as much slipped away. The pottery clanked and broke.

"Father, stop! Please!"

"Sheng-kun!" Takumi's voice pulled me from the dream. The ground rolled beneath my sleep-mat. The breaking pottery from the dream merged into tumbled crashes as cups, bowls, and tools jostled each other. Takumi grabbed my arm, "Get out of here!" A bowl of paint fell from the table and splashed yellow along the wall.

I stumbled to my feet and pushed the sliding door open. Early morning cast enough light to see Ōkami cowering on the porch. The masks swung on the outside wall. A red demon face leapt from its peg and crashed at my feet, breaking its long nose. Takumi grabbed me and pulled me from the porch to the middle of the shifting path. "Get down, cover your head."

I dropped to my knees, pressed my forehead to the ground, and linked my hands over my neck. I'd been through many earthquakes in my life. But none this big. Ōkami pushed his nose underneath me. The ground shifted and jerked and rolled. The road plumed dirt. I coughed and spat. Wood screamed. I glanced up. The porch's straw thatched roof hung tilted forward at one corner. A support beam lay on its side.

"Get your head down." Takumi pushed my head back to the dirt and covered my head and neck with his body.

Another scream of wrenching wood. Did the whole porch fall in? What about the masks? I tried to look up, but he held me firm.

Finally, the ground stilled to only a gentle back-and-forth sway. Takumi released his hold. "It's safe."

Grit stung my eyes. I wiped them on the inside of my sleeve, then looked up. The porch roof hung against the house wall, both supports lying on the ground. "The masks!" I lunged to my feet and stumbled toward the house.

"Wait."

I froze.

"The masks remaining will wait an hour. We must first check on the living." He whistled and Ōkami padded beside him as he jogged into town.

I glanced back at the slumped porch roof. Below it, three masks lay on the ground: the red demon, a noble-lady, and a kitsune. Behind me and drawing away, Takumi's off-key whistling shrilled. I bowed my head and followed Takumi from one house to the next. The after-tremors shook the ground. Some villagers were injured. None badly. Some accepted our help. Others sent us politely but firmly away. But he continued until we'd visited each in the village. The midday sun finally warmed the dust-filled air as we walked back to his masks.

"Why did you help them?" I muttered as I trudged beside him. "They didn't need our help. Many didn't want it. None asked about you, nor would they care if we've lost all the masks. You are nothing to them."

He walked silently beside me, growing slower with each step. His rough pine house stood in the distance with its sag-roofed porch. He was too poor to purchase the paper and framing to make a proper house; too poor to get a proper porch, one that didn't collapse in a quake. The other houses were light and strong; only the sliding doors fell. His was heavy and held together by lashings.

We stopped in front of his house. He picked up the kitsune and traced a broken fox ear. The snapped-off piece wedged between porch floorboards. He slipped the piece into his sleeve and finally looked up. His jaw hardened and his lips thinned. "Do you think you are strong enough to shove a bracing under the porch roof when I lift it?"

I had to be. I wouldn't subject him to begging for help when he'd helped everyone else and none offered.

The dry post slivered against my grasp as I pulled it upright. *Let there be some masks still whole. Please.*

He knelt with his back to the wall, placing hands and strong shoulders under the porch roof. With a shout, he lunged upward and outward, lifting the pine frame and thatching.

His masks—most of them—hung from the wall, *undamaged.* Takumi groaned, and I remembered the post in my hands. I shoved it under until the weight of the roof rested on the post.

Together we shoved in the other post and he lashed them to the roof. Then he stepped to the wall and touched each mask. "The kami bless us."

I looked to the kitsune mask with the missing ear. *Honored zenko, tell Inari thank you. Takumi deserves these blessings for his kindness.*

It took us the rest of the day to adjust and re-secure the wall and roof lashings before Takumi allowed us to tend to the masks. Six of his masks were damaged—one was Takumi's sun-kami, the one that could be many emotions.

I fingered the ragged crack that ran from outside of the right eye through the cheek, splitting the lips and ending at the chin. Why her? She was the most beautiful and mysterious of all the masks.

Takumi knelt next to me. "She'll be even more beautiful when gold streaks her face."

9

____

Broken, scarred by life.
Brush gold in each crack—embrace
flaw's glowing beauty.

The earthquake after-tremors were less by the next day. Takumi stood at his cluttered work table mixing lacquer with gold dust. He sang quietly:

River runs constant,
different water flowing
through same river banks.

But sky takes away,
pulling water into heavens,
leaving river dry.

This time the song was serene and not sorrowful. His words changed.

*Polished stones shine
where water once danced and sang:
memories of joy.*

He looked up. "Sheng-kun, it's time."

I held the mask as he filled the crack with liquid gold. It flowed into the ugly gash, crossing white skin and red lips, underlying dark-rimmed eyes. When the gold hardened, he tilted her so I saw anger, sorrow, and finally joy, each streaked through with a wild brilliance. "She's beautiful."

"She's powerful and now bears a history, just like the kami she represents."

"Will the Nōgaku theater still use her?"

He hung the mask on the wall where the joyful face, streaked with gold, smiled on us. "Perhaps. However, if not, we have a little more than a week before they come for the commissioned masks. If we hurry, I'll be able to replace it." He looked around at his workbench. "Crush more shells."

I ran outside to the little shed where he stored supplies. Clay sat in clumps on the bottom shelves. Above that sat baskets of shells and sheaves of sekishu-washi paper. We'd just finished cleaning up the mess from the quake the day before.

A crash and a bellow echoed from the house, followed by barking.

I ran, shoving the door to the side. Takumi knelt on the ground, clutching his left hand in the folds of his kimono. Ōkami chased the four-tailed white kitsune, who jumped on the workbench and then out the door. Ōkami followed.

"Sensei!" I ran to his side. "Are you hurt?"

"Stupid, clumsy fool," he hissed through gritted teeth.

I stumbled back at his words.

He grimaced with a pain-white face. "Not you. Me. Tripped."

His hand! The kitsune! I jumped up to chase the kitsune with Ōkami, then dropped to my knees again. My chasing wouldn't help Takumi. "Are you bleeding?"

He shook his head and withdrew his hand from the folds of his kimono, wincing as he moved it. The two littlest fingers sat askew from the rest. "I tripped. Hit my fingers against the edge of the table. Broken. I need bracing and cloth."

I broke one of my chopsticks in half and wrapped his two fingers next to a non-broken finger, bracing all three with the pieces of chopstick. His usual muttering was silent.

I looked at Takumi's wrapped hand and blanched. *Sheng, what will we do now?* He had his masks for the commissions, but the quake damaged some. He couldn't mold clay with one hand. Would the gold-mended masks be accepted? Why did the kitsune trip him? Didn't he favor Takumi? He helped him heal when he was ill. "Trickster field foxes," I cursed. Especially the four tailed one.

"It isn't so bad now," Takumi grunted. "Get the shells while I mold the mask."

"But sensei, your hand."

"I'll do it one-handed. Now go, before you lose us any more time than is already lost."

An hour later, Takumi's wrapped hand was thick with clay and his face deep with wrinkles. He threw down the lumpy form of clay with his good hand. It looked as much like his other creations as my first sketch of Ōkami had looked like Takumi's fine drawings. "Sheng-kun," he yelled, even though I stood hovering at his side. "It's time you learned to mold clay."

I backed away. My words stumbled between trembling lips. "I can't."

"I can't either. You showed skill with drawing. You can see the picture in your mind. You'll just have to figure how to put it into clay."

"And when I don't?"

"Then, we'll have a dull couple of weeks doing nothing and a lean winter for lack of yen because we didn't deliver the full promised commission."

"I'll try." I picked up the bowl-shaped clay. "But I know not where to start."

He pointed to my sketch of my mother and sisters. "The sun-kami sent you the image, and you must form it."

My shoulders ached from hunching over the table for a third day. The clay lay in a bowl shape with a clumsily formed face. *Sheng, this is nothing like what I sketched. How does my sensei do it?*

Takumi grunted as he set down another of my malformed masks. Pain etched his face and clay crusted his braced hand. "You try too much with your mind. Shape the clay like you traced the chalk."

I took the mask and pushed the clay to form a space for the nose and created a yam-shaped crater. "It's impossible. The cherry trees are already beginning to bud."

His good hand slid over top of mine. "Close your eyes."

I closed them and focused on his teaching fingers.

"Now, see the face."

"How? My eyes are closed."

"You saw the face before you drew. See it again and feel it under your fingers."

I looked beyond the cool grey of my closed eyelids. The kami with my family's faces formed, first a mist, then softly glowing water. It grew to a solid brightness. I reached out and traced my fingers over the forehead, along the chin, brushed the lips and eyebrows. The folded skin at the eye corner crinkled under my fingers.

"You see and feel it. Now pull the clay around it." He guided my hands to the clay and to feel where I'd molded.

"But the face is looking at me and the clay face is looking away."

"Then turn the face you see around and look from behind it."

"Oh, like a mask."

He chuckled, though it was the tight laugh of one who needed a master artisan and only had a trembling apprentice. But maybe, with the face glowing in my mind, I could do this.

I turned the glowing face around and found I could see through it, like ice formed on a koi pond, though it glowed like carved sunlight. Then tilted it downward till it fit against the clay in my hands.

I felt along the clay. The cheeks were too high and sharp. I smoothed them against the face. Takumi let go of my hand and I formed the clay around what glowed in front of me. I only had to fill or remove clay to fit against what was there.

But some parts were too fine for my fingers to form. I bit my lip as I pinched at the creases along the eyes and dulled them instead.

A rounded stick about the size of a chopstick was pressed into my hand. One end was pointed, and the other wedged. Takumi used it for the finer work. I traced the pointed end along the crease and pressed the wedged edge to form a soft ridge between the lips and nose. My fingers saw the clay in a way my eyes couldn't have. I couldn't see with the stick and had to rework many parts I formed with it after I felt it with my fingers. Still, I kept my eyes shut. Would the face disappear when I opened them? If so, I'd keep them shut until I'd fully formed the mask to the face.

Pinch, pull, fill, move, crease, smooth.

"Sheng-kun."

I shook off the word. I needed to stay focused.

"Sheng-kun, you must stop before weariness and hunger make your fingers sloppy."

"I'm almost there."

"Sheng." His voice came stern.

"If I stop now, the face will disappear."

"You will see it again. It is inside of you. Now open your eyes."

I stared long at the glowing face before me, then opened my eyes. The glowing face disappeared to be replaced by the mostly formed clay face. The room was strangely dark. I'd started working on the mask in the midmorning, but now only firelight and lanterns lit the room.

"How late is it?"

"The sun set an hour ago."

"How?"

Takumi spoke with quiet reverence. "When you see like you did, time pours past like water from a teapot. You have the talent that all mask makers seek—to see the spirit and create a physical copy."

I traced the lines of the mask. "I had no ability before becoming your apprentice. Do you brush in gold, mending my brokenness and filling me with talent?"

"I could not give what was never there, only uncover what was unseen before. Your mother's kitsune mask also showed this talent. Maybe she guides your hands."

I studied the clay mold. A light pulsed softly within it, like moonlight through cloud. I sucked in my breath. "Sensei?"

He nodded.

"The clay mask mold seems to glow."

His eyes widened. "I have sometimes seen them glow when a kami accepts the work. You are truly kami-blessed with talent."

A kami had blessed and accepted my work? A shiver of both fear and excitement ran down my back. The sketched merging of my mother's and sisters' faces gazed from the table. All my sisters had talents.

Sheng, do I have this talent because of you? Or can Shisei create something other than death?

10

Masks conceal the heart,
blinding others from seeing
truths lying beneath.

I swept the cherry blossoms from the porch. Soon the director of a Nōgaku theater would arrive for tea. He'd be the third we'd had this week. The other two bought all their commissioned masks, even a few that bore golden repairs.

The gold streaked sun-kami still hung on the wall above the work-table, and my mask with my family faces hung beside her. Takumi asked that I paint mine, but though I could see what colors I needed, making those colors from the layers of paints was harder. So he painted it with his good hand while I held the mask in place. My mask sat in poor comparison to the other. A commoner's face, beautiful to me for the familiarity, but not a powerful kami lighting the skies. Though both glowed. Since I first saw my clay mask mold glow, I could see many other kami-accepted masks amongst Takumi's work. I shivered each time I glanced at mine glowing beside the gold streaked Amaterasu.

The coming director would choose one sun-kami mask along

with other masks for the Kagura performance of the sun-kami hiding away from a demon. He was the only one who'd commissioned masks for that legend.

Ōkami barked as three figures walked down the cherry-tree-lined road. The shortest of the three dashed forward.

I dropped the broom as my youngest sister, Nanai, threw her arms around me. "I told you I'd come back," she whispered.

"Who's this?" Takumi's bemused voice startled us apart.

I focused on his brows, avoiding his eyes, and tried to form a lie. "She's my, she's a, she's—"

"I'm her sister!" Nanai finished for me.

Takumi's brows rose. "And?"

"And," Nanai rushed on, "she's mine."

I clamped my hand over Nanai's mouth. "I'm Sheng."

Her blue-grey eyes challenged me above my hand.

Takumi touched my shoulder. "I knew you were a girl."

I released Nanai and spun around. The world spun faster. "You did? Why did you take me on as an apprentice?"

"I'll tell you when our guests are gone. Get the tea ready."

Nanai knelt between the theater director and his wife. Nanai was the first lead actress, playing the sun-kami, Amaterasu. She sipped her green tea and ignored me as I served the sakura mochi with its pickled cherry leaf wrapped around rice and red bean paste.

Takumi brought over the two sun-kami masks, cradling them carefully with a good hand and a bandaged one. He dropped the honorific greeting as he did in all his conversations. "The earthquake damaged the first mask. This second is of the same quality, though it invites a different feel. Which do you want for your performance?"

Nanai fixed her stormy eyes on the mask I made.

The greying director took the gold-streaked one and tilted it to see the different emotions. He traced his finger along the gold streak. "This is the finest quality mask I've ever seen of Amaterasu, and the gold only adds to its beauty."

"I won't wear it." Nanai stated.

The director's lips thinned. "I allowed you to come to help choose the masks, not to make demands."

"Sensei, you allowed me to come because I'm the finest actress in your theater and the only one worthy of playing Amaterasu."

"You are the only one with the proper colored eyes."

She lifted her head in defiance. "I will wear the other. It is the seven virtues of theater embodied in one. Serenity and wild energy, skill and wisdom, grace and confidence, all unified by sacred poetry."

She saw all that? Or did she just want to wear the mask that bore our family's faces?

The director frowned as he studied the mask again. "I begin to see elements of each. They grow stronger the more I look. Yes, my tensai—my prodigy—this is the one for the sun-kami. But *I* will choose the other masks."

Nanai bowed her head, "Thank you, sensei." When the director turned back to Takumi, she darted a triumphant glance at me before finishing her mochi.

By the end of tea, the theater director had chosen the rest of the masks.

Nanai lingered behind while the others stepped onto the porch. "Shisei, we perform in two weeks. You must come."

I shook my head. My voice would betray me if I spoke.

Her jaw tightened. If she were still a toddler, then the next moment would mean a storm of kicking and screams, but instead she grabbed my arm. "Shisei, I'm not asking you to leave your apprenticeship. I just want to see you again. And the others do too."

"Nanai," the theater director called through the sliding door, "we must go. Bid farewell to the apprentice and come."

Her grip tightened on my arm. "Promise me."

"I promise—" the words caught in my throat— "to do what is best for our family."

"Nanai, come!" he called again.

She stomped a foot, slipped on her geta sandals, and left.

I couldn't go back with her, not even to visit. My eldest sister already lost a baby because of me. *Sheng, where will we go? I can no longer apprentice to Takumi. He knows I'm a girl, and girls can't apprentice to men—ever. It is not allowed. I cannot stay.*

Takumi set three pouches on the workbench, one from each of the theater directors who'd commissioned masks. He rubbed his neck, then scratched his fingers through his tangle of hair while he studied them. "Sheng-kun, we have enough to build a proper house, if you'll help in the construction. We'll be safe when next time Namazu shakes the earth."

My hand flew to my mouth. Had he forgotten? "Sensei, I'm not Sheng. He was my twin. I'm a girl."

He studied my face, and my form, like he studied clay. "Yes. However, you are strong. You've chopped wood and dug clay. You can help build the new walls."

"But I—I can't be your apprentice."

His eyebrows rose. "Why not?"

"Because I'm a girl."

He laughed. "I knew you were a girl from the moment I helped you into my house the first night."

"If you knew I was a girl, why did you treat me as if I was a boy?"

"You were playing the role of a boy. Who am I to tell the actor their part or ruin the play?"

My head hurt. He'd known the entire time, but had still apprenticed me. Why? I dropped my gaze to the floor. "What will you do with me?"

"Do with you? You are my apprentice. You will keep working and learning and developing your talent."

"But—"

He grasped my shoulder with his good hand. "Look at me."

I looked into his face, searching for a lie.

His face was as serious as when he molded clay. "I know that traditionally girls don't apprentice to men, but you have a talent that cannot be taught, only nurtured. I'll not find another with such talent, even in the emperor's court. You may keep pretending to be a boy, if you like. I'll treat you the same either way."

A tremor of relief flowed through me, like the settling of the ground after an earthquake.

I bowed. "Thank you, honored sensei, for keeping me as your apprentice, even after I deceived you."

He laughed again as disbelief flickered across his pocked face. "You didn't deceive me any more than an actor deceives the audience by wearing a mask. You've been honest in everything that is important. You've worked hard. You've listened and learned."

My stomach clenched at his words. I hadn't been honest. I hadn't told him of my curse or of the kitsune who broke his fingers.

As if he could read my thoughts, he said, "Sheng-kun, I would hear Shisei's story. The full one."

The tremor of relief changed to warning of an earthquake yet to come.

The firelight flickered on the walls and over Takumi's solemn face as I told of my twin, Sheng, who died at birth, my mother's death with my next brother's stillbirth, and my nephew's death. Takumi molded a small piece of clay in constantly moving fingers of one hand, while his braced hand sat motionless in his lap. His brown-and green-eyed gaze stayed fixed on me. The clay changed from bird, to grasshopper, to fox, and finally formed into a human face.

When I finished speaking, he looked down into the clay nestled in his fingers, then back to me. "You bear scars inside, more painful than the ones I bear on my skin. The kami some-times break us so we can grow into something new. I'm sorry it was this way for you. You are safe here."

"I'm not." I bit my lip, not wanting to continue, but I had to. "And you're not safe while I stay with you."

His eyebrows rose. "There is none here who can be harmed if you truly bear a curse against infant sons."

I closed my eyes, bracing to tell the rest, then looked into his face. "A kitsune follows me and torments me. He is the one who tripped you so you broke your fingers."

Takumi sucked in his breath and stared down at his braced and bandaged hand. He still winced when he put pressure on his fingers. The fire flared as a piece of wood burned through and fell in halves. "A kitsune?"

"Yes," I whispered.

His jaw hardened. "Well, I know now."

"I'll leave. Please forgive me for bringing trouble into your life."

He laughed, a hard, bitter sound. "Trouble has always followed me, just as it follows you. You will not leave. We'll face that trouble together, be it cursedly blind people or a trickster field fox."

At Takumi's words, the four-tailed kitsune sauntered into the room.

I gritted my teeth. "Sensei—" I began. The kitsune glanced at me, then curled up next to Ōkami. The wolf-dog sniffed him and laid his head back down. I sighed at the reminder. He wasn't completely bad. "Sensei, the kitsune helped you heal when you were so ill I thought you'd die."

Takumi laughed. This time the rounded laugh filled the room. "I would thank the capricious spirit. See, it isn't only trouble that follows you. Come, we will go to your sister's performance. You can bid your sisters a proper goodbye and let that wound heal."

My hands knotted around my kimono. "Go back to my sisters?"

"Only for a short time." His eyes brightened. "Then we will travel from theater to theater creating masks until all Nihon knows your kami-blessed skill. And not even a kitsune or a curse can stop us."

My hands knotted tighter in the kimono cloth. Ichia was no longer pregnant. I couldn't hurt her more. I would go say goodbye and then be free—as free as I could be, carrying my curse and shadowed by the kitsune.

11

———

Kami sing and dance,
call forth the sun from hiding,
light the world again.

Hundreds of people dressed in their best kimonos pressed together on the rows of benches that surrounded the Kagura stage. The raised platform of the stage with its arched roof sat in front of a shrine to the sun-kami, Amaterasu. The painting of an old pine tree, the Kagamiita, covered the back wooden panel. White gravel spread around the stage like a river and reflected the afternoon onto the stage. A narrow bridge ran from the left side of the stage back to a curtained room. Five small pines lined the bridge, with the largest pine closest to the stage and the smallest at the far end of the bridge.

Mother's whispered explanations from the first time I watched a Kagura performance tickled at the back of my thoughts. *The bridge is a passageway between the world of living and dead. The trees show where the actors are in those worlds, the smallest tree being furthest from us and closest to the kami. We see mostly in the living, but glimpse the world of the spirits.*

Takumi tugged on my arm, bringing me back from my thoughts, and pushed his way through the crowd of hundreds of people. If Ōkami had been with us, the crowd would have parted, but Takumi left the wolf-dog in the care of a crippled girl back in his village. Though I didn't really fear Ōkami anymore, my shoulders had finally untensed after days of not having him around.

We reached a ribboned-off second-to-the-front bench. Takumi spoke with a man wearing a lion-dog mask, reminiscent of the stone lion-dogs that guarded the shrine. The scowling mask dipped in a nod as the man untied the ribbon.

Takumi took my elbow. "Being the mask maker carries certain privileges."

I touched the kitsune mask that sat over my right ear. I'd like to place it over my face. But only the theater troupe would. All the audience wore their masks on the side or back.

Takumi didn't seem to notice the startled glances at his bi-colored eyes, crooked nose, and pock-marked face. Could I be as strong if my sisters saw me? If Sheng were here, he'd be brave. I pushed my kitsune mask more to the front, so it half-covered my right eye.

Takumi stretched his legs under the front-most bench. "You'll miss half the performance covering your eye like that."

I ducked my head.

He chuckled. "Are you the least interested in seeing our masks bridge the physical and spiritual? The Kagura—the dance of the Kami—will make the masks that once hung on the wall glow like you've never seen before. Watch. See which masks seem alive and which are but paper and glue."

I glanced at the many other masked people. An old man with a laughing priest mask sat brightly in the middle of an otherwise dark-masked family. A gaijin woman lifted her bear mask and tucked a curling lock of black hair back into a knot. The bear mask smiled with the same knowing look as the wearer. She disappeared in the crowd as a harried mother tugged along three wiggly boys while her glowing red hannya mask glowered over them with its sharp horns and leering mouth. A child ran up to her father, and he swung her up onto his shoulders. Her flat, child-painted mask of a monkey glimmered on the side of her head like the moon reflecting off a pond.

"Sensei. Why do some of the simplest masks glow?" I pointed to the monkey mask.

He cocked his head and studied the child and the mask. "On festival days the spirits are much more amongst us, causing both mask and person to glow. By tomorrow they will be back to mortal glow and blame their exhaustion on the excitement of the day." He looked at me. "You glow brightly right now."

"I glow?"

"Hush."

The rich and high harmonics of the nohkan flute floated from the bridge, and the audience silenced. The flutist crossed the tree-lined bridge and stood at the back of the stage. His trilling notes wove with the freedom of bird twitters and the low sighing of river song. Each note contained echoes of many other notes, as if the ghost of ten other flutes played alongside his.

I closed my eyes and let the music pull, taking me far from fear and regret. Drumming joined the flute. A soft beat, gentle as bare feet across a wooden floor, intermingled with a sharp higher thumping. The shuffling of the chorus taking their place along the right-hand edge of the stage underscored the music.

Takumi nudged my elbow. "The masked players are entering."

I opened my eyes. Susanoo, the kami of storm and ocean, entered first. His proud, scowling mask framed with wild black hair flickered like lightning hidden in a black storm cloud. I caught my breath and scooted backward. I'd watched Takumi make the mask from sketch to painted finish. It was always powerful, but now I feared it.

"What do you see?" Takumi whispered.

"Lightning and storm."

Amaterasu, the sun-kami, entered next. My youngest sister, Nanai, floated across the bridge, her white and pink kimono edged with red rippling with her smooth steps. An embroidered red sun marked each long sleeve. But even without those symbols, I'd never doubt that she represented the kami of sun and heaven. The mask that bore all the faces of my family burned with a noon sun. I squinted, then widened my eyes. Despite the brightness, my eyes didn't hurt and I could still see the details. One face flowed to another: Ichia, Nichika, Sanaho, Gomako, Rokue, Nanai, mother, and I. Mother's face stood most prominent. Was her spirit here?

"What do you see?" Takumi's voice jarred against my ears.

I closed my eyes for a moment to clear my thoughts. "Summer sun and family."

And the performance started.

"When the earth and heavens were new," the chorus of eight black-kimonoed singers intoned, "Amaterasu and her younger brother, Susanoo, quarreled."

Amaterasu danced in graceful movements, counterpoint to the wild pride of Susanoo. Their fight, narrated by the chorus, floating on the flute's ghostly notes and carried forward by the drumbeat, took them from her winning the argument to his devastating anger. He destroyed her rice fields, broke her heavenly loom, and killed one of her beloved attendants. With each attack, Amaterasu shrank further and further from the stage front.

I shrank with her. The lightning from Susanoo's mask flickered and his eyes glowed with demon intensity. He flowed towards her like the tsunami wave, ready to swallow both sun-kami and day.

"Amaterasu," the chorus intoned, "in fear and grief, hid inside a cave, plunging the earth into darkness and cold."

Amaterasu fled across the bridge and disappeared, followed by the triumphant Susanoo.

Flute and drums filled the emptiness, slowly pulling the emotions from grief to expectation. The knot in my chest loosened. It was just a play, and they were just actors. Yet they'd captured yūgen—a subtle grace, a beauty only partly seen but fully felt.

An unmasked actor trudged onto the stage wearing a farmer's kimono and carrying a market basket. Behind him crept a white-robed actor—a ghost. A smile tugged at my mouth. The mid-performance interlude was always my favorite part of the Noh-performance. Today I needed it for more than its humor.

Scattered laughter punctuated the audience as the farmer convinced the ghost he was a new ghost so the ghost wouldn't harm him. The laughter grew as the farmer had the old ghost carry him partway to the market, the ghost grunting beneath the man's mortal weight. Finally, the farmer tricked the ghost into changing forms—a monkey, a wild dog, and finally a sheep—and the farmer spit on the sheep, trapping the ghost forever in the animal form, which the farmer sold at the market.

I heaved a shuddering breath to still my laughter as the two comics exited. I was ready to see the rest of the kami-touched performance.

The flute and drums music flowed, starting out light-hearted and growing darker until my heart thudded again.

"The world lay in darkness," the chorus spoke. "The crops froze, the people shivered in their homes, the land fell to chaos. The other kami had had enough."

Masked players representing the kami of war, agriculture, medicine, wisdom, and revelry crossed the bridge to the stage. Uzume, the kami of revelry, sauntered at the front.

"I will convince her to come out," Uzume boasted.

"But we have pleaded," said the kami of agriculture.

"And we have threatened," said the kami of war.

"I will convince her where your pleading and threats have not." Uzume stepped to the center stage and moved into a slow dance. The flute music floated around her movements and the drums matched her steps. Her mask didn't glow, but even if it had, her movements would have stolen my attention. Her dance quickened and became more powerful and playful. The other kami joined the dance, their clapping almost overpowering the music.

Amaterasu appeared at the far end of the bridge, her mask shining, her movements both hesitant and curious. Uzume continued to dance. Amaterasu crept forward until she entered the stage and openly watched Uzume.

My skin prickled with the returned warmth and brightness, though the temperature had not changed.

The chorus concluded the play. "Amaterasu, drawn forth by curiosity at how the kami could be happy and dance when all was dark, found that joy can bloom even in the soil of grief."

Amaterasu joined the dance. Whereas Uzume's dance had pulled and quickened my heart, such that I wanted to dance beside her, Amaterasu's movements flowed with the sad beauty of suffering. I ached with her as she chose to shine again on a scarred world, bearing the marks of her loss. The world glowed with gold-mended brokenness.

Sheng, our sister should have chosen the other mask. Its line of gold through the cheek and lips would have honored the sun-kami's loss and return. Our mask is but of common faces. My vision blurred, and I blinked away tears. Those common faces glowed more brilliant with each flowing movement of my sister and each ghostly note of the flute. The faces overlapped each other. Each one familiar and forever cut off from me. Including my own. I was no longer Shisei. That life was gone.

Nanai should have chosen the other mask.

The dance ended, and the music disappeared beneath thunderous clapping. One young nobleman, in a dragon-embroidered red silk kimono, rushed to the stage calling out, "Arigatou!" He bowed in the white stones at the base of the stage and held out a mandarin orange, something he had to have bought at a high price from the warmer islands. "Please, Amaterasu," he said, his voice carrying over the applause, "accept my humble offering. You are the sun, and all the world is darkness without you."

Nanai removed her mask. Her smile was proud. "Your offering is summer sweet, but common. Does not the sun-kami deserve something uncommon—a branch from a cliff-clinging pine or snow from the mountain peak?" She reached for the orange. "I will accept your *humble* offering."

Nanai! I leaped to my feet to reprimand her. Though I didn't care for Daichi's boldness, he was still the son of the noble Kazoku. His father funded the theater, dance school, and many other arts.

Takumi caught my arm, "Not now. Let her enjoy her day of glory. She'll learn soon enough that she isn't the sun to the world."

My movement must have caught her attention, for she looked over at me and her smile warmed, melting away the proud frost. She motioned for me to wait.

"We should go," I whispered to Takumi.

"We will if you so desire—but will you find peace if you go without having let go?"

I found my seat and waited.

The nohkan flute cried, weaving through the sea of voices congratulating the actors, a memory of the world that had slipped away with the ending of the performance.

How much memory and hurt would I carry away when I spoke with my sisters again? I'd found my place of safety. Would my sisters try to tempt me away, like the dancing kami? Nanai would, and possibly Nichika. But unlike the sun-kami, I had no light to shed on them. I only brought them sorrow. It would have been better if we'd not come.

The flute's voice trilled, rising in a shrill note over the voices of the crowd, then died away. Nanai descended the stairs into a cluster of five women—my sisters. Where had they sat? Had any of them noticed me yet?

I moved my kitsune mask to cover my face and stood. "We must go."

Takumi shrugged and followed as I pushed my way through the crowd, away from them, deeper among those who didn't know me. Elbows and shoulders met. Quiet murmurs of apology. Then we were beyond the crowd. I quickened my pace.

Paws landed on my shoulders, the mask slipped from my face and clattered to the ground. I spun around. The four-tailed kitsune leaped from shoulder to shoulder through the crowd like leaping stones in a stream, his laughter trailing behind him.

Takumi chuckled beside me. "Was it him?"

"Yes."

He picked up the mask and handed it to me. "If you want to escape, you'd better hurry. They're coming this way."

I shoved the mask over my face, but it was too late to leave now.

"Shisei, you're back." It was Nichika's quiet voice.

Sanaho's voice pushed in. "Nanai and her flare for drama. I knew she was keeping a secret from us for weeks."

The rest of my sisters overlapped their words.

"You've cut your hair."

"Why are you dressed as a boy?"

"Where have you been?"

"What happened?"

"Why did you leave?"

Ichia's voice cut in, "Shi, if it is really you, then look at us."

Shi—death.

I shifted my mask and looked into their faces. "I came to say goodbye."

My throat tightened to see them, familiar but changed. Grief had thinned Ichia's face. A weight bowed Nichika's gentle shoulders. Sanaho, always so confident, stood open-mouthed with surprise. Gomako and Rokue clasped each other's hands and stared at me as though I was a ghost.

Only Nanai laughed. "Goodbye? But you just arrived. Ichia has prepared a feast for this festival day. You must come. And you, master mask-maker," she said, turning to Takumi, "are invited as well."

Ichia seemed to see Takumi for the first time. Her eyebrows rose in a silent question. "Please, forgive our rudeness. I am Ichia, eldest daughter of the potter Asahi, and wife to the potter Yahito. They are both at the imperial court. In their absence, may I offer our most humble hospitality?"

Takumi bowed solemnly, though his bi-colored eyes crinkled in the corners with contained laughter. "I most gratefully accept."

Wait—we are staying? In my shock I found my hands in my sisters' hands and my feet walking the familiar path back to our home.

Ichia stopped at the market square corner and placed two yen in the hand of a blind beggar. I sighed at the familiar action. She always helped the beggars and the injured. Even now with her own loss of child she looked beyond herself to tend to the needs of others.

"Are you well?" Nichika asked, walking at my side.

I swallowed. I thought I'd only have to say goodbye, not speak with them and answer questions. "I am well. I'm apprenticed to the mask-maker."

Rokue gasped. "You're his apprentice? But you can't be. Girls don't—"

"She pretended to be a boy." Takumi laughed. "And I couldn't just let her wander off in the snow. She was nearly frozen when I found her. And a good thing too, or else I'd never have gained my talented apprentice."

Nichika paused on the path. Her brows furrowed. "Who made the mask that Nanai wore?"

"My master painted it."

"But you created it."

I nodded.

Her eyes widened and her mouth dropped into a soft O. "I wondered if the maker of that mask had spied on our family to capture us within its lines. But the maker knew us, grew up with us."

"But," Rokue said, "you really shouldn't be pretending to be a boy, nor apprentice to a man. What will the neighbors think?"

I ducked my head.

Sanaho nudged Rokue. "You think too much of what the neighbors think." Then she turned to me. "I think it's good that you are making masks, and I always thought that rule about apprenticeships was ridiculous."

"Of course you would," Rokue muttered. "If women weren't allowed to study the naginata, you'd have disguised yourself as a boy to learn it."

Sanaho grinned, and a smile tugged at the corner of my mouth. It was good to be with my sisters again, if only for a short time.

"Why didn't you tell us where you were?" Nichika asked.

"Forgive me. I was busy with my apprenticeship and had no time to spare."

Takumi chuckled behind me. "I'll attest to that. I kept her running from task to task so she was like a spring-swollen brook, always tumbling forward—sometimes in the right direction."

We stepped onto the wooden porch that wrapped around our shoji-walled house. Home.

Ichia slipped off her geta sandals and slid the door open. The warm, starchy scent of steamed rice combined with the clean sea scent of raw fish. Floating on these came the scents of sweet green tea, earthy shiitake, rich tempura, and some others that I couldn't tell just by the smell.

Nanai opened her mouth and breathed in through both mouth and nose. "Ichia, this smells better than the feast my sensei's wife made last week. I can almost forgive you for missing most of my performance to make it."

"Nanai!" I reprimanded.

She just laughed.

What had happened to her to make her so rude? She'd always spoken her mind, but now her words cut.

12

Feast welcomes with scents,
eldest sister's offering.
Is there room for me?

We knelt around the low table. As the hostess, Ichia knelt nearest the kitchen entrance, ready to serve us. Takumi, as honored guest, knelt at the far end, in front of a tokonoma of flowers. He'd offered the place to Nanai, as the feast was to celebrate her success, but Ichia firmly insisted. Instead, Nanai knelt to his left and I to his right. I'd been given the third place of honor. My other sisters knelt by age, eldest closest to our end and the youngest next to Ichia.

Ichia had prepared a feast to rival any Mother had ever made: rolled sushi arranged in shapes of flowers, hand-molded sushi topped with thick pieces of raw tuna, grilled scallops darkened with shoyu, golden shrimp crackling with tempura, small bowls of vinegary sea vegetables, and steam wafting above delicate sakura-painted cups.

We pressed our hands together and looked to Ichia. "Itadakimasu."

She nodded and waited until Takumi took his first bite, at

which point we all ate. For long moments I lost myself in the beauty, tastes, textures, scents, and even sounds of the foods—quiet sips, muffled crunches, appreciative sniffs. A contentedness settled in the room and I relaxed into the feast.

When Ichia had cleared the last of the food and we'd savored our tea, she set down her tea bowl and fixed her gaze on Takumi. "Honored guest and master mask-maker, please tell us of our sister and how she came to apprentice to you."

He leaned forward on his knees. "I am Takumi, the maker of masks, not yet master. I needed an apprentice and Sheng, I mean your sister, sought work. When I saw the quality of her kitsune mask and found that her mother had made it, I hoped that the skill of the mother had passed to the child. She has surpassed my hopes. If she continues in her apprenticeship, she will become one of the finest mask-makers in all Nihon."

I glowed with his praise, as untrue as it was. Then his words sank in. *If she continues her apprenticeship.* Why?

"Shisei." Nanai's voice broke through my worried question. "Tell us about mask-making."

I forced a smile. "It starts with seeing a picture in the mind, then sketching it on a slate. I was buying my sketch slate when we first met at the market. I—"

"Nanai, how long ago did you see her?" interrupted Gomako. "You should have told us!"

"Hush," Ichia cautioned. "Let Shi speak while she is here."

I bowed my head at her stern voice and my name. Speak while I was here, because I would not stay long. How could I? Ichia sent me away. And she was right to—though I left too late to protect her baby from my curse.

"What is next?" Nanai pressed. "Or must I ask your master?"

Takumi nodded his head to me. "Carry on, my tensai."

I pushed the regret and sorrow from my throat down to my stomach, where it disagreed with the meal but allowed me to speak. "I saw each of you and Mother in my mind, so I sketched, then molded your faces into clay. Once the clay was fired, I layered glue, crushed shells, and *sekishu-washi* paper in the clay mold. The hardest part is not forming the mask, but breaking the mold. My fingers trembled to break the art that my sensei created, and my heart cracked with each piece I broke away from the mold of your faces."

"Could you not remove the mask without breaking the mold?" Rokue's ethereal face scrunched with confusion.

I shook my head.

Takumi answered for me. "The fine details of the paper mask would be ruined by pulling it from the mold. A bird cannot be born without the egg cracking." He stood. "And as for me, I must excuse myself to stretch my legs. I am made for standing and working, not long conversations on my knees. They will crack if I kneel much longer, and no bird will emerge from that."

Several of my sisters covered their shocked mouths. I held in a laugh. This was the real Takumi.

He turned to Ichia and bowed low with his hands pressed together. "Arigatou gozaimasu. The feast was delicious." And he left.

As soon as the door slid shut behind him, five of my sisters clustered around me, pushing up against my sides and touching my hands. Ichia quietly moved to join them, though she didn't touch me.

"What a strange man," Rokue said, giggling. "What happened to his face and eyes? Is that why he makes masks—to make up for his own face?"

"Rokue—he is my master and a good man. Do not disrespect him."

"I don't think he would care." Nanai leaned her head on my shoulder. "He doesn't seem to keep to politeness, and I like it. What is he like as a master?"

I thought for a moment, trying to put into words all that I'd experienced the last months, and then taking out the parts that they wouldn't understand. "He's an artist. His entire world is perfecting his skill in making masks. He expects me to give my best, and though he is patient with my many mistakes, he makes me retry until I reach a level he is satisfied with."

"What does he do when he's angry?" asked Sanaho.

"He huffs and mutters and creates some of his most frightening demon masks."

Nanai shivered, her head shifting on my shoulder. "I saw some of them when we went to buy the masks. We had no demons in the Amaterasu play, but if we had, it would have given you nightmares. The storm-kami's mask was frightening enough."

"Are you happy there?" Nichika leaned forward.

"Yes." I looked at the closed door and thought of my sensei's home two days' walk away. "I never thought I had any skills. Each of you is so beautiful and good at your talents. I couldn't even live up to the simple tasks of chopping wood and taking care of the garden. But—"

"But you've found your talent," Nichika finished for me. "If I hadn't seen the mask, I'd not have believed anyone could capture our family so beautifully. You truly see what others cannot. You are as Mother named you, our sacred poetry, our bridge between the seen and unseen."

Sacred poetry. Bridge. I can create and not destroy. If Takumi will keep me as an apprentice. Why did he say that earlier?

More of my sisters' questions poured over me, but they slid by my ears, blocked by thick thoughts—Mother, my name, Takumi, my apprenticeship, Ichia, my curse.

"Shisei? Shisei?" Nanai patted my knee. "Are you listening?"

"Forgive me." I stood. "My heart is full and I must think."

Several protested, but Nichika held up a hand. "Go, Shisei. We'll talk tonight."

I slipped out and found Takumi strolling by our koi pond.

"Sensei? What do you mean by *if I continue as your apprentice?*"

He studied me as he studied a partially molded mask, his eyes taking in details that were there and details not yet made. "As your master, I need your full focus. You are divided. Your kami-light snuffed when you saw your sisters. All people have a slight light, like banked coals, but yours is almost gone. I will leave in the morning. When you have found peace with your sisters, then return to me and perfect your skill."

I bowed my head, shame heavy upon my shoulders. "If you take me tomorrow, I'll find that light again. I won't be divided."

He knelt by the koi pond and placed his hand in the water. An orange and white koi knocked its head against his hand, then nibbled at his fingers. "Did you know the koi swim upstream, even jumping waterfalls, to reach their home? If I took a koi from the stream and carried it, it would die. It needs the water and grows stronger because of the fight."

I bowed my head further. He was asking me to be brave, but fear climbed from my stomach and lodged in my throat. "I love my sisters too much to hurt them again."

"If you truly carry a curse against unborn sons, then Ichia won't be hurt again while her husband is gone. Use this time. Find peace with your sisters. Then return quickly. I have much yet to teach you, Shisei."

I placed my hand in the water, and a golden and black koi nibbled my fingers. *I will seek peace with my sisters and forgiveness from Ichia.*

13

____

Old wounds ache beneath
broken soul hidden by skin.
Bring scars to surface.

Takumi stood at the open door with the grey evening dimly outlining him and the cool breeze whispering around him. "Who will come with me to see the moon rise and hunt ghost crabs?"

"Oh," Nanai cried, "we could build a fire and tell stories of kitsune and kami. Sanaho knows the best ghost stories, ones of warriors and treason."

Gomako grabbed a flute from its hooks on the wall. "I'll provide the music and Rokue can dance. Maybe a kitsune will join us."

"I'll carry the wood for the fire," I offered.

Takumi scowled. "Would you leave your eldest sister to clean up after such a feast by herself? No, you stay and help. I'll take the younger ones out from underfoot."

"But I'm older than—" Sanaho started.

Takumi spoke over top. "I want you along to protect us from bandits. I'm a mask maker, not a warrior."

Sanaho grinned and grabbed her naginata from above the door. She stood ready with the staff gripped in one hand and sword-bladed end curving above her head.

I shivered. Takumi was giving me time to speak with Ichia.

Nichika stepped away from the excited cluster. "I'll stay and help Ichia, too."

He nodded and turned from the door with four of my sisters trailing after him. I stood in the opening and watched their forms grow faint in the dusk. A single paper lantern bobbed a glowing circle. Takumi's voice carried indistinct on the wind, followed by their giggles.

I longed to follow, to not face Ichia and ask her forgiveness. But if not now, then when? I had not the strength to ask it in front of all my sisters and let them also know my curse. And if I asked tonight, I could leave with Takumi in the morning.

As their voices died away, I slid the door shut and followed Nichika to the kitchen where Ichia knelt by a knee-high stove, warming a basin of water. Ichia didn't look up as she scrubbed a glazed tea bowl in the water and set it on the sunokoyuka, a slatted floor made with split bamboo. The water dripped off the teacup through the floor to the gravel beneath. Cups, plates, and platters filled most of the rest of the slatted floor.

I dippered water from the kitchen well into a pot and set it to warm on a second stove. Nichika, Ichia, and I worked silently as we scrubbed, dried and put away the dishes of the feast into chests. Instead of words, our conversation was the scrape of a wooden paddle pushing food scraps into the garden bucket, the swish of a cloth on a plate, the clink of stacked pottery, and the slosh of old water dumped.

How long would Takumi keep my other sisters? How much more time could I enjoy the quiet companionship of my two eldest sisters and pretend that no wound stretched between us?

I watched Ichia bend her weight to scrape the remnant

tempura from a pan, her sleeves pushed up to her elbows and a cloth tied across her front to shield her kimono. Even in such a mundane task, she was graceful. She was always the epitome of elegance, perfecting each of the home skills, always saying the right words. And though she'd called me Shi all my life, she'd also helped me learn proper manners and how to serve others. I owed much to her teachings.

Nichika settled to her knees beside me and dried a pot. Her shoulder pressed against mine, and her comfort brought back many memories. She was my first confidant. I told her first when I found a drowned fox kit. And she'd let me cry on her shoulder without shame. She had studied when the rest of us sisters hunted shells along the ocean's edge. While all felt Ichia enter a room, Nichika could slip in without notice, yet when she was gone, I missed her silence. She was safe. I could speak in front of her.

I gathered the sorrow and regret from where it churned in my stomach and carefully brought it upward to form words. The words jumbled in my head and throat. Anger at Ichia found a place amidst the regret. She'd sent me away. If only she'd gone to live in her own home, she'd not have lost her baby.

I bit my lips to keep the words from coming out too soon. No, I could not blame her for protecting our family and hers.

I turned to Ichia and pressed my forehead to the bamboo floor. "My eldest sister, I beg your forgiveness."

Long moments of silence pressed onto me. *Can she forgive me?* The fire popped and crackled. *Do I deserve forgiveness?* The nighttime wind brushed against the paper walls. *My curse has brought four deaths.*

Ichia's quiet words cut into the air. "Will forgiveness bring back my son?"

I kept my head pressed against the floor. "I am filled with sorrow that I did not leave sooner. I should have gone as soon as I knew you were with child. I know I am Shi—death follows me.

First my twin, then Mother and our baby brother, and now your child. I promise that when I leave, I will not let my cursed shadow fall again across your feet. While you are not with child, I want to pay for my hurt against you. I cannot bring him back, but I will make a memorial mask for him."

Nichika's hands took mine and gently pulled me up from my bow. "Shisei, you are not death, you are sacred poetry. How long have you believed this lie? Children die. And you are not the cause." Nichika turned a reproving look on Ichia. "Is this why you shortened Shisei's name to Shi? I wanted to assume you meant fourth. You blame her for your child's death?"

Ichia lowered her gaze until it rested on her clenched hands in her lap. "She's not the same as the rest of us. Even as a small child she felt different. The demon that took Sheng follows her like a shadow. She knows it, I know it. I've tried to ignore it, tried to care for her as I have the rest of our sisters. But I will not put my own children in danger. She is kitsune-mochi to a fox demon."

Kitsune-mochi? The bonding of a fox to a person. Stories told of entire families ostracized for a fox bonding. No one would marry into such a curse. No one would buy land from the family.

Understanding crushed over me, each new thought a wave beating a rock. Ichia was right. She was the only one I'd told about seeing the kitsune. I'd told her when I was little, and that was when she started to call me Shi and treat me coldly, so I never told another. She knew then what I should have guessed.

Sheng, I'm not just a pastime amusement for a trickster field fox, and my death-followed curse isn't separate from his teasing. A fox demon claimed me as his plaything at birth. He's not only made my life miserable with his tricks, he also took you and our younger brother. Is he so jealous of his kitsune-mochi that he can't share me with brothers?

Takumi. My stomach knotted. *The kitsune saved Takumi's life once. Is it because the kitsune wants me to learn the mask-making skill?*

But when I've reached the level the kitsune is satisfied with, what will he do to Takumi then?

The anger that I'd pushed away sparked forward—but not at Ichia. If it weren't for the four-tailed white fox, I'd have brothers and a mother, I'd have my twin Sheng. If it weren't for him, Ichia would love me. If it weren't for him, I could develop my skill of mask making under Takumi. The four-tailed white fox was the reason for my curse, my broken dreams, my torn family, and my exile from those I loved.

It wasn't right. I couldn't sit by and let the fox destroy the rest of my life. My jaw hardened and my brows pushed down. "Ichia, Nichika, now that I know where my curse comes from, I will fight it. I will break the kitsune-mochi bond. I cannot bring back Ichia's son or the others, but no one else will be hurt by me."

Ichia lifted her face and looked into mine. A flicker sparked in her soft, sad eyes. "I'll know when you are free of it. You'll feel different. When that happens, then I will trust you. But if it doesn't happen before my husband returns, then you must keep your promise and never return."

I bowed. "I promise."

Nichika looked between Ichia and me, her eyes wide and her jaw slack, confusion mixing with distress and melding into fear. "If Shisei is truly kitsune-mochi, then our entire family is. They bond themselves to a family and a land; that is why it is so difficult to break the bonding."

Ichia's face blanched, and she fled the room.

I shuddered. It wasn't just me, but my entire family. Even if I left, they'd still suffer. Fear shuddered through my body until the tatami mat rustled beneath me. "What if I can't break the curse?"

Nichika placed her arm around my shoulder. "Shisei, what Ichia said earlier is not true. You are not responsible for those deaths. We will break this curse together. You are my sister—our beloved sister."

Beloved sister. I tried to pull her words in and let them sink deep. They sat on my skin, over older words repeated until I knew them as sure as I knew my sisters' faces. *I am Shi. Death follows me. Sheng should have lived, not me.* I shoved at the old words, digging my fingers under their weight. I'd break the curse and death would follow me no longer.

14

———

Potter's hands form clay,
soft, fluid under fingers.
Fire makes eternal.

I stood on the cliff beside Takumi. The sky lightened as a promise of the sun to come, and a cool salty breeze tugged at my hair.

He swung his woven rice-straw pack over his shoulder. "It's time I head back."

I didn't want him to go. I bowed to hide my traitorous face. "I'll come as quickly as I can."

"Good, because if I don't see you back at your apprenticeship before the first snowfall, I'll come get you."

Snowfall? Did he think it would take a full season to mend the relationships with my sisters? Would it take a full season to break the kitsune bonding? I trembled and looked up. "Sensei?"

He met my gaze, his eyes studying mine.

Could I tell him of the kitsune-mochi bond that I planned to break and plead with him to stay? He would. He valued my skill and would try to protect me. But if he did, the kitsune could hurt him. No, I had to make it seem as if nothing more

90

was wrong than my need to glue together the breaks with my sisters. I took a slow breath. "I will seek peace with my sisters."

His brow furrowed, and his lips parted as if in question.

I pushed down his conical straw hat, so it covered his bi-colored eyes. "Go. I'll find peace with my sisters quicker with you gone. Besides, Ōkami must miss you, and I need a break from his nightmare-inducing bulk."

He laughed behind the hat. "You were so serious, I thought you were going to reveal another deep secret. I'll go, and I'll give Ōkami an extra good scratching behind the ears for you."

My throat tightened. "Thank you for teaching me."

"I'm not done teaching you. You are far from a master." He reset his hat and placed a hand on my shoulder. "Until kilned, you can still change the form of the clay. Your relationship with your sisters is not kilned." He turned up the path that would take him into the forest and then northwestward.

Ichia looked up as I slid the door open, her face carefully blank of anger or fear. Only sorrow creased her eyes. She knelt at the table spread with a breakfast of steamed rice, summer peas, tofu, and tea around which my other sisters sleepily ate. Ichia's food lay untouched.

"Welcome, sister." She motioned to an empty place between Nichika and Rokue. Ichia wasn't calling me Shi, but neither was she using my name. *Will she finally forgive me if I break the curse?*

Nichika poured me tea and spoke softly. "I will visit my tutor today and seek further knowledge on what we discussed last night. I would invite you to come with me, but my sensei is protective of her knowledge. All our other sisters, except Ichia, have their own studies and will be gone from the house."

My throat tightened at the prospect of spending the day with Ichia, especially now.

"Where is the mask-maker?" Rokue asked.

"He left this morning. He's given me time to spend with my sisters before I return to my apprenticeship."

Nanai clapped her hands. "This is wonderful! You can come with me to the theater and see us practice and study the years of masks from other performances. You'll like that."

"You can't keep her all to yourself," protested Rokue. "She's my sister too."

Nichika took my hand under the table. "Shisei is sister to all of us and we all get to spend time with her." She turned to me. "Will you spend the morning with Nanai and afternoon with Rokue?"

"What about—"

"We'll work on that together this evening."

I wanted to protest, but Nichika was our scholar, and I needed her knowledge and wisdom to unravel the kitsune-mochi binding. I could spend the day with my sisters—the ones who didn't know my curse and were not afraid of me. "Yes, if their masters will allow, I will happily follow them."

"Tomorrow you'll come with me." Sanaho lifted her chopstick and flourished it in the air. "I'll refresh your skills in the naginata."

I groaned. I didn't want those skills refreshed, especially at her hands.

"And me," Gomako said. "You'll enjoy listening to the flute much better than watching women thrust sword-bladed spears at each other."

Nichika squeezed my hand. "Ichia and I will get her in the evenings."

Arigatou, I mouthed, my voice not working. *Arigatou.*

Nanai skipped along the path, her straw summer sandals sending up little puffs of dust. "I don't understand why you're still dressed as a boy. You are my sister."

I studied the ground. "I don't want my master slandered by having a girl apprentice. The theater director must continue to think I'm a boy. And so must everyone else."

"If you want it so. Though sometime people will realize you are my sister, even though you're a reclusive shrew-mole."

"Shrew-mole?" I scowled at her, though a smile tugged at my mouth.

"Yes, shrew-mole. You avoided the shopping. You always hid your face at the village celebrations. You—"

"I didn't always hide. I delivered Father's pottery."

She shrugged. "Fine. I'll introduce you as my cousin. I can't wait to show you the Namazu mask. His long catfish whiskers are just like—" She stopped skipping, her jaw hardening as she looked down the path.

A young man approached, carrying a basket. He wore a red dragon-embroidered kimono. As he drew closer, I recognized him. It was Daichi—the nobleman who praised Nanai at her performance. His father, the Kazoku, funded the theater, the dance school, and many other arts, making our village a place where thousands flocked to each festival. Yet the rest of the year we remained a quiet village because he owned most of the land and didn't want it ruined by crowded streets. I appreciated what the Kazoku did with our village, but not what his son had become—a lover as changeable as the ocean, moving from one woman to the next with beautiful poetry and broken promises.

Daichi held out the basket with barely a glance at me. Mandarin oranges nestled on top of each other. Despite my aversion for him, my mouth watered—we only had oranges once a year and had had none since Mother died. He bowed. "Oh, kami of the sun and sky, please accept my humble offering."

Nanai lifted her chin. "Daichi, give your fruit to those who've given you their bloom."

He stood from his bow, his lips thinned, then he spun away. The dust billowed under his feet as he stomped off.

I swallowed. "Nanai, was it wise to speak so proudly?"

She sighed dramatically. "I know. He's the Kazoku's son. I shouldn't offend him. But because he's the Kazoku's son and because he has power, money, and manners, he thinks he can get whatever he wants."

"Has he hurt you?"

Nanai dropped her gaze to the ground. "Not me. He ruined my best friend in our acting troupe. He got her with child. Her father drove her out when he discovered it. But Daichi, who had once showered her with gifts and promised her lifelong happiness, only handed her a bag of yen and murmured a hollow apology that his father forbade their further association. So she became a shrine maiden. She isn't the first."

I hadn't heard of Daichi fathering children. "Are you safe? Has he tried to..."

"He has too much honor to force me," Nanai said with a bitter smile, "but he also speaks the sweetest words and is richly hand-some. I know what will happen if I give in just a little, I'll fall for him, just like all the other fools did, and then his honor will disappear. He'll realize he doesn't love me enough to go against his father's wishes." She huffed. "I just want him to leave me alone. If I insult him enough, he'll lose interest. It's better than what Sanaho suggested."

I raised my eyebrows. "What did Sanaho suggest?"

Nanai laughed, her face clearing. "You'll have to ask her." She returned to her skipping. "We start learning short skits today. I hope we do the *Luck Cat* or the *Tanuki who Makes Himself into a Drum*."

I walked behind her. *Sheng, I wish you were here to protect Nanai.*

We arrived at the open yard behind the stage where all the other actors gathered in groups of three or four, their quiet conversations mingling with expressive hand motions.

"Sensei," Nanai called, "my cousin Sheng, the mask maker's apprentice, would like to see our other masks."

The tall man who'd visited us a few weeks before looked at the two of us. His narrow face pinched. "Cousin?" Then he laughed. "Cousin, indeed. I see the family resemblance." He bowed to me. "Welcome. Your master makes fine masks, and I hope you will follow in his skill." He pointed to the room that stood at the end of the stage bridge. "The masks are in there. Come Nanai, you are late."

I slid the door partly open and hundreds of shadowed faces stared from the dim room. None glowed. I'd lost the ability to see that when I spoke with all my sisters. But the room was thick with unseen spirits. I brushed my fingers through the air, half-expecting to touch a mist.

Nothing. I pushed the door the rest of the way open and stepped in. Moth repellent camphor stung my nose. The sunlight reflected off the pale wood floor, brightening the room.

Masks covered the wood-gridded walls in uneven rows, a large red demon mask nestled next to four smaller masks of monkey, dog, kitsune, and tanuki. A samurai glowered above a white powdered lady. Lion-dog, water spirit, old priest, farmer, catfish with long whiskers—each mask stared. Takumi's work stood out as the best of them, save for a few older ones. On my right, at shoulder level, a carved tiger mask snarled. His nose wrinkled and his teeth overlapped the edges of his hungry grin. Red covered his skin while carved golden stripes curved along his jaw and over his eyes. Each line vibrated with frozen movement.

Who made him? I reached out to lift the mask from the wall and see if the maker had left his mark on the inside. Before my fingers could brush the wood, something soft but strong pushed against my legs. I stumbled back. But nothing stood in the room other than the masks and me.

Was the trickster fox here? If he was, would he listen to my plea that he release our family? I would have to be polite. I gritted my teeth against the words I wanted to say and spoke the ones that felt false. "Honored kitsune?"

Nothing.

The voice of the theater director carried through the open door. "You must act with shizen—without pretense. The audience must forget you are acting but be pulled into your world as if it is the natural world. They must feel the dirt itching at the farmer's neck and rough woven cloth sticking to his sweating back. You cannot do this if..."

White flashed at the corner of my vision. I spun to face the open door. The white darted away into a dark corner opposite the tiger mask, then disappeared near an old kitsune mask, its faded paint merging with the wall behind.

I blew out a breath. I'd speak with him the next time.

I knelt. It was simple and small. A child's mask. Wobbly lines defined the eyes and a blot of black marked a nose. I took it from its hook and turned it over. Two large simple characters, ink blotted and shaky, marked the inside cheek. *Watashi*. The child who'd painted the mask had only identified himself as *me*.

Why is this child's mask hanging with the others?

I carried it out and watched Nanai and the others practice until the director noticed me. He motioned for them to carry on and came to stand beside me. He glanced at the mask and raised his eyebrows.

"Master director, why does this mask hang with the others?"

He took it from my hands and turned it over so the fox face gazed at us. "It will sound foolish to your ears, but I will still tell you. Years ago, when our village became large enough to build a theater, we commissioned a mask maker to create the masks for the first performance. He came to live in our village with his little girl. Day after day he created masks, while his daughter ran, trailing laughter and mischief through the construction of the theater—a wooden beam painted with flowers; planed wood stacked in a cave-like bundle and her voice making up stories within."

The director traced his finger over the kitsune's perfectly shaped face, a sharp contrast to the childish painting. "The builders called her their trickster field fox, come to hinder their work, but they laughed as they sanded the paint from the beam and restacked the flooring, then offered her treats."

"Why?" My brows furrowed. If I'd done any of those things, I'd have been lectured or even struck across the hand with a bamboo shoot.

He shook his head. "This was long before my time. But they say she scattered joy like sunlight, and none could stay angry with her. Then one day as she ran over the nearly finished stage, she tripped and cut her leg on a saw. The doctor cleaned and sewed up the wound, but it took infection. She grew feverish and weaker each day. Finally, the mask maker gathered her in his arms. 'I will take her to Sukunahikona's shrine. If she heals, we both will return. Keep the masks I've made to pay for my breaking of our contract. Take this one too, to remember.' He handed a mask he'd made, but she'd painted. The people of our village never saw him or the child again."

The director's gaze pulled back from the far-off look, and he half smiled. "The theater prospered, and each theater director instructed the new one to always keep the child's mask and always remember the story. I honor the promise of the first theater director." He handed me the child's fox mask. "Though it is time we commissioned a new mask maker to live in our village. I've asked your master, but he refuses to move. Ah, like many artists, he is stubborn. But his art is worth the travel." He glanced shrewdly at me. "When you have completed your apprenticeship, if you've gained his skill, come be our mask maker."

He wanted me to be the theater's mask maker. My head spun. If—no, when I'd broken the kitsune-bonding, I had a future as an artisan, and I'd be with my sisters. Ichia would accept and love me then.

I bowed my thanks to the theater director and returned to the mask room. Could I force the fox to return? Could I catch him this time? He'd pushed me away from the tiger mask before. I reached out my hand and laid a finger on one curving, golden strip. A shock of fear rushed up my arm. I jerked my hand away and stumbled backwards. My arm tingled.

A four-tailed white fox crossed in front of me and sauntered toward the wall.

"Wait! You must break the bond with my family!"

He glanced over his shoulder and sniffed.

"Please, honored kitsune, I beg you to remove the bond."

He disappeared through the wall.

The room dimmed with the loss of his white light. *Sheng, how am I supposed to talk with him if he won't listen?*

"Shisei," Nanai called. "You've studied the masks long enough. Come join us in the next skit. I need a partner."

I stepped onto the porch. The actors had paired off. Nanai motioned me over by her. "Just read your part—you are the father and I am the foolish son."

I glanced at the script. "I think we should reverse our roles."

"You just want the more interesting part."

"No, I'm more foolish."

Nanai laughed. "Just read your part."

"Very well."

"That's not part of it," she said.

I stared at the script and read, "Which is farther, the emperor's palace or the sun?"

Nanai let her face fall into comical idiocy. "The emperor's palace. I can see the sun. But I can't see the palace even if I climb the mountain."

Did the things I didn't see seem farther? What if they were close by?

"Shisei," Nanai whispered, "your part."

"E-Eto," I stuttered, then read, "it is true. I can see the sun, but not the spirit world."

Nanai stifled a laugh. "Palace."

"Palace." My face heated.

The theater director laughed from the side. "I appreciate the improvisation, and I shall ponder the question. Which is further: the sun or the spirit world?" He clapped his hands together twice and all the skits stopped. "It is time to practice the different basic characters from trickster to pious to proud. I will assign each of you a role you have not performed before."

I settled on the ground at the edge of the open yard.

The director called a name. "You are the frightened child shivering in a thunderstorm."

A tall man stepped to the middle of the hard-packed ground. His square face and broad shoulders spoke of enough strength to cause the thunder, not cower from it. He crouched on the ground, wrapping his arms around opposite shoulders. His face crumpled, his brows drawing down at the outer corners of his eyes and pinching over his nose. His lower lip quivered and his mouth opened slightly. A quiet wail extended and grew into a windhowling cry. As he shivered and howled, a transparent image of a boy child, his round cheeks wet with tears, took shape over the man's face. It was like when I saw my sisters' faces and formed the mask.

The next actor was a girl even younger than Nanai. She took on the role of a sharp-tongued widow. Another mask image formed of a pinch-lipped, wrinkle-lined, white-haired woman.

My fingers moved as if forming clay but met only empty air.

When I break the curse with the kitsune, I will make many masks. All that I can see. Soon.

~

Nanai and I knelt on the porch at the back of the stage and ate a bento lunch of nori-wrapped rice balls, pickled daikon, and rolled slices of thinly-cooked egg.

Nanai set down her chopsticks and giggled. "Can you believe the tengu took the polite twin's hump and gave it to the rude twin? Wasn't it funny when the rude twin sputtered and protested? Oh, I don't know which I like better, the grand stories of the kami or the silly stories of the people. Which performances do you like best?"

"The ones you are in."

"Arigatou." She grinned as she bowed her head. "But truly, which do you like best?"

"Forgive me, Nanai, I am tired and can't think well enough to decide."

It was true. I couldn't sleep the night before. And that morning, after I'd met the kitsune again, I'd formed many masks in my mind. After imagining the twentieth mask, my thoughts pulled through my head like a cart through mud.

"Shi-Sheng." Rokue ran down the path with light, dancing steps and settled next to us. "Did you enjoy your morning with Nanai?"

I nodded and tried to smile, but a yawn interrupted.

She glanced at Nanai; her face a wrinkled question.

Nanai threw up her hands. "Sheng stayed up late last night and now is ready to fall asleep as we talk."

Rokue's face wilted. "Are you not coming with me this afternoon?"

I forced a smile past the yawn. "I'll come. I promised. And I desire to see how you've improved in your dance."

Rokue led me down the path to a large paper-walled building. Laughter twittered from the open doors. We entered and Rokue pointed to a tatami mat along one wall. "You can watch from there." She skipped over to join the other dancers in orange kimonos with red sashes.

A white-haired woman stood from her mat, and the room fell silent. She nodded to the drummers. A lively beat echoed through the room as dancers boxed their lunches, set the bundles along the walls, and formed into three lines.

Without words, she led them through fluttering steps of the sparrow dance, their fans creating the wings. Their blue and orange fans became sweeps of color. The tumbling beat of the drums merged into the beating of wings.

And the white fox stood before me.

Sheng, if I flatter him, will he listen? He's no zenko, but isn't that an honor that kitsune seek? Maybe. "Honored Zenko." I bowed with my hands pressed together.

He twitched his nose and turned to walk into the midst of the dancers. None noticed him as he passed through their dancing legs. He looked back at me.

I stood.

My body remained kneeling on the mat, my body's eyes closed and my head bent forward as if in sleep. How? Was he taking me into the spirit world? I shivered to see myself and not be in myself. But he was here. If I followed into the spirit world, would he listen when I asked him to break the curse? This was my chance. I had to go.

I turned my eyes from the kneeling figure, gulped three times at the fear that seared my throat, and followed.

He led me through the dancers, their movements passing through me like a warm breeze through my core.

Rokue stepped in front of me, her walnut-brown eyes lit with joy in the motion, the rest of her face a graceful calm.

The white fox waited by the wall, his head tilted.

I stepped around Rokue and followed the fox through the wall.

A smooth river of wind lifted me into the air. I screamed and crouched in a ball as the ground fell away. The kitsune floated on the air ahead of me, and his body shook with laughter. What new trick was this? Where was he taking me? "Please, put me down."

We sailed over the village and into the forest, and, after a time of many held breaths, descended by a small red-and-white building with a green tile roof. It was too small for a person, only coming up to my waist. It was a shrine to the sun-kami, Amaterasu. Ichia knelt in front of it.

I huddled on the ground, digging my spirit toes into the firm soil.

"Please," Ichia whispered in prayer, "free us from the kitsune-mochi." Insects settled in the folds of her kimono and on her hair, and crawled across her face, but she didn't brush them away but continued to pray.

The white fox walked around her, brushing his tails against her and sending the bugs flying. At his touch, her tight shoulders relaxed slightly, and her fisted hands softened in her lap.

Why was he comforting her? Had he a twisted, possessive love for the women in our family as well as a delight in tormenting us?

"Zenko." It came out too strong. I tried again. "Honored zenko. Please, if you truly love our family, then release us from the kitsune-mochi bond and leave us."

He nodded his head in a slow bow, then walked away.

Did he break the bond?

No river of air lifted me to take me back to the village.

Is our family free?

I walked through the woods. Ribbons of tree-filtered light

brushed against my skin. My steps glided over the pine-needled ground. The forest ended in our village and I skipped between villagers washing clothes and weeding gardens. None could see me as I danced with clumsy joy. *Sheng, our family is free. It was as simple as asking with respect.*

The home of the dance master vibrated with the dancers inside. I slipped through the wall, found my still kneeling form and touched my hand. The world shifted from seeing myself to seeing the dancers in the afternoon light from slow-blinking eyes. My body ached as if I'd walked a day and a night without stopping, but we were free.

The dance continued, as if nothing else in the world mattered.

15

Grey emptiness whips
memories across my face,
stinging with harsh truth.

I stumbled through dinner and the after-dinner chatter, glad to let my sisters carry the conversation. Exhaustion hung from my limbs like a wet kimono even as excitement ran through me.

Nichika watched me carefully but said nothing about my silence. Finally, when all our sisters were asleep, we sat down to the books behind the screen.

"Nichika," I said, my voice carrying. I bit my tongue and whispered, "I think I've broken the kitsune-mochi."

"How?" She leaned forward.

"The white four-tailed fox came, and I asked him to break the bond. He nodded and left."

Nichika's eager face fell. "Maybe."

I fell with her.

"He may have broken the bonding with our family. And I hope he has. But I learned much from my sensei today. Kitsune-mochi bonds are difficult to break. The only successful breaking has been through a ritual cleansing at one of Inari's shrines."

"What kind of ritual?"

She looked down at a page covered in her writing. "There are many methods. The least dangerous is being licked by hunting hounds."

"Licked by hunting hounds?" I trembled. Takumi's dog was the only dog I'd ever grown comfortable enough to touch. But if that was what it required— "We'll go tomorrow."

She shook her head. "My sensei said it is best to do when the moon is full, a time of change and enlightenment. That is in two days. Spend tomorrow with Sanaho and Gomako."

"May I spend the time just with Gomako?"

She laughed. "Sanaho's lessons are painful. But she is right. You live away from home and should be able to protect yourself."

The night breeze from an open panel tugged a lock of my short hair loose. I brushed it back. "I'm sorry I left without telling you where I went. I—" I stumbled to silence.

"You were trying to protect our family. I understand that now. Though I am grateful you came back and that we can break the curse on our family together. I will miss you when you return to your apprenticeship."

"I'll visit when I can. But..." I paused, uncertain if it was right to speak, but then Nichika was safe to say this to. "I am happy there."

She nodded. "I can see that. I've never seen you as alive as when you sat next to your master at Nanai's performance."

"You knew I was there?"

"I saw you when you walked into the village."

"Why didn't you come to me?"

"You didn't seem to want to be known, and I felt I should wait for you to reveal yourself if you chose."

"Thank you, Nichika."

She put an arm around my shoulders and pulled me close. "I

am happy for you in your new talents and apprenticeship. Though I hope you can be happy here too."

Maybe I could be. When the fox no longer endangered my family.

~

Sanaho woke me from a dreamless sleep. The room was still dark. "Come on, Shisei. I'll give you a few lessons with the naginata before I must meet with my sensei."

I groaned and turned over, exhaustion from the day before nested in my shoulders and forehead. I'd been on the receiving end of her lessons before. Her natural ability made her quick and sure in her movements. And I, being her first younger sister and one who did the brother's chores, was whom she'd tested all her newly learned skills on. "I'll come after breakfast—" Maybe.

Sanaho grabbed my shoulders and pulled me to sit. "If you are going to be apprenticed to a mask maker who doesn't know one end of a naginata from the other, then you have to learn to defend yourself and him. You should have seen him on the beach. I tried to teach him a few simple forms, and he nearly stabbed himself."

"He broke his fingers two weeks ago. He only took off the bracing the day before Nanai's performance. He shouldn't even have tried holding the naginata."

"Ah, so that is why he favored his right hand. Even so, you already know the basic forms, and you are fair enough in your skill, or were before you left."

I groaned again, but her words slipped under my grumbles. *Who knows what I'll face in the coming years, and Takumi's dog can only protect us so much.*

I slipped on a kimono and added the leather shielding apron that Sanaho handed me. She stepped around our sleeping sisters and lifted two practice naginatas from the wall before handing one to me. Instead of a sharp blade curving at the end, each was solid oak, hardened and dangerous even without the cutting edge. The curved edge could still hook me. And any part would leave bruises.

We slipped outside into the cool pre-dawn.

A shadow stood from the porch.

I stumbled back while Sanaho lowered her naginata and took a firm stance.

The shadow held up his hands. "Don't strike. I have a gift for your youngest sister, the beautiful ocean-eyed Nanai."

Sanaho stepped forward, gripping her naginata, her eyes squinting. "Oh, it's you, Daichi. She doesn't want to see you. Let her be."

He held out a folded bundle. "Give her this silk kimono. It will match her eyes."

Sanaho lifted the fabric with her naginata. It unfolded around the oak tip, flowing down and shimmering in the grey pre-dawn. She tipped the naginata so the kimono fell back into Daichi's arms. "She won't take it. Go home."

He clutched the silk to his chest and glanced at the closed door. "I'll return. Tell her I will always return." He trudged into the grey early morning. When he'd disappeared, Sanaho led me to a flat open place before the house.

"Sanaho? Is he here every day?" I stood with my naginata, the tip tilted down to the ground.

She stepped across from me, putting more than a naginata's length between us. "Of late, yes. He'll grow bored and find someone else to bother." She bowed to signal the start of the spar.

I bowed back. "Will she be safe?" Nanai had said he wouldn't force her, but this daily persistence was unnerving. Again, I wished Sheng were here to protect her.

Sanaho snorted. "He knows I'd gut him if he hurts her, no matter who his father is. Now focus. We only have a few hours.

And I'll not let you get hurt by someone just because you are away from my protection and don't know how to protect yourself." She raised her naginata and lunged.

I raised mine just in time to sweep away her strike. She danced back on light feet, then forward again, striking the curved end of her weapon against mine. The rapid clack of oak on oak rang out as I blocked her quick strikes. Then she swung the naginata up and swished it down on my shoulder.

Pain burst under the blow and spread down my arm. "Oi!" She'd lightened the blow, but I'd bear a bruise there. She circled me and flipped the staff so she stood with the naginata to her left instead of her right. The motion was fluid, but it gave me enough time to tighten my grip. I met her next strike and locked the curved end with hers. She strained against me, but I'd been chopping wood and hauling clay. I held.

She slipped hers from the lock and tapped my bare foot. I returned with a blow to her hip.

"Oi, that was good." The sky had lightened enough for me to see her grim smile. "But you should have followed with another blow. Never back away when you have the advantage."

We sparred until sweat slickened my hands and the early sun burned away any morning chill. My body was a mass of aches, and by night my skin would be multi-colored. Though Sanaho would bear her own marks.

"Sanaho, Shisei. It is time to eat." Nanai stood on the porch.

A movement flashed, and I turned in time to semi-stop another blow from Sanaho. It slid along my naginata and scraped my fingers. "I wasn't ready."

"You must always be ready."

I twisted around and cracked the side of my naginata into her ribs. Her "Oof" was satisfying—for a moment. The blunt end of her staff drove into my stomach, the leather apron only partly absorbing it. I fell, gasping for breath.

"You opened your weakest point to attack. Always guard your core." Sanaho's words came broken between wincing breaths. She grasped my hand and pulled me to my feet. "But you'd do well enough against the common criminal."

She bowed to me and I bowed back, gritting my teeth against the movement over my bruised middle. The fight was over. She wouldn't attack again.

Nanai came to my side. "Shisei, what did Sanaho say to get you to spar with her? You said you'd never do it again."

I leaned on Nanai and limped to the porch. "She said I'd better learn to defend myself because my sensei couldn't."

Nanai laughed.

I didn't join in. *If I'm enough to fight a common criminal, am I good enough to fight a curse? What if the hounds and other methods don't work?*

Sanaho left for her naginata lessons and I stretched back on my sleep mat. Weariness deafened me to my other sisters' departures. Shadows walked at the edge of my sleep, fleeing whenever I focused on them—a fox, a tiger, a little girl running over a stage, a brother, then darkness. A melody wove, gentle and multi-voiced as a breeze through the forest pines, pulling me upward.

A high note hung in the air and died away, leaving the soft rustle of leaves. I opened my eyes. Gomako knelt by the open door, a nohkan flute pressed below her lips, her fingers dancing over the bamboo tube.

"Gomako, why are you not at your lessons?"

She set the flute in her lap. "I sparred with Sanaho once, and I didn't want to move from my sleep mat for several days. You are stronger than I, but I assumed you wouldn't want to walk to my sensei's home. So I'm staying here and spending the day with you."

"Gomako, you dishonor your sensei by not attending your lessons."

Her voice dropped to a whisper, and her lip quivered, "I gained permission. But if you don't want me, I'll go."

Why had I said those words? Gomako was quick to learn and quicker to wilt under rebuke.

"Forgive me." I rolled to my knees. "I want to spend the day with you, and your music is beautiful. Will you play more?"

Her shoulders came up a little. "My sensei said I'd understand the nohkan flute better if I taught someone else."

"You want to teach me?"

She nodded.

"I have no talent—"

"You made the mask."

"No talent with music."

Her shoulders stooped again.

I held out my hand. "I'll try."

She smiled as she came to kneel next to me. "I've only been learning nohkan a week, so I won't teach you anything difficult. It is easier than the koto or the shamisen." She handed the flute to me. "Hold it sideways and blow across the mouth hole, not into it."

I pressed it to my lower lip and blew. All that sounded was my breath.

"Place it below your lip and blow across so your breath skims the hole."

I tried again and again, adjusting the flute, the direction and strength of my breath. And each time I created a breathy sound and no notes.

"May I show you?" She reached for the flute, which I gladly handed back. "Like this." She placed the flute just below her lower lip and reached her upper lip slightly over the lower. Then she blew a note as haunting as a winter wind, rising and falling. She handed the nohkan back. "Try again."

I wanted to refuse, but Takumi's words with the masks echoed. I'd told him I had no talent, yet he kept teaching me until I learned. I could honor Gomako enough to try again. At least until I could create a note. I placed the flute and blew. Again, again, and again.

Gomako knelt, listening. Did she cringe inside with each breathy attempt?

I set the flute down, my head light and the room slightly tilting. "I can't."

She laid it back in my hands. "One more time, then we'll eat the midday meal and I'll play for you this afternoon."

I glanced around our home. All the sleep mats and quilts were folded except for mine. A wrapped bento sat on the low table. We were the only two in the room. "Where is Ichia?"

"She went to visit the Amaterasu shrine. She'll be back this afternoon." Gomako tilted her head and added in a quieter voice, "She's not been the same since she lost her baby. I hope she will heal in mind before her husband returns."

A chill ran along my arms. *Forgive me, Ichia. I will break the curse. I have to.* I lifted the nohkan flute and blew my fear and grief through pinched lips. A single high note sounded. A broken cry.

"You've found it," Gomako whispered. "Try moving your fingers to different holes."

I blew and shifted my fingers. The flute cried, jagged partial notes dipping down low and rising high. A part of me moved with them. Each one was a war cry from my soul. The notes wavered, my breath spent.

Gomako took the flute. "I would that my sensei could have heard you."

"He'd have covered his ears in pain."

She shook her head solemnly. "No. I only know how to imitate what another has made, but you have created."

She said no more as we ate. Then she took the flute and played.

I closed my eyes and let the music wash over me, dancing through the air like a dragon, weaving, dipping, flying high again, twining within its own secondary notes.

The dragon took form in the darkness of my closed eyes. He carved patterns in the sky, then shifted. The kitsune landed by my knees.

"No," I whispered, my voice muted under the sound of the flute. "You weren't to come back. You agreed to go away."

He tilted his head.

Frustration bloomed into anger. "Take me to the place that binds me. If you won't break the bond, then I will."

He met my gaze, his eyes bright. He nodded, turned and walked through the walls of my home.

I followed.

Emptiness swallowed the ground, the trees, the sky. Only roiling grey remained—damp, silent, and gritty—shifting like ocean-sucked sand beneath my feet, buffeting my face, tearing at my hair and kimono.

"Kitsune!" My voice sounded inside my head, vibrating in my mouth, but fell silent as it pushed between my lips. The grey swallowed it. "Kitsune!" I stumbled forward. Where had he taken me?

A stink pushed its way back to me. Rotten fish, bloated seagull. The stink grew. I gagged as a scent from childhood overpowered the others. A memory hid in the empty grey. *Walking the beach after a storm. A fisherman's body broken on the sand. Death. Shi.*

I covered my nose and mouth and crouched, trembling. "Stop!" I screamed, and it whipped away on the silent wind, never adding a sound. "Please, take me back. Or take me into the spirit world.

But do not leave me here in the nothingness surrounded by—" I gagged again. I couldn't speak the word. It followed me. "Please," I whimpered, "don't leave me here."

"You demanded to come here." The voice came from within me, penetrating the silence, but it was not my own. It was resonant, mocking, and male.

"I d-didn't mean to," I stuttered.

"Oh, so now you can hear me?"

"Who are you?"

"I am your family's guardian."

It was the trickster kitsune. Anger at his mockery rose inside me. The wind grew hotter and whipped my hair against my face. "You are no benevolent zenko!"

"I'm not?" His voice shook with laughter.

"You took my twin, my little brother, my mother, and my nephew!" Each screamed word fell silent as it left my mouth, swallowed up in the stinking grey.

"Why would I do that?"

Oh, he was a trickster fox, every word a riddle.

"You wish to be free of a curse?" His voice took on an almost serious tone.

I lifted my head. The wind peeled my eyelids open, stinging my eyes, and still I could only see grey nothingness. What would be the cost? A lifetime of servitude to him? It didn't matter, if he'd break the bond with my family. "Yes! I'll do anything."

"First, stop thinking death follows you."

"Death does!" The winds whipped to a torrential strength. Death surrounded me, sucking at me with its silent decay, filling me with its stink. Soon it would tear me apart.

The fox huffed. *"You can hear me, but are you ready to listen? No, not today. When you are ready to let go, call for me with the flute. We will revisit this place and then I will tell you."*

"Shisei," a girl's voice called from far off through the silent, grey wind. "Shisei."

"You will leave now."

The grey solidified and pushed me backwards. "Wait! Tell me how to break the curse!" Grey wind turned into waves of grey water. Pushing me back, back, under, under. The scents of decay disappeared into brine. And grey turned black.

"Shi."

I gasped and heaved my body against the black.

Two hands pressed against my flailing. "Stop it. Lie still." It was Ichia's voice.

I sucked in more air. It was clean—free of brine, grit, and death.

"What happened?" Ichia's voice carried distantly.

I sank back towards blackness. No, I couldn't. I had to pull free. I struggled again, but hands held me firm.

"She fell asleep and I couldn't wake her." Gomako's voice trembled. "Should I send for the doctor?"

"No. Get our sisters."

Blackness closed over me.

"Shisei, come back to us." A cool cloth pressed to my forehead.

"Nichika?" My voice came out a rasp. I blinked, and even that motion ached.

"Thank the kami," she whispered. Her face hovered over mine, a blurred brightness backed by haze. Other indistinct faces pressed in around hers.

I blinked again, and they took shape into my sisters; all six of them. They stared at me with a mixture of concern and fear. "I'm sorry," I rasped.

"Just rest." Nichika smoothed my hair away from my face.

"But the kitsune came again. There is a way to break the curse. I have to return."

"Kitsune? Curse?" Four of my sisters' voices overlapped. Only Nichika and Ichia seemed unsurprised, though Ichia's brows deepened into creases and Nichika's mouth parted with unsaid words.

"Are we cursed?" Gomako's face paled.

I swallowed to moisten my throat. "Yes." I shuddered as I remembered the tearing emptiness.

Ichia leaned closer. "How will you break it?" Her voice was small, pleading like a child and not an oldest daughter and leader of seven sisters.

I closed my eyes against her intensity. "I don't know."

"You said there is a way!"

"Ichia, let her rest," Nichika's soft voice said. "We'll talk in the morning."

"No!" I opened my eyes again and met Ichia's pleading, demanding gaze. "We'll talk about it now. I need to return." I shuddered again. Would I again follow the kitsune into that place? What would the kitsune demand to break the curse? But if I didn't return, what would I do? Let the curse destroy everything I held dear?

My sisters waited in silence. And the silence deepened as I haltingly told of the kitsune who'd followed me since my first memories, his jealousy causing the deaths of the boys in our family; the grey void and the hope that I could break the kitsune bond if I returned.

Laughter broke the silence. Sanaho laughed again, her mouth widening in loud disbelief. "Did you drink spoiled rice wine?"

Gomako looked between me and Sanaho. "So, there is no curse?"

"Shisei is drunk," Sanaho said. "Or I struck her too hard when we sparred this morning. Let her rest. The only things we have to fear are in this world, and I'll protect our family from those."

"Enough, Sanaho," Nichika warned.

Sanaho's mouth twisted as she grabbed her naginata from the wall and strode outside. Evening air rushed in, filling her place.

The room darkened as the door slid shut. Sanaho had never believed in the kami, but I'd hoped she'd believe me. I'd never lied to her.

My three younger sisters clung together. Finally Nanai spoke, "Even if we are bonded to a fox, what can we do about it? I wouldn't go into a place of silent wind and stinking death. Shisei shouldn't either. Or do you think she'll come back?"

My throat tightened at her words. The fox had said, *when I was ready to let go.* Let go of what? My freedom? My place in the mortal world? What if the fox made me stay in the grey world in payment for removing the kitsune-mochi bond from the rest of our family?

Memories of the stench-filled grey pushed against me. Death dwelt there. Hidden, indistinct, silent as a beatless heart and suffocating as a tsunami. I gasped for air.

Nichika laid her cool hand on my brow. "Shisei. The fox is tricking you. Don't return. We'll drive the fox-spirit away through the ways we've already discussed."

My constricted breathing eased. I didn't have to return. We could break the curse without going back there. I caught hold of that hope and let my mind fall into a dark and heavy sleep.

16

───────

Pine clings to cliffside,
shaped by wind, twisted by storm,
gift for sun-kami.

Men's voices slapped me from my slumber. The room was filled with the muted light of early morning.

"Be careful with his head."

A low moan issued.

Another voice answered, "Not much further. We're almost to the potter's house."

Heavy steps stamped onto the deck.

Ichia stood at the door, and Sanaho stood beside her, gripping the naginata.

A deep voice called, "The Kazoku's son is injured. He desires you tend him until the doctor comes."

Nanai's breath hissed through her teeth. "Daichi."

Ichia slid the door open and bowed. "Please accept our humble help."

Four men carried Daichi in and laid him on the sleep mats that Ichia had piled together.

Daichi's once proud face twisted with pain, blanched against the sand-crusted blood on his left cheek and temple. His left arm lay at a broken angle while his right hand grasped a small twisted pine, the roots still clinging to bits of rock.

Ichia knelt by him, dabbing at the blood and sand. Two of the young men knelt on the other side, wealthy friends, by the look of their sand-covered silk kimonos. One bent close. "Hiromu and Tomeo have gone for a doctor."

"Nanai," he moaned.

She slipped further into a dark corner of the room.

"Nanai."

Ichia looked up and gave a small jerk of her head. Nanai crept forward and knelt by him. Her own face had turned polished-rice pale.

Daichi turned his head toward her and cried out. He clenched his jaw and took long breaths through his nose. "I've brought a gift worthy of the sun-kami." His right hand fluttered and one of his friends lifted the uprooted pine from his chest and handed it to Nanai.

She clutched the pine. "What happened?"

Daichi's two friends glanced at each other. Daichi winced as he shifted his head to glare at them. "Tell her."

The younger of the two, his shoulders still narrow with boyhood, bowed slightly to Nanai, though his eyes were hard. "The Kazoku's son has lowered himself to seek the love of a potter's daughter. When she rejected his many costly gifts, he sought to prove himself by bringing her a cliff pine."

Nanai's grip tightened on the small pine.

I remembered her words to Daichi after her performance as Amaterasu. *Your offering is summer sweet, but common. Does not the sun-kami deserve something uncommon—a branch from a cliff-clinging pine or snow from the mountain peak?*

The young man continued, "He climbed the cliff to a small

pine. Instead of cutting a branch, he carefully removed each root from the cliff. But like you, the tree mocked him, the last roots resisting and then giving way. He fell backward, and we were too slow to catch him." His gaze dropped back to the tatami mat.

"I protected my gift for you." Daichi's voice cut. "May both you and it live crane-long lives."

Nanai stood, the tree tumbling from her lap, and fled through the open door. I stumbled after her. Nichika's murmured prayer followed: "Please, Inari, protect our family."

Nanai ran towards the cliff, her unbound hair whipping in a black flag of retreat. I pushed to a shuffling jog, my muscles pulling from the sparring bruises and the journey with the zenko. She stopped at the edge and fell to her knees. Muffled sobs rose above shaking shoulders.

I knelt next to her and wrapped an arm around her shoulders.

She leaned into me, her words muffled in my kimono. "I didn't mean to. I didn't mean for him to fall."

"It wasn't your fault."

"But it was. I told him to bring me a cliff pine."

I held her tighter.

Her shoulders shook beneath my arm. "I should have accepted his gifts and his offer."

"No." My voice came out a harsh whisper. "He'd have satisfied his desires and left you."

"But he fell because of me. He's the Kazoku's son. I'm just a potter's daughter. What if he's crippled? Is my virtue worth more than that?"

"Yes. Much more."

She lifted her head and gazed over the ocean, her body shuddering with each broken breath.

I blinked away angry tears. The sun floated a finger's width above the grey waters, casting a white path. Waves rolled onto sand and sucked away. If I leaned forward, I would see down the rough cliff face, speckled with ancient pines and new birds' nests.

"No one made Daichi climb," I said. "He chose to not listen when you said no. He chose to climb that cliff. He is the reason he fell, not you."

She hiccuped and sniffed. "But he still fell."

I nodded.

She leaned into me again. "I didn't mean for it to happen. He didn't deserve this. I just wanted him to stop asking."

The salty breeze pushed against us, drying my already tear salted face.

Nanai quieted and tightened into a stone stillness. "What will happen to me? What will happen to our family? Will we lose our home?"

I froze at her words. Daichi was the Kazoku's son. Even though we owned our own land, he could make life difficult for our entire family.

The soft clop of wooden sandals approached. Nichika knelt next to us. "The doctor came with the Kazoku's servants. They've carried him away."

"How is he?" Nanai asked.

Nichika's face creased. "I don't know. Ichia is preparing a basket of food for the Kazoku family. When she is finished, we will go with our apologies and prayers for his recovery. Will you come?"

Nanai wiped her face with the back of her hand. "I'll do whatever I need to to help him recover and keep his father's wrath from our family."

They walked back to the house, but I stayed rooted to the cliff edge. *Sheng, this is but another part of the curse. The kitsune protected Nanai by making her rejected suitor fall from the cliff. I have to break the kitsune-mochi bonding.*

Inari's closest shrine with priests lay a quarter-day's walk south. I returned to the house and slipped on my sandals from the porch. My sister's murmured voices carried through the paper walls, the words indistinct though the fear and worry clear. They'd try to stop me if I told them where I was going. Especially Nichika. She didn't even ask me to help with the apology to the Kazoku family. She must have thought I was too weak from my journey into the grey world.

But I had to go.

The village was usually quiet that early in the morning, but this day women stood whispering on their porches and men huddled in small groups in the village square. I hobbled past, my body slow to respond even to the simple motion of walking. Muttered words snatched at me, almost tripping me—*Kazoku's son —proud and hard girl—poor boy—she should—*

I hummed one of Takumi's songs to block any more words.

River runs constant,
different water flowing
through same river banks.

A servant with the Kazoku's bamboo symbol embroidered on his kimono ran past me, bearing buckets of ocean water. Infected wounds were often washed with the salty, cleansing water once it had been boiled. Were Daichi's wounds already infected?

Always, yes always,
different water passing swift
through same firm clay banks.

I turned south on the path that led to Inari's shrine and passed close to the Kazoku's hillside estate, which sat above the village. The tall walls concealed all but the triple-tiered roof, its corners curving up. The red gate stood open and a gravel path led between weeping pines and lace-leafed maples, over a stream, and past a rock garden with the gravel raked into flowing patterns. The servants running to and fro on the path were in sharp contrast to the meditative garden. A moaning from an upper window mingled with the jangling instruments to drive away demons who would make the injury worse.

But sky takes away,
pulling water into heavens,
leaving river dry.

I broke into a stumbling jog as I sang the words to block the sounds.

I tumble through life,
bound by river walls of earth.
Spirits float above.

The forest closed in around the path, and the rushed and broken sounds muffled into the silence of pine, sweet breeze and unconcerned birds. I let Takumi's song fade from my lips, and my jog fell back to a shambling walk.

The morning hours stretched between thousands of slow steps. A walk that should have taken but half the morning pushed into the noon heat, though the forest kept most of it from my unsheltered head. The forest path ended at the red torii gate. Its two thick pillars and double lintel, the upper one curving at the edges and capped with lacquered black, marked the transition from mundane to the sacred—the entrance to Inari's shrine.

She was the kami of foxes, both the benevolent and malevolent foxes. If anyone could break the kitsune-mochi bond, it would be her.

A white kimonoed priest with a narrow black hat bowed as I passed under the torii gate. I returned the bow. My body still ached, but the walk had loosened the muscles. "I humbly request your help to break a kitsune-mochi bond."

"Where is the person?"

I bowed my head. "Me. The kitsune follows me, but he has caused much grief to my family. Please. I'll do whatever is necessary."

"I see. Driving away a fox is difficult and sometimes dangerous. Have you considered feeding him more? Kitsune can be helpful if you are careful."

"Helpful?" A clash of memories tumbled before me. "He helped my master heal once from an illness, but he also broke my master's fingers. He comforted my mother as she lay dying of a difficult childbirth, but he took my younger brother. He's tormented me with cruel tricks my whole life. My twin brother died at birth. My sister just lost her baby boy."

"Ah. Not just a mischievous trickster field fox, but also a malicious one. I don't believe feeding him will stop him troubling you. All kitsune are unpredictable, and this one sounds especially so. Come, we will do what we can to drive him away."

He bent his head in thought as he led me over the slate path, past stone foxes, through the red-pillared shrine building and a long walk beyond it, through pines and maples into a mossy clearing walled by bamboo.

Aw-rhoof!

I jumped sideways, my chest tightening as a massive dog placed his forepaws against a shoulder-high bamboo gate. The dog let out another bone-vibrating bark.

"Down," the priest ordered. The dog dropped back behind the bamboo.

I gritted my teeth to stop their chattering and blew out a breath through them.

The priest raised his eyebrows. "We will start with the tosa inu hound. He only responds like that when a kitsune is nearby. That is why he is so far from Inari's shrine."

"What must I do?"

"Kneel in the center of the yard while the hound licks you.

Kitsune fear dogs, especially the tosa inu. When the fox spirit flees beyond the bamboo walls of this yard, he cannot reform the bond."

"Will the hound bite?"

The priest chuckled. "He won't hurt you. He's gentle to humans. I'd trust him to watch over a baby."

I knelt in the middle of the mossy yard and squeezed my eyes shut. My shoulders scrunched up around my neck. My kimono fabric crumpled in my tight fists. *I can do this. I learned to trust Takumi's dog. I'm brave enough to let the hound lick me. He won't bite. He's gentle.*

The quiet scrape of a bamboo latch sliding broke the silence, and then a panting, thumping force raced towards me.

I tightened for the impact. But it didn't come.

A low, rumbling growl washed over me with the fishy stink of warm breath. *Aw-rhoof! Aw-rhoof!* His voice jarred as I clamped hands over my ears. His spittle splattered across my face.

I can do this. He'll just lick me. Don't run. Soon our family will be free.

He growled then barked, but nothing touched me. I squinted open one eye and fell on my back, both eyes wide open. A massive deer-colored hound growled an arm's reach from me, his black-gummed mouth vibrating with the sound. He barked and jerked his head forward, snapping his teeth, then jerked back.

The four-tailed white kitsune stood between the hound and me, baring his own teeth. The hound tried to circle the fox, but the fox moved between us again.

The priest grabbed the folded skin at the hound's neck. "Down, back!" The hound pulled against him. "Run child," the priest called, struggling against the hound's lunges.

I rolled over and rose shakily to my feet, then stumbled through the bamboo gate, slamming and latching it. The gate vibrated as the hound thumped against it.

The four-tailed fox bristled beside me, the hair along its back standing on end.

I slumped to my knees. What had gone wrong? Why had the hound attacked?

Other priests came running. One helped me back to the main shrine and offered me tea. A time later, long enough for me to worry about the priest but not long enough to still my shaking limbs, the first priest came. Moss and paw prints dirtied his rumpled white kimono. His black hat was crushed.

I rose. "Sensei, are you injured?"

"No." He looked at me guardedly. "Are you?"

"I am unhurt."

"Good. Sit, child. Tell me what happened with the hound."

I swallowed as the scene played before my eyes. "The kitsune didn't flee the hound. He stood between us and bared his teeth. I think he was defending me."

The priest nodded solemnly. "I've never seen our hound attack a person. It must have been your kitsune that angered him. Your kitsune may burden your family, but he saved your life today."

My trembling doubled. The priest had said what I feared. The hound would have torn out my throat.

The priest sipped some tea. "Will you still try to break the bond?"

"Yes. I have to." The kitsune may have protected me, but so many others had died because of him.

"Then we will try driving him away with the smoke of fresh pine needles. It will make you ill, and you already seem weak. We will wait until tomorrow. Rest."

I protested, but my shaking limbs agreed. I fell asleep as soon as I lay on the mat in a small room off the side of the shrine.

I knelt in a windowless, domed, clay-walled room with only a small doorless opening leading into it. I'd crawled to come through it. It was like the inside of Takumi's kiln, though big enough to stand hunched over in. The early morning birds twittered in the trees outside. White-kimonoed priests piled pine needles in a deep ring around the edge of the room.

The priest knelt next to me and handed me a damp cloth. "Before we light the needles, take ten deep breaths, then wrap the damp cloth around your mouth. Before the smoke grows thick, lie on the ground near the opening to breathe the fresher air. We will fan in more air, but it will also make the smoke thicker. When you see your kitsune leave, call and we'll finish the breaking of the kitsune-mochi bond. However, if the smoke becomes too thick for you, call for help, and we will pull you out, even if he hasn't left."

I took slow breaths while my heart raced against the flickering brand handed through the opening. The priest took it and laid it in the pine needles on the far side of the dome from the door. Smoke trickled upward. The priest grabbed another fire brand through the opening and laid it in the needles to my right. The first needles smoked like a dark waterfall flowing upward. After a third and fourth firebrand lay smoking in the needles, the priest crawled out, lifting his knees over the pine pile so the ring was unbroken. I pulled the damp cloth over my mouth and nose, then laid my head against the cool clay floor. The ceiling turned black, and the air thickened into grey. Even with the cloth, I coughed as the acrid smoke pushed closer to the ground.

White flashed to my left. The four-tailed fox scattered the smoking pine needles from in front of the opening. *Sheng. He'll leave. We'll be free.* But he didn't leave. He scattered the other needles, spreading them out so they couldn't feed each other, stamping on the glowing, smoking green.

I crawled forward to catch him, but he danced away from my fingers, though he limped. Blackened needles stuck to his paws.

"Please," I coughed, "just go." The smoke made everything blurry and my thoughts slow.

"Child." The priest's voice carried through the door.

"The kitsune is stopping the fires," I called back.

A young priest crawled in, glanced at the scattered needles, grabbed me under my arms, and pulled me out.

I coughed until I vomited. A priest stood ready with a bowl. I wasn't the first who'd exited the pine smoke to do such. As I knelt, panting over the foul substance, the priest who'd led me to the hound handed me a cup of tea.

"It will help soothe your throat."

It helped my throat, but not my heart. "He wouldn't leave."

The priest knelt quietly, his eyes gazing into the distance. Finally, he turned to me. "Unless Inari intervenes, I see no way to break the kitsune-mochi bond. Please accept my most humble apologies."

17

Curse bound, curse harassed
sister blamed for fox's crime
innocent condemned.

Unless Inari intervenes, there is no way to break the kitsune bond. The priest's words followed me as I stepped under the red-arched torii gate, whispering in my head, pricking at my tight chest.

The forest closed in around the path, cool green lit by filtering late morning sun. The sharp scent of cedar tickled my smoke-tender nose. I coughed against the raw tickle in my throat and lungs left by the pine smoke. The smoke should have driven away the kitsune, but all it did was leave me weak and coughing. A grey squirrel chattered a reprimand for my noise.

Unless Inari intervenes. But how? Her messengers are the zenko. Would the kitsune that follows me stop a zenko, just as he stopped the hound?

Anger rose like the wind from the ocean, sending me into hacking, breath-stealing coughs. I leaned against an oak, gasping in air between coughs until they subsided. *I will ask Inari directly.*

I strode through the forest, my muscles warming up with the

movement, my lungs growing less irritated with each cool, smoke-free breath. I scanned the edges of the forest path. Broad-leafed oaks and pale lime-leafed beeches shadowed the soft-needled cedar. A dormouse ran upside down along the underside of a branch. The musky tang of wolf wafted from my left. I shivered and quickened my steps. The kitsune would probably protect me from the wolf, but I didn't want his protection or the wolf lunging inches from me like the hound had. *Where is the path-side shrine? I* squinted down the winding path, hunting for the red of painted wood. I'd seen one on the walk the previous day, but where?

Dragonflies floated and dipped over a stream to the right of the path, and a quail darted under a large fern. The *hoohokekyo* of a bush warbler danced carelessly over the sound of my rapid foot-falls. If only I could be such a bird; to sit in a branch and sing all day and never worry about kitsune or sisters or the capricious kami. *Will Inari hear me? And if she does, will she care to intervene?*

The sun slipped from its center balance and slid slowly into the afternoon. Red showed through the ferns at a bend in the path. I stumbled forward. A red roof, waist high, nestled under weeping branches of a cedar. A knee-high stone fox sat in front— one of Inari's small shrines. Hornets buzzed around a food offering of sake, honey, rice packed into tight triangle balls, fried tofu, and thinly sliced raw beef—diving in to sip at the honey and carving off pieces of beef. *Beef?* Usually an offering was less expen-sive. *Is the Kazoku making offerings at all the shrines for Daichi's return to health? Has he grown worse? No.* I fell to my knees before the shrine. *No, I have to break the curse binding me to the kitsune before the fox hurts Daichi further and destroys our family.*

I pressed my forehead into the waxy cedar needles layering the ground. "Inari, I know I've always sent my prayers through the kitsune, but I can't trust them. Please hear me and break this bond with the kitsune that follows me. He's only caused my family sorrow. He made the Kazoku's son fall to protect my sister, but if the Kazoku's son dies, then my sister will suffer. I've done all I can, all that I know to do. I will give you anything to protect my family. I know more than when I promised to cut wood for you to preserve my mother's life. I can make beautiful masks for your sanctuaries and for plays to honor you. I'll dedicate my life to you. Please hear me and help."

The breeze brushed over my neck, playing with my short hair. Something, maybe an ant, crawled along my arm, over my shoulder and across my cheek. Another followed. I kept my forehead pressed to the cedar needles and listened. The sweet and musty decay of forest floor layered with pine needles, crumbled leaves from last autumn, and damp soil filled each breath against the ground. The scurry of rodents, the chirping of sparrows, the hop-thump of a rabbit. And then a caw. I started to lift my head, then pressed it firmer to the ground. Crows were a sign of divine intervention. Was Inari answering? A flapping of wings and then a clawed weight landed on my shoulder. Another caw echoed in my ear, and I scrunched my face against the noise. *Please be a messenger from Inari. Please speak and tell me she's freed me of the kitsune-mochi bond and that our family is safe.*

A sharp tugging at the back of my head brought tears to my eyes. I held my hands pressed together under me to keep from snatching at where the crow pulled at my hair. He cawed again and pulled harder. Several strands ripped free. His wings beat against my head as he pushed against my shoulder and launched into the air. My eyes watered. *No message. Just a crow seeking soft nesting material.*

I waited, reaching out all my senses for some answer. More of the same sounds and scents. The ground pressed against me. The light flickered in grey variations beyond my closed eyelids. The sun's warmth moved in bands from my head, across my neck, and down my back, until it disappeared into the cool of dusk and the whirring evening call of the nightjar. Nothing changed. No whisper from my mother's spirit, no brightness of kami glory, not even the crow's return. Nothing.

A heavy weariness pressed me to the ground. *Kitsune-cursed, kami-rejected, family-exiled, death-followed. I'll dedicate myself to one of Inari's shrines—one far from here. May the kitsune follow me and leave our family in peace.*

I stood and brushed the needles from my knees and forehead and felt a cross-hatch of lines above my eyes. My head ached with unshed tears. I trudged through the forest as mosquitoes whined and lit upon me. Night cast its dark net over the sky, each knot a shining star, then the stars faded as a mostly full moon rose, casting blue shadows of trees across my path. The mosquito whine expanded into pitched cries.

I broke into a jog. Keening carried through the forest, growing louder with each step. The forest path opened onto the road and Daichi's family estate sat behind large closed gates illuminated with stone lanterns. Moans and cries rent the air. It wasn't the sound of distress over one injured, but of one dead.

The shrill voices hounded me, biting at my heels as I sprinted past the closed gates, skirted a village filled with echoes of the gated cries, and came to a panting halt on my family's dimly lit porch.

The paper door slid open, and arms enveloped me. Nichika held me tight. My other sisters stood staring, their hair disheveled and their eyes red and puffy. Ichia, Sanaho, Gomako, Rokue, and — "Where's Nanai?"

"They took her." Ichia turned her gaze downward and bunched her kimono in her hands. "Daichi died this afternoon. The Kazoku demands Nanai's life."

The world slipped under my feet, and Nichika steadied me. "When?"

"Tomorrow. After they cremate him."

I pulled from Nichika's arms. "Tomorrow! We have to free her tonight."

"Exactly." Sanaho grabbed her naginata from the wall. "Shisei understands. We go tonight, kill the guards and escape."

"No." Ichia lifted her eyes, and they burned with bloodshot intensity. "We've already discussed this. I'll not lose my other sisters to certain death. We will offer the Kazoku our land to spare Nanai's life."

"And when he doesn't," Sanaho retorted, "will you carry out the rest of your plan—offering us as bondservants?"

"I'll give myself as a servant to spare Nanai's life," whispered Nichika.

"So will I," said Gomako, though she bit her lip.

Rokue kept her gaze on the tatami mats, tracing the weave with her bare toe.

Ichia locked eyes with Sanaho. "I'll only offer my own freedom. You can do what you will with yours."

A shiver ran down my back. *Sanaho will offer her freedom as well. We all will to save Nanai. But will the Kazoku even accept our servitude to spare Nanai's life? He demanded the life of the herd boy who let his cow get into spring clover and die of bloating. He'll demand someone's life for Daichi's.* "There has to be another way."

"There is none," Ichia said.

The kitsune could help, whispered a thought. *He protected you from the hound.*

No, I argued back. *He's a trickster field fox.*

What if he would help? Are you willing to risk Nanai's life because of your fear of asking?

What if? I looked at each of my sisters, their bodies crumpled in despair—even Sanaho's defiant stance slumped at the shoulders.

Nanai would die tomorrow. All of us could be enslaved. Could the kitsune make it any worse? The night breeze rustled through the maple outside our house, whispering like the spirits I couldn't understand. I had to try. "I tried to break the kitsune-mochi. But the priests at Inari's shrine couldn't. Since we are still bonded with the white fox, I'll ask his help to free Nanai."

Sanaho snorted. "We don't need any mystical fox to help us. We could free her ourselves if any of you had more courage."

"Enough, Sanaho," Nichika reprimanded, then turned to me. "So that is where you went. Perhaps it is good that you couldn't break the bond. We need his help now. Call the fox."

I nodded. "Gomako, may I use your flute?"

She nodded, her eyes wide and her face blanched, and handed me the bamboo flute.

I blew across the hole. A raspy breathy sound came, but not a note. Sanaho stood in the corner, running her whetstone over the blade of her naginata. The scrape of stone on metal rasped in unison with my useless breaths across the flute.

We had little time. It was drawing close to moonset, when it would be easiest to free Nanai.

"I can't in here." I slipped between my sisters, stepped onto the porch and down into the garden by the koi pond. Night-dark water lapped at the edges as koi came to the sound of my steps. I lifted the flute and blew across it. A single semi-pure note sounded, then a second.

A softness brushed against my leg. The four-tailed white kitsune sat down between me and the pond. His eyes glimmered in the moonlight. He tilted his head as if waiting.

"Honored kitsune."

He sniffed as if my words were putrid. I'd tried everything to get rid of him, and now I was calling him honored.

"Please accept my most humble apology for trying to break the bond with you. I know I am bonded forever to you. I will not try to break the bond again. Please forgive me."

He glanced up at the sky.

"No," I rushed to say, "I know I called with the flute, but I cannot return to the grey place. It would tear me apart. Please, I need your help to free Nanai."

He turned away from me and walked towards the village, not even looking around to see if I would follow. If I followed, where would he take me?

"Did he come?" asked Nichika from the porch.

"Yes."

"Will he help?"

He had to. I needed him to. He wouldn't release me from the bond. He'd protected me from a hound. He seemed to protect the women of the family, even as he played with us for his amusement. *Please let him help us save Nanai.* I dashed down the path after him. My spirit stayed firmly in my body and my feet stayed on the ground. My breath loosened. He wasn't taking me into another world, only along a mortal path.

"Thank you, honored kitsune. Thank you," I whispered as I caught up to him.

He turned his head and seemed to smile. Was it in acceptance of my thanks or mischief?

Minutes later, sandaled feet slapped the ground behind me. Sanaho fell into stride beside me, carrying two naginatas. "Here." She shoved one naginata into my hands, the sharp blade glinting in the moonlight. "You'll need this before the night is through." She clapped me on the back with her now empty hand. "Clever plan to get Ichia to let you go. She couldn't stop me from aiding you and even bringing weapons. You are a better actress than Nanai—kitsunes, kamis, worlds that are silent wind and full of decay. Better yet, be a playwright or a storyteller. When we get Nanai free, you can write a play for her to act in."

Sanaho's voice prattled on in a low whisper. She'd not spoken in so many disjointed thoughts since the time before her first competition—six years ago. She was afraid. "When we get her free," Sanaho continued, "we'll meet our sisters by Mother's shrine. They are packing food and supplies. We'll flee northward. Maybe to your sensei until we can contact Father. We don't need any imaginary fox. We'll get Nanai free, you and I."

She still didn't believe in the kitsune. Or maybe she did, but she acted as if she didn't because she was afraid of it, just as she was afraid we'd fail to save Nanai. I stepped sideways, closer to her, letting my arm brush against hers. She didn't move away. So we followed the four-tailed kitsune through the dark of the fields behind the village, crossing over the paths between rice paddies, the low moon glinting off still water and thin stalks of green. An owl swooped, a silent shadow. My fear lessened with her beside me, even if she was as afraid as I.

Then the kitsune crossed back toward the road that led to the Kazoku's estate. He looked over his shoulder at us and growled.

"If we stay with your sensei, we must make some other sleeping place..." she said.

"Sanaho," I whispered.

"... or sleep outside. That won't..."

The fox growled again, and the hackles along his back rose.

"Sanaho." I stopped walking and placed my naginata in front of her to bar the way. "We need to be quiet now."

She tightened her grip on her naginata and lightened her steps so we moved like ghosts over the road. The moon lay close to the horizon, and the first light of pre-dawn would be a couple hours away.

The kitsune led us up a steep hill to the back wall of the estate where the shadows were deepest. He touched my feet with his nose and then touched the wall. I would follow him over the wall. I bound my kimono up between my legs to give them more freedom. Sanaho followed my example, her movements sure as she knotted the fabric around her legs. The kitsune touched her feet and touched the ground.

"Sanaho, you need to stay here. I'll bring Nanai to this point and we'll escape together."

"How do you know?"

I don't know. I spoke in my head, not ready to tell her my fears, just as she wouldn't tell me hers. *I'm just guessing what he means. If I could speak with him, then I'd know, but I can't. I'd have to go to the grey place of nothingness and death. And we don't have time for that.*

Maybe, whispered a different part of my thoughts, *you don't have time not to go.*

B-but, I stuttered internally as Sanaho watched me. *No buts.* And I spoke to Sanaho, "The kitsune led us here and wants me to continue alone. You don't have to believe me, but if you want to help Nanai, you will stay here until we return."

She opened her mouth, then closed it and bowed. "I will wait until an hour before dawn. You had better hurry."

18

The moon dipped below the forest trees as I slipped off my straw sandals and handed them to Sanaho, along with the naginata. I'd not be able to climb with clad feet, let alone a weapon, and the naginata would do me little good against many guards. I had to trust that the kitsune would protect me as he had against the hound.

The wall stretched above, three times my height, protection against an ancient time of roving bandits—a black solidness in the now moonless night. I placed my hand against the wall and tried to find what the darkness hid—handholds to carry me over and to Nanai. But the wall, though rough like lava stone, had been flattened and fitted together, so there were no handholds deeper than the tips of my fingers. I'd chopped wood and hauled clay, but could I bear my weight by fingertips?

The kitsune brushed against me, his fur warm against my night-chilled ankles, and then placed his paws against the wall and sauntered up the side as if it were a curving path along the forest floor. He glowed white against the dark wall and left behind him a faint trail, each footstep a small spot of grey-glimmering stone in the black wall. I placed my hands where he stepped and gripped rough hand holds, deep enough to hold most of my fingers.

Dew slicked the stones. I moved upward along the glowing grey path, not leaving my fingers or toes long in any spot. *Seek a hold, grip firmer, push upward, seek, place, pull—you're not that tired, look up, don't look down, keep going.* My half-thoughts directed my trembling motions. I was more than halfway. The kitsune sat on the line between black wall and dark sky. His tails wrapped around him and his bright white washed out the stars above even more than the moon had.

Would anyone be watching the wall? They wouldn't see him, but they would see me.

My fingers cramped as I clung to the wall, the question freezing my movements. But if they caught me, was it any worse than not trying to help Nanai?

"Please, honored kitsune," I whispered, "Please help us free Nanai. Don't lead me into a trap. I'm trusting you."

He glanced down at me, his eyes bright and his mouth grim.

Sheng, should I trust him?

I shook my head. No, I didn't trust him, but he could save my sister, and it was worth the risk.

I climbed the last of the wall and rolled onto the top, hugging the stones to make my body as small as possible. I slowed my breath and listened. No shouts, just the night breeze whispering through the garden trees and the burble of a stream over stones. The grounds were dark and the only light came from the three-storied, arched-roofed home of the Kazoku, sitting downhill from me. One room glowed through the paper walls. Daichi's body would lie there, watched over by his family. The reverberating keening from the evening had ceased, leaving behind an empty, aching silence.

Tomorrow all the gardens, streams, and ponds would be alight with paper lanterns to guide Daichi's spirit after they cremated him. But not tonight. Tonight darkness lay in a protective blanket between the wall and the house. Where were they keeping Nanai? In darkness or light?

The kitsune walked down the other side of the wall as he'd walked up the first, his four tails waving behind him. I followed until my feet met the branches of a bush. The kitsune danced over it to the ground, but its narrow branches wouldn't bear my weight. I tried to inch sideways to the bare wall but slipped. The branches snapped, scratching my already abraded arms and legs, and sending up the hazelnut scent of corylopsis.

I crouched in the middle of the broken branches. No alarm sounded, no running of feet or the swinging light of a carried lantern. Dark mounds, squarish shadows, and tall leafy walls surrounded me. We were in the kitchen gardens.

The kitsune wove his way between bamboo-staked kyuri and bushy kabocha. I padded over the cool packed-dirt paths. The dark mounds of vegetables ended at a bamboo fence. While the kitsune leaped over it, I opened the gate and followed.

If the grey world was filled with death, then this place was filled with life. Though everything was blacks and greys under the moonless sky, stars rained droplets of light and a pond splashed the starlight back onto bamboo, pines, maples, and flowering camellia. The air filled with a blend of lemon, apple, and jasmine. The soft *hwoo-hwoo* of a night heron thrummed over a laughing stream. Stepping stones made black pockets in the pond, zig-zagging across to a willow. A turtle—a symbol of long life—dove into the water, sending ripples through the starlight. Not even Inari's shrine had held so many spirits and life. Water, stone, plant, animal. And my sister, somewhere, preparing to die.

I followed the glowing kitsune, his light illuminating the winding path of smooth stones set in moss. We climbed over a moon bridge guarded by a stone crane, descended a dark passage of stairs between trees that blocked the stars, and passed under a pergola dripping with wisteria, the sweet scent enveloping us. Waxy leaves and twisting tendrils of the wisteria clung to my hair. On the far side of the pergola, a low light flickered from a knee-high stone lantern at the edge of a new pond, catching on the water and the flat stones bridging it. I hadn't seen it from the wall, but the short bristled pines, yew, and cypress that seemed to dance in the lantern light would have blocked it.

Why the lantern now in the early morning hours—unless? I pushed forward and stumbled, catching a vine of wisteria in one hand, as the kitsune blocked my path. He growled and gazed to the right of the path, across from the lantern.

I froze.

In the shadows by the edge of a pond stood a statue—grey kimono and grey sheathed katana, the upper half lost in darkness. It stood more still than the trees; it didn't even appear to move in the flickering light. Until it did. The kimono shifted. The statue stepped across the path, bent down to the lantern, and lit a long pipe. His face pinched with anger as he clamped the pipe in his teeth. He stood, his top disappearing back into the shadow, only a small glow coming from the bowl of the pipe. He was one of the men who carried Daichi to our home after his fall—the young man who'd berated Nanai.

A whimper came from a fence behind him. "Please, a little water."

"Ask it of the man you killed."

It wasn't her fault! It was mine and the trickster fox who plagues me! The wisteria creaked in my tightening grip and I froze again.

A low rumble came from the kitsune's throat. Was he laughing? It was his fault. But he was helping me now—I hoped. Did he read the complaints in my face? I bowed my head and bit back even my thoughts.

Another mocking rumble came from the kitsune's throat, and he strolled toward the guard. Was he going to give me away? The wisteria creaked again in my grasp. He sniffed, then circled the guard. The lantern flickered with the kitsune's movement, dancing yellow squares of light on his white fur.

One circle, a second. The man stood unmoving, shadowed and filling the air with bitter smoke. The wisteria's strong perfume tickled alongside the smoke. I squinted my eyes and pinched my nose. My neck tensed.

The kitsune circled a third time. Wisteria scent and smoke entered my mouth and traveled upward. The kitsune began a fourth circle, his four tails fanning patterns in the air.

I gritted my teeth, and the sneeze exploded.

The guard turned and drew his katana.

No. Please turn around. It was a tanuki. Nothing but a tanuki. What is the fox doing? Do something! I have to do something! One of Sana-ho's lessons pushed to the front of my clamoring thoughts. *If your opponent has a weapon but you don't, surprise him.* How? Leap on his back? He was much taller than me. He'd throw me off and sever my head with his katana.

He strode toward me, and the kitsune widened his circle.

Should I try to wrest the katana from his hand or strike his head? If only I had the naginata. I bent over, scrambling in the dirt path for a stone or a pruned vine thick enough to use as a club. The ground was bare.

The guard quickened his steps. "Who's there?"

I scooped up a handful of dirt. I'd fling it in his eyes, then dart around and grab his knees, tripping him. Maybe he'd fall on his own katana.

He stepped under the pergola.

I flung the dirt.

It flew over his head as he lunged at me. A scream lodged in my throat, my feet rooted to the dirt. His katana clattered to the ground as he toppled to his face and lay still, his hair resting across my bare feet. The kitsune came to a stop at my side. He'd completed the fourth circle.

My knees buckled, and I flopped to kneel beside the young man. *Has the kitsune's fourth circle killed him? Please, no!* His katana lay to his side where he'd dropped it. His pipe, sticking from under him, flickered and went dark. I turned his face from the dirt and felt the soft brush of breath across my hand. *Thank the kami he's alive. Daichi's death is too much already. How could I have believed Sanaho that I could kill the guards? Death follows me, but I will not create death.*

I flung the katana into the pond and ran to the fence where Nanai had spoken.

Was it kindness or a final cruelty to enclose her where she could feel the richness of life that she'd leave behind? "Nanai."

"Shisei." Her voice wobbled. "You came."

"Are you hurt?"

"No. Where's the guard?"

I glanced back over my shoulder. The kitsune sat by the fallen guard, glowing in smugness. "He's unconscious. Be ready to run when I find the gate." I touched the bamboo fence, feeling along it for hinges or a latch. The fence was taller than me with bamboo set in crossing diagonals and lashed to horizontal pieces.

Nanai reached through and grasped my hand with fear-cold fingers. "There is no gate. They lashed the fence to the walls of a covered bench. Did you bring a knife?"

"No. Can you climb over it?"

"The fence goes all the way to the roof, but if we can push the fence out enough, I'll try to fit through." Her fingers and toes pushed through the fencing as she climbed. I peered into the dark above the fence. A roof blocked the sky a handspan from the bamboo. I pulled at the fencing. It wouldn't move, even with Nanai's weight to help lean it.

The katana! I ran to the pond and waded in, searching for the blade among water lilies. Koi darted around my legs. A snake slithered from beneath a foot. Then my fingers brushed a narrow smoothness and a sharp edge. I hissed against the sting of a sliced finger as I walked my fingers along the blade to the cord-wrapped handle, snatched it up, and dashed back to the fencing. "Nanai, get down. Where's the wall that the fence is attached to?"

She leaped back to the ground and guided me to the wall that backed the covered bench. Five ropes bound the fence to the slatted wall. I swung the blade against the first knot and the tip sliced through. As the last knot severed, Nanai pushed against the fence and it swung towards me. She dashed out, the lamplight illuminating her dirtied lower half while her upper half was but a shadow in the dark, but she moved without the stumbling of injury.

I took her hand and led her to the kitsune under the wisteria. Nanai edged away from the fallen guard as we ran past. The kitsune watched us pass, then rose to his feet and dashed ahead.

He'd helped me thus far. I dragged Nanai as he ran, winding over new paths and taking us closer to the house.

"Where are you taking us?" Nanai whispered as we skipped from stone to stone across a stream.

The same question thumped inside me. *The kitsune led me to free Nanai. Why is he leading us this way?* "Hush," was all I answered Nanai as we raced down stone-stepped hills and between boulder-shaped bushes, and wove through crooked planked paths—always downward and closer to the house. Our path ended at a large pond—or a small lake—with a single dock pushing out onto the dark waters.

The kitsune ran onto the dock and hopped into a flat-bottom boat. Across the expanse, the arched three tiers of the house silhouetted against the brightening pre-dawn sky. The stars faded to a few bright spots overhead. The *kyokyokyo* of the crake-bird knocked against the air. My hand tingled in Nanai's tight grip. The kitsune nudged the pole in the boat with his paw and looked at us. If we got in the boat, we'd be visible to anyone looking from the house or any edge of the pond.

"Honored kitsune," I whispered, "please lead us along the shadowed paths to freedom. We are not invisible like you."

Nanai's grip tightened. "Are we following the fox that cursed our family?"

I nodded.

"Why? He's tricking us, just as he tricked you to go into the world of death."

I shuddered. What if he was tricking us? What if this was just a game to him?

"Shisei, let's go back to the wall. I don't trust him."

The kitsune growled at her words and nudged the pole again.

The first hints of a servant's morning trailed across the lake—the clank of a pot, smoke from a cook fire, and then a shout followed by the deep peal of a gong. They'd discovered Nanai was gone.

I jerked her around and we ran back up the path along which we'd come, tripping up the stone steps of a hill. The kitsune dashed in front of us and growled, his four tails erect behind him. I pulled Nanai around him again and continued our climb. The shouts from the house increased and new shouts took up to our right. We darted left and leaped over a low wall, landing in sand. Wave-carved rocks sat in the middle of spiral-raked sand. Our feet left whirlpool prints as we dashed across to the opposite wall and climbed over.

The voices drew away, going north, but our tracks showed us going south. East led back towards the house. We turned west. The kitsune ran beside us, no longer hindering our steps nor leading us. The land rose steeply into dense foliage. A waterfall misted the air as it tumbled between stones and evergreens. The path ended at a bench.

"Nanai, we'll hide in the trees until tonight." I pushed her ahead of me. We scrambled upward, grabbing roots and branches, until we found a hollow of space in the middle of a lacy maple. We settled on the uphill side of the trunk, bracing our feet against rocks to keep from sliding downward. The curtain of red leaves brightened with the rising sun. The kitsune curled up on my feet and closed his eyes. I pulled my feet away, and he opened one eye and glared. I blew out my frustration. I'd promised never again to try to break my bond with him so he would help me, but he only helped sometimes. Capricious fox.

Trying to ignore his weight as he resettled on my feet, I pulled Nanai closer. Her trembling faded into soft whimpering breaths of sleep. I shifted, and she muttered, "Daichi. I'm so sorry. I didn't mean to."

I brushed her hair away from her face. "It wasn't your fault." Then even her whimpering silenced.

The waterfall blanketed us in mist. My head dropped forward. And I jerked it back up. The pounding falls combined with the breeze-rustled leaves lulled me. My kitsune-warmed feet relaxed, and I leaned my head on Nanai's.

Baying bounced off the hillside. Men's voices followed, drawing closer. "He's scented her," called a deepset voice.

Nanai stiffened in my arms. The kitsune stood in front of us with tails bristled.

I pressed my hands together and bowed around Nanai. "Please, honored kitsune, protect us."

He touched my hand with his nose, then ran from under the

curtain of red maple leaves. The baying intensified and then turned away from the hill. He was leading them away. The men's voices faded as they urged the hound on.

"Come, Nanai. It's no longer safe here. We'll find a new hiding place." We crawled upward from the maple's shelter, through pines, and finally to a wall at the top. Two men stood along the path, the morning sun glinting off spear points. We had to go back. We started our downward climb, and a stone dislodged, crashing through the trees.

"Did you hear that?" asked one man.

"Hai," agreed the other.

Tall pines surrounded us, the lowest branches out of our reach. Dense bushes mounded like boulders between the pines. Our maple hiding place sat halfway down the hill. We ducked on the downward side of a squat evergreen bush, hidden from above but exposed to anyone below who looked up.

Branches broke as a heavy form skidded down the hillside. They'd find us. "Stay here," I whispered and crawled from behind the bush.

"Stop, boy!" Halfway between the top of the hill and me, a man in the rough cotton kimono of a servant braced himself with his spear against the ground, and clung to a branch with the other hand. He glared. "What are you doing here?"

"Don't hurt me." My voice cracked. "I'm a runaway. My sensei beats me. Please don't return me to him."

His scowl deepened. "A runaway? You picked a dangerous place to hide. I'd beat you myself, if I didn't have to look for an escaped murderer. Now get off the Kazoku's estate and don't come back."

"Escaped murderer?" I trembled, only partly pretending. "May I stay with you, please? I can help. I thought I saw someone up that way." I pointed uphill towards where Nanai had been imprisoned. Then I shook my head, "But it couldn't have been him. The shadowy figure was small, like a girl."

"That's the murderer." He reached out for me. "Hurry, boy, and show me where you saw her."

I scrambled up to him and set my palm in his meaty hand. As his thick fingers closed over mine, I sent up a prayer and a hope, *Please protect Nanai.* I didn't direct it to any of the kami or zenko. Whom could I trust? Instead, I let it float away from me. *Please, someone be listening and protect Nanai.*

The servant pulled me to the path at the top of the hill, grunting curses under his breath as his sandal-shod feet slipped, leaving trails of brown through the moss. My bare feet kept a slightly better grip.

After I clambered over the wall, an awkward action with the servant still holding my hand, I nodded with my head up the trail. "That way, near a statue of a crane by a moon bridge."

The servant's hand tightened on mine. "You will show me."

We walked the same paths Nanai and I had stumbled over in the dark. The gardens were even more beautiful in the morning sun, but worries dulled my eyes, and instead I kept seeing Nanai crouched on the hillside, waiting. Had she crept back under the maple? How soon could I beg my leave and return to her? Or would they throw me out of the estate, or worse, send someone to return me to my master?

I stumbled on a root pressing up in the path. "Forgive me," I murmured as the servant roughly pulled me back to my feet. "I've lost my way. Where is the moon bridge?" It was true. I didn't know where we were going, except further from Nanai.

He snorted. "Useless runaway. This way." He jerked me to the right and up a different path. "I should have left you with Haru."

Haru? The other man? The one who was there with him on the path? I turned around. He wasn't following us. I set my heels on the path. I had to go back. "Please. Let me go. I—I—" What could I say? "I told you where I saw the person. I can't help you anymore. Please. I'm frightened."

"And you'll be less frightened wandering by yourself? No, you'll get a good beating as it is. Don't cause me to give you one right now." He lifted a massive fist and shook it in my face. I shrank back and then stumbled forward as he yanked my arm. "Come on."

So we climbed higher, passing through banded light and cool green, crossing streams and stepping across stone-pocketed ponds. Koi followed our steps, splashing hungrily around the stones. A moon bridge spanned a smooth pool, its reflection completing the circle. A crane perched on the left, its long neck grey stone. Another crane stood in the reeds beneath the bridge, dipping its head into the water. Long life. Nanai should have the crane's promised long life. *Please keep her safe.*

The servant pointed to the bridge. "Where did you see her?"

"She was—" A gong silenced my words. It rang over the garden, vibrating through my bones.

The servant grunted. "She's found. Now get you gone." He turned down the path without a backward glance.

Sheng, they found Nanai. Why couldn't I get her to freedom?

Because I am Shi—death. My legs trembled. *But let my curse end with me. I'll offer my life in her place, something I could not do for you.* The gleam of sunlight off the stream was sharp, like the katana that would sever my head if I traded places with her.

I slunk after the servant, dipping into the shadows any time I thought he'd turn around. But he never did. Instead, he strode with an unhurried step. He followed winding paths, the house appearing and disappearing behind trees and walls, until we came to the largest pond. He followed the gravel path around the pond to a stone wall surrounding the red three-tiered house. He passed under an arched wall and into an open courtyard. The house loomed on the far side like a tiger and held at its claws two forms with long black hair flowing in tangles down their backs. Two. Nanai knelt, head and shoulders bowed, her arms bound behind her. Sanaho stood nearby, straining against the hold of two samurai in black layered armor.

No one glanced over as the servant joined the masses of other servants along one side. Their gaze fixed on the man standing with his back to me, facing Nanai. He was a short man, rounded with the labors of others. His green silk kimono shimmered, and his bald head gleamed. The katana he held in his hand gleamed brighter. He raised it.

"Stop!" I darted past the servant toward Nanai and Sanaho. Hands grabbed me. I stumbled to my knees, but kept my eyes fixed on the blade, paused at the top of a swing. "Please stop."

The Kazoku turned, his katana arcing sideways through the air over Nanai's head. "Who are you? Another victim to this vixen?"

"Her sister. Take me in her place."

Bitterness pinched his eyes and down-turned mouth. "It won't bring my son back."

"Nor will her death." I kept my eyes on his. He seemed a stone frozen mid-motion, his katana extended, his knotted fists around the hilt, his red-rimmed eyes locked with mine. Only his long silk sleeves swayed, as if continuing the swing without him. If I looked away, would he finish his killing strike?

His heavy lips tightened. "She caused it. She shall pay for it."

"Then let me pay the debt." My pulse hammered in my neck, stifling my words. I forced them out again, the sounds rasping through my tight throat. "Let me pay the debt with my life."

His eye twitched. Would he accept my offer? Could I truly take Nanai's place? Acid ate away the seconds as he studied me. My whole soul screamed to take back the offer, to tell him I was mistaken. Life throbbed hot through me. But it did in Nanai, too. She shouldn't pay for Daichi's mistake or the kitsune's malice. I strengthened my face into the calm that masked the storm tearing beneath.

His face strengthened into hatred. "No. The debt is paid when my son's scorning kitsune is dead."

He wouldn't take my life. Traitorous relief flowed over my shoulders, loosening the stone choking my breath. "Please, have mercy. She's just a child."

The tip of his katana dipped as his brows creased over his nose, but then his jaw hardened. "She is the reason he climbed the cliffs. Unless the kami show me they wish to preserve her life, she will pay for my son's."

The kami. They only come down in stories. No kami will beg for her life, especially when they have done nothing to help me free her. A tremor shimmered over my hopelessness. But the kitsune might help. He could create illusion. Just as our masks create the illusion for the theater.

He asked me to return to the place of grey death. If I did, would he save her? Would he make it appear as if a kami came down? What will he require in payment? What must I let go? Will I have to stay in the grey world with him? Death would be better. At least death would release me to the spirit world where family awaited me. But if I don't go, Nanai will surely die.

I let my eyes drop to the ground. If he swung now and ended her life, I would not have to choose. Instead, I'd live with her death the rest of my life, just as I already lived with Sheng's death.

No! I can do something for her. If I do nothing now, it is as if I swung the blade. "Master, give us a day to petition the kami. And then we will bear with your judgment."

He lowered his katana, slipping it back into the sheath behind him. "A day. She stays a prisoner and we will meet at the gates at noon tomorrow to see what the kami say."

Whoever held me let go. I ran to Nanai's side, wrapping my arms around her trembling form. She crumpled into my embrace.

Sanaho joined a second later, wrapping her arms around both of us, as if trying to shield us. "Shisei, how could you offer your life?" Sanaho's voice cracked.

"Because Nanai is our sister."

Sanaho swallowed. "You are brave and good as Momotarō. I will help you in whatever plan you have."

She trusted me. Maybe she'd believe me too. Though I had no assurance for her or Nanai, only a hope. "Nanai, hold strong."

She didn't speak, and her body shook like a rudderless boat when servants grabbed Sanaho and me, shoving us away from Nanai. Sanaho tensed to fight.

"No," I whispered. "We will do more good if we go now and petition the kami."

The gates clanged shut behind us, and a white kitsune with four tails came to stand beside us. I bowed my head. "I am ready."

19

Grey world, wind-torn.
Trade own life for sister's chance,
hope that she may live.

Storm clouds darkened the sky as Sanaho ran beside me to our mother's shrine. Wind whipped hair against our faces. Summer dust filled our eyes. The kitsune ran ahead of us, his tails streaming out behind him. We ran through the center of town, the shortest path. Neighbors stepped toward us, but their words—questions, pity, or condemnation—whipped away on the growing wind. The forest closed in around us again. A branch groaned as it swayed. Two more branches rasped against each other. Still rain didn't fall, and the sky grew darker.

Our sisters huddled around Mother's shrine with bundles of clothing and straw baskets, ready to flee northward with all seven sisters. Ichia was first to stand as we dashed over the dirt path. Nichika met us partway, pulling us close. "Is she...?"

"She's still alive," I yelled over the howling wind. "We have one day. Let's get back home where we can talk."

The wind stole away Nichika's sigh. Relief softened her tense body.

The first fat drops of rain splashed against the back of my neck as we scurried back to our home and pushed inside. The kitchen fires were cold; no scents of meals lingered. They'd waited by Mother's shrine the whole night while we'd tried to rescue Nanai. Would they now wait beside me as I tried to rescue her another way?

"What happened?" It came from several sisters at once. Ichia slipped away into the kitchen, hopelessness carving deeper into her already grief-lined face.

"I must speak with Ichia, then I'll tell you."

Nichika stopped the others from following as I stepped down into the kitchen. Ichia knelt by one of the low ovens, holding a burning twist of rice-straw. It cast flickering shadows across her face.

I knelt next to her. "Ichia. I know I've brought much sorrow to you and our family. I tried to right it today. I offered my life for Nanai's, to die in her place."

"No." Ichia dropped the twist of straw and it snuffed out, leaving us in darkness.

I rushed on, speaking words that she'd said to me, needing her to say them again so I could be honorable to do what I must. "I am kitsune-mochi. I'm cursed and I should pay for the harm my curse brings on our family."

"No. Not even you. You are my sister."

I stumbled on my next argument, as my nose stung with tears. *Her sister. She claims me. Why does she claim me now? I need her to push me away so I'm strong enough to leave.*

I reached for her hand in the dark. "The Kazoku wouldn't accept my offer, but he said if the kami pled on her behalf, he would let her go. I think we can trick him. I'm going to speak with the kitsune."

Her hand tightened around mine. "Do you think he will help?"

"I don't know. I hope he will. I must return to the grey world where I can speak with him. Kitsune are masters of illusion. He could help."

Her voice tinged with hope. "Please ask him."

"If I die in the attempt, bury me next to our mother." I needed that assurance before I went. Ichia was the only one I could ask. She would promise without asking me to stay.

Silence throbbed in a pulse between our hands. Rain pounded the roof like evil spirits trying to get in. A flash of lightning turned the paper walls white and revealed Ichia's wide eyes. The room darkened as a boom shook the thin pottery on the shelves. Then her voice came a quiet stream through the pounding overhead. "No, I was wrong. You are different from the rest of us, but you are still good beneath your curse. You offered your life for Nanai's when none of us would. Sanaho was willing to fight for her. The rest of us would give up our freedom. But none of us would trade places with her. Forgive me for my blind words. You can't go. Nanai will still die if you speak with the kitsune. I won't lose two sisters."

Anger rose with frustration. Ichia was supposed to help me be strong enough to go, not plead for me to stay. "When Momotarō left his home and faced an island of demons with only his animal companions, did he shrink because he couldn't win? I won't either."

I pushed past her into the main room. My other sisters stared as I pulled Gomako's flute from its wall pegs and ran out into the torrent. The rain muffled their calls into the dark. I continued running until their voices faded, then settled under the dripping limbs of a pine. If I survived this visit, my body would be more protected from the storm and I'd recover quicker.

My first note came clear, and the second. The four-tailed kitsune settled in front of me before I could draw breath for a third note.

I bowed and followed him.

The grey of the pounding rain silenced to the grey of tearing wind. I huddled, hiding my head in my arms. Putrid death stung my eyes and nose, stifling every breath. A new scent laced it. Was it Daichi's perfume? Did every death follow me here?

"Are you ready?" As before, the voice came from within me, penetrating the silence, but was not my own. Reproof vibrated with each word.

"I will give up anything, even my life. I will stay in this place if it will free my sister. Keep me as your kitsune-mochi." My words fell silent as they dropped from my lips, but he chuckled in response.

"Then listen. You call this a place of death. It is not."

"I know it isn't the death that leads to the dwelling of the kami. This is a frozen death, a place of demons."

"You are not ready to listen yet. Will you let your little sister die before you do?"

I pulled into a tighter ball as the wind ripped the tie of my kimono loose. The sleeves pushed up to my shoulders and my arms flattened with the force of the gale. "Forgive me. I will not speak again."

He huffed, a disbelieving puff. *"You will. And you must. But listen first."*

I waited as silence engulfed the minutes. He didn't speak again. How was I to listen if he wouldn't speak? Was there someone else that I couldn't hear? I listened, seeking sound outside the suffocating silence. If this place was not death, what was it?

A small sound slapped in the distance. I'd heard it many times over the last six months with the mask maker. It was the first throw of a block of clay on the table as he prepared to form a new mask. Clay. Why that sound?

Another sound in the storm, this of singing. I knew the tune and felt the words reach for me.

Paper pressed in mold,
ground seashells and horse-hoof glue,
form mask for spirits.

Was Takumi here? He couldn't be, but if he was—

"Sensei!" I screamed. My voice carried, muffled, through the wind. It wasn't death silent anymore. Takumi had followed me here and broken part of the curse. If I found him, together we could break the rest of it. Was that what the kitsune meant?

"Listen and look." The kitsune spoke. His instruction warred with my need to find Takumi.

I crouched, ready to run, listening for where Takumi's sounds came from. But his voice faded away.

Listen and look? The grey sat thicker than a fog. What was hidden behind the nothingness?

The grey thinned and a small shack of a building stood at the end of a cherry tree-lined path. Masks hung along its wall. A bark preceded the red wolf-shape of Ōkami, bounding up onto the porch.

I stood. The wind died to a gentle whisper against my cheeks. I stepped down the path. The sweet of cherry blossoms mixed with the smoke of the kiln.

"How?"

The four-tailed kitsune walked beside me. *"Interesting. But not surprising. So this is closest to your thoughts when they are not consumed with death? I thought you'd first see your sisters, as you were willing to give up your life for the youngest. But then, that was tied to death. And this is not."*

"Is not what? Where are we?"

"Do you not remember? This will be difficult."

"Who are you?"

He turned and dipped his head in a low bow. *"I am Torikkusutā."*

I laughed. Torikkusutā. He was named trickster.

"You came to ask me a favor, but you have not asked it yet."

I paused on the path, trying to think of what he meant. We were walking a beautiful path, soaking in the sun as cherry blossoms danced around us. Something dark lingered behind, but it was shadowed like a nightmare scattered by morning. The little house ahead held much more interest with its many masks. Even the wolf-dog seemed friendly.

"Torikkusutā, if the question is important, I will remember it when we've finished our walk."

"Shisei." His voice turned serious. *"You must try to remember."*

"Then give me a hint, sensei trickster." I spun through the blossoms, sending them floating from the ground back into the air.

"Ichia, Nichika, Sanaho," he said.

Faces flashed in front of me. Beautiful, carrying many of the same lines, but each filled with a different spirit. Did I know them?

"Shisei."

A woman with thick eyebrows and eyes bright with thought twirled before me, just as I had spun through the blossoms.

"Gomako, Rokue, Nanai."

Grey crushed over me with memories. I fell to my knees. Takumi's house and the path disappeared. Nanai would die if I didn't help her. "Honored kitsune, how could I forget so quickly?"

His warm fur brushed against me. *"This place is confusion, even for a trickster who knows illusions. It creates what is only possibility—a bridge to what can be."*

"I don't understand."

He curled up at my feet. *"Think of someplace pleasant while I tell you of my sister. Maybe that koi pond outside your childhood home. Or even the shrine where you always left tasty offerings for your family zenko. Well, sometimes tasty. Your mother didn't teach you well."*

The grey cleared, and we knelt by the small shrine for our family's zenko. The crispy brown packets of inarizushi sat on the stone base. Wisps of steam and rich scent drifted upward in the crisp autumn air. Mother had taught me to cook and make offerings for our family zenko, but I never developed the talent beyond the basics. What sat before us was made by an artist, just as I imagined they should have been, but never were.

My thoughts drifted back to lessons by Mother's side. Her voice called in the distance, "Shisei, come gut the fish while I make the rice." I jumped to my feet.

The kitsune caught my sleeve in his mouth. *"You must focus on listening to me. Put all other thoughts from your head, or the possibility of them will interrupt us so much that it will be a year before I finish."*

I tried to gather my scattered thoughts. They whispered around me like spirits, some enticing me to follow them, others warning of danger. Each made it hard to think or even remember why I was here. I grabbed the memory of Nanai, her need. "Honored kitsune, Nanai will die unless you use illusion to free her. Please help her. I will serve you in this place for as long as you desire to pay for your help."

The kitsune fanned his tails around him. *"I can help her, but only if you listen. Stop thinking about Nanai for a moment."*

I cleared my head and the grey mist returned, but it was calm and did not hide the kitsune.

He sniffed the mist. *"Well, I suppose I must forgo the inarizushi, though what you created smelled delicious. At least your thoughts are gathered.* He settled with his chin on his paws. *My sister was a powerful kitsune. She could create illusions that would fool a hound to chase a dandelion fluff thinking it was a hare, or send the miser flinging away his gold because he thought it was spiders. He laughed. She created this space to experiment on her illusions before she used them in the mortal world. Here, her slightest thought became real to the senses. When I grew older, she brought me here. But I never learned how to manipulate the possibilities or create illusion."*

"Then you can't—"

"Wait till I finish."

I bit my tongue.

"She, like too many powerful kitsune, fell in love with a mortal and wed him. She bore a daughter but never told her of her heritage. And so that daughter could never tell you."

"Me?"

"Your grandmother was a nine-tailed kitsune. A favorite zenko of Inari. And you have inherited her skill in illusion."

"I am kitsune?" The grey mist around me exploded in a blinding white. Heat stole my breath. *I am kitsune. Kitsune.*

"Only a quarter," he said. *"Now calm down or we'll both be uncomfortable."*

I breathed searing breath after breath until the cool grey returned. *I am kitsune. I'll never break the kitsune-mochi bonding because I am kitsune.* A strange peace settled over me. I couldn't be rid of the kitsune. But maybe I could use my kitsune heritage to help Nanai, just as I hoped the zenko would.

He twitched his ears as if shaking off the last of the brilliant heat. *"Only a quarter kitsune, but you influence this grey space too quickly for our good. You may even be a more powerful illusionist than my sister."*

I blinked. "I'm more powerful than a nine-tailed kitsune?"

"More powerful in illusion. But you lack control. Your ability to create is so strong that when you walked into the space of possibility, you filled it with the stink of your fears and prejudices against yourself. I could not change what you created in this mist, but only hoped if you listened long enough your thoughts would catch hold of something else

and then you'd be able to think clearly. I wonder at where you keep your thoughts to make such a dismal place."

A dark understanding pushed forward. I created that place of death. I was more powerful than a nine-tailed kitsune. Had my power to create from what I thought caused death? Bile rose in my throat as the stink and wind rushed forward. "Tell me. Did I cause the death of my mother and brothers by creating death in this place?"

I gasped as sharp teeth pierced my hand.

"Stop it. I will not stomach more of your morose dramas. Keep your thoughts on my story, or I'll send you back out of this world and we'll never finish this conversation. Nor will you save Nanai—whom I also care about. If you didn't notice, I'm her uncle. I've watched over your family since my sister married. So stop it."

I stilled my thoughts, and the grey turned back to mostly calm, though a lingering scent like rotten egg stung each breath. I rubbed my hand where he'd bitten.

"That will have to do." He covered his nose with one paw. *"No, you didn't cause their deaths. All mortals die; it is part of life. You only create illusion. And no illusion killed them."*

"Daichi? I had many ill thoughts for him."

"He made the foolish climb on his own and fell on his own. You can claim no part in his death. Now are you ready, or will you play over every memory of anyone who died?"

He was right. I pushed at the clinging, insinuating thought that had followed me since I first knew my twin brother had died and I had lived. The thought had strengthened every time Ichia called me Shi. It was a lie.

I gritted my teeth. "What can I do?"

"What do you imagine you can do?"

What would help most? We needed to free Nanai. An army? Could I learn to make one by tomorrow? I'd created Takumi's hut and his wolf-dog. I'd created the merging faces of my family for the Amaterasu mask. But the first was unconscious, and the second took days.

The faces of my family. What if? "Can I create the illusion of Nanai?"

He tilted his head. "*How would that help?*"

"If I create an illusion of her, I can sneak in and leave the illusion in her place. The illusion would be executed, not her."

"*True. She'd have to move, and speak, and tremble, and then die. It is a difficult illusion you speak of, especially for your first one. You've already created much without knowing. You could do it.*"

"I have to."

"*Nanai must leave the village when you free her. If the Kazoku learns that she's still alive, he will pursue and kill her.*"

"Then we'll leave. We'll make a new home northward. We'll write my father and let him know. Do you have any *helpful* words?"

He shrugged. "*Stop talking and start creating.*"

I bit back a retort. My kitsune uncle was curt, but his words were true. I needed to create. "Forgive me for my rudeness."

He chuckled, and I set to work.

I pictured Nanai, forming a rough outline of her in the grey. She shimmered like a chalk sketch in the air, radiating heat, and her faint lines glowing with the colors of sunset.

I turned to the kitsune. "Honored zenko?"

"*I'd rather you call me Uncle or Torikkusutā. I've not been an honored zenko since my sister and I left Inari's service. But ask your question and work while I answer.*"

"If you are our family guardian, why did you torment me?"

He laughed, his thought laughter deep underneath the high-pitched fox laughter. "*Torment you? You are a stubborn girl who wanted to be your twin brother and wouldn't develop your own talents. Stagnant water only breeds mosquitoes. I just stirred the water occasionally.*"

"Stirred the water? Helped me? How was it helping when you stole my mother's mask and I had to chase you all day?"

"You found the mask maker."

"Oh." I thought of the other times. I'd grown happy with the little jobs of the apprenticeship and wanted nothing to change, then my uncle tripped me so I broke the mask mold and Takumi had me finish the job. When I was afraid to break the mold away from the tengu mask, my uncle startled me into burning the food so Takumi required I finish the mask while he cooked. Even as a child, each of the kitsune's teasing tricks ended up with my learning from my father, mother or sisters.

Each memory now looked different. It was like Takumi tipping his mask so that it took on a new expression. "I suppose that you knocked over the ladder when I was mending the roof so I had time to create my first haikus."

"Actually, that was mostly an accident. But your first haikus were hilariously horrible. I still laugh over them."

I swatted at him, and he danced away sideways. He was a trickster kitsune, but mostly a good one, except— "It was wrong for you to hurt Takumi so I'd have to make the next mask."

He ducked his head. *"I didn't intend for him to break his fingers. And I used my healing ability to make sure they mended straight. But yes, you needed to move forward, and you weren't."*

His healing ability. "Uncle, you healed Takumi. Why didn't you save my mother?"

This time his head dipped all the way to the ground. *"She lost too much blood. I saved her at the birth of your twin and you, but I couldn't that time."*

"Oh." His words fitted the shards of my life into a picture opposite of what I'd believed. He had watched over and protected our family. He'd saved my life at birth as well as my mother's. He'd pushed me to grow. And now he was teaching me yet a new skill so I could save Nanai.

I bowed my head. "Thank you for everything you've done for our family and for me. Please forgive me for pushing you away."

He brushed against me. *"There is no need to apologize. I did nothing to gain your love or trust. Work on the illusion. The time is short and you have far to go."*

Nanai stood before me, solid and mostly formed. No sun or moon showed the shifting of time, but hours must have slipped by. I added the sea color to her eyes. They stared ahead with the woodenness of a carving.

Even if I could create an illusion to look like her, how would I get it to move? Takumi's words echoed in my mind, *Just try. The worst you can do is never pick up the chalk. Any line will be better than emptiness.*

It would have been much easier if we'd freed her that first night. "Uncle, why did you lead us to the pond? We would have been free if we went to the walls."

He huffed. *"I was leading you to freedom. If you had stepped onto the boat, the lake would have concealed us."*

"You said you can't create illusion."

"True, but the water spirit that lives in the lake can, and he owes me a favor. He'd have carried the boat to the water gate under the wall, and then you two could have slipped away. You never entered the grey space, so I couldn't tell you any of this."

I ducked my head. The grey heated, and the air grew acrid.

"Shall I send you back?" He bared his teeth.

I tucked my hands into the folds of my kimono. I didn't want to be bitten again, nor sent back. I breathed slowly through my nose until the grey returned to almost a comfortable temperature, and the biting scent of shame only whispered through the air. "Can the water spirit help us free Nanai tonight, when I replace her with the illusion?"

"No. He was offended when you refused to enter the boat. Shouldn't you be working on your illusion?"

I pushed my thoughts back to the shimmering image of Nanai. She looked too young. Like before I left home. Not the woman she'd grown into in the last half-year. I pulled the image to match Nanai as she'd huddled beside me under the maple tree, hiding from the Kazoku's search. The illusion stretched and snapped into a muddied figure, not quite her before nor her now. I scowled. "Any line is better than emptiness? Unless it convinces the Kazoku, it won't be enough."

The kitsune circled my illusion. *"You should know that what you are creating looks like Inari."*

I scowled deeper, struggling to fit the illusion to Nanai, when his words sank in. "We look like Inari?"

He flicked an ear. *"You needn't shout."*

I softened my voice. "We look like Inari?"

"More so than most."

"Uncle, how is it we look like Inari?"

His ears swiveled while he looked around in the mist.

"Has she commanded you to not tell us? Are we related?" As the words slipped through, I realized the truth. Some of Inari's zenko were also her children or grandchildren.

He glanced around once more. *"You said it, not me."*

Hope surged through my chest. *I'm related to the kami Inari. That is why my grandmother could create such illusions, and so can I.* Plans blossomed with the knowledge. If I made an illusion that Nanai was executed, then we'd all have to leave our village to maintain the trick. But if we convinced the Kazoku that the kami favored her, she'd truly be free. "I'll create an illusion so powerful that the Kazoku will beg for mercy and never bother our family again. I'll bring down an illusion of Inari and—"

"Careful."

I bit my lip. Would the kami punish me for making an illusion and having it speak as if for one of them? "I won't offend the kami. Instead, I'll create a dragon."

"Hai. You just may. But remember, you are still mortal. Even my sister had to work days to create a dragon, and you are still struggling to just make an illusion of your sister."

"We don't have days."

"Then you'll have to think of something else."

But what? If only my sisters could help. Could they? They also were part kitsune. "Do my sisters also have the talent of illusion?"

"Them, illusion?" he laughed. *"They have their own talents, but not that one."*

I grasped my short hair near my forehead. I needed days, or more ability, or, or— "Please help."

"I have. I brought you here and told you of your ability. I don't know what you can create. You must figure that out yourself." He closed his eyes as if in sleep.

"Trickster fox," I cursed.

The corner of his maw turned up in a smile.

20

Seven aesthetics
seven sisters' deception
trap set for freedom.

I woke to a cool cloth on my forehead, soft light filtering through my eyelids, and the arguing voices of my sisters.

"The storm is over and she's still not awake. We should call the doctor."

"What can a doctor do? We should call a shrine priest to drive away the demon."

"Shisei already tried. And now she's caught firmly in the demon's world. Why, Ichia, did you push her away?" It was Nichika's voice, gentle even in rebuke.

"I didn't. I pled with her not to go to the kitsune."

"You must have said something. Now we'll lose both Nanai and Shisei."

"Stop. Both of you," Gomako said, her voice tight with tears. "Our arguing will only invite more demons to torment us."

I rolled to my side and opened my eyes to the evening sun making our paper walls glow red. "I'm fine." And surprisingly, I was. The deep aches and slowness from the first time I visited the grey world were absent. Instead, a vigor ran through my limbs, as if I'd soaked in a hot spring. Was what I created in the grey world of illusion so impactful on my strength? Thoughts of death drained while creating life invigorated? Or was it knowing that Inari was one of my grandmothers?

My sisters were huddled on the far side of the room, their eyes intent on each other. "I'm well." I spoke louder as I stood. "And I have a plan for how to save Nanai, but I need your help."

In the confusion that followed, my sisters pressed a cup of broth into my hands, wrapped me in three blankets—each from a different sister—and buffeted me with questions. I laughed in answer, which only made Ichia's frown deepen and Nichika's arm tighten around my shoulders, as if to support me. I was not cursed and I had power to help. How could I not laugh with the lightness of a burden dropped?

"Please, I'm not hurt or ill," I finally said. "I learned from our uncle how to create illusion, and we will trick the Kazoku into thinking the kami favor Nanai."

"Our uncle?" Sanaho asked. "One of our deceased uncles taught you how to make illusions?" She spoke with a hint of disbelief, but not the full mocking tone from before.

They didn't trust the kitsune. How could I explain? I sipped the broth, avoiding Sanaho's questioning eyes. I'd explain our kitsune relation at a different time.

I turned to my second-youngest sister. "Rokue, what are the seven aesthetics of a kami-touched maiden?"

Rokue blinked and knelt in silence for a moment. "The seven aesthetics? Serenity and wild energy, skill and wisdom, grace and confidence, all unified by sacred poetry." She whispered. "Shisei, you are one of the seven."

"As are each of you. Nanai said the Amaterasu mask had each aesthetic. I created it from us. Together, we seven sisters are kami-touched, or could appear to be." My kitsune uncle's silence had given me time to realize this. He was a trickster who knew the best help he could give was pretending to sleep. I almost laughed again at his feigned deafness to my pleas for help.

"But how will this help Nanai?" Gomako asked.

"We will ask the Kazoku to give Nanai seven tests to see if she is kami-touched and thus kami-protected. We'll each complete one test. A different one each day. And by the last day, he'll be convinced to let her go." If he wouldn't, I'd use the dragon. It would drive terror into him if reverence for the kami didn't work. Seven days of tests would give me enough time to create the illusion.

"But we can't pretend to be her," said Gomako. "Even though we are all around the same height, we have different faces. Besides, she has blue-grey eyes and we all have brown."

I closed my eyes and pictured again the mask I made in the grey world, one I'd carefully formed like the molding of clay with Takumi. Nanai's sea-colored eyes smiled at me and her mouth turned up in a mischievous grin. It was her face when I found her eating a sakura-mochi before the cherry blossom festival. I settled the mask over my face, feeling it nestle against my skin like plum blossoms.

"Shisei," gasped some. "Nanai," gasped others.

I opened my eyes and smiled, though the mask stayed frozen in the one expression, forming my mouth into Nanai's grin. The illusion dissipated. I'd have to work on adding flexibility to the mask, so it moved with my sisters' words and expressions. "I'll work on it more so all will think you are Nanai. Will you each be tested for her?"

Sanaho clapped me on the back. "I never thought you were the clever one. But this is fit for a kitsune tale. What test will I do?"

"We'll all do it." Ichia's face blanched, but her words came firm. "It is a hope to save her when we had none before."

"Thank you for your courage." I bowed to each. "We should plan."

Sanaho leaped to her feet. "I am confidence and I will spar with the naginata to prove it. I'll go first."

Nichika shook her head, her face even paler than Ichia's. "We should carefully plan what tests we do and who goes when. Shisei, how long can you hold the illusion?"

"I'll hold it as long as needed," I said. "You just do your best in your test so the Kazoku has to believe you are kami-touched. And I will do the same."

I stepped out onto the porch. There was one other person I needed to talk to. I passed through the darkening garden until I knelt in front of our family shrine. I unbound my hair from the boy's knot and laid the leather strip on the stone. "Sheng, our uncle was right. I kept trying to be you. I promise never to forget you, but I know now that I need to be Shisei."

The sun had not yet warmed the path when the six of us knocked on the Kazoku's southern gate. A samurai opened it. "You are early."

I stepped forward, dressed as a woman and trying to be brave. It should have been Ichia, but her voice trembled so much that the Kazoku would never have listened. Sanaho was too brash, and Nichika deferred to me. Oh, to have a mask of courage and calm, but I'd have to fake it with my own face. "We have petitioned Inari and received an answer through Inari's priest. We wish to give the message to the Kazoku."

The samurai led us to the stone-paved courtyard where Nanai had almost lost her life the day before. The cold of the stones seeped through my sandals as we waited while the inner court wall shadowed us. On either side of Ichia, Gomako and Rokue twined their fingers around hers, her sleeves hiding their gripped hands. Nichika stood close to me, offering silent support. Sanaho, with her wide stance, stood slightly in front.

A door slid open, and the Kazoku strode out. "You've come early."

I bowed. "Inari's priest gave us a message. Inari will show that she favors Nanai by giving her seven divine gifts. Each day she will give her a different gift. Each day you may test her."

His eyes narrowed. "Inari's priest? Seven tests?"

I bowed again. He needed to believe us. Oh, to have a little of Sanaho's confidence. "Seven tests. Starting with the naginata."

He snorted. "She'll not be able to fight her way free if we give her an oak bladed weapon."

"We understand. We only ask that you give her seven tests so Inari may show that she favors her. If the priest was wrong in his interpretation, she will fail them. No maiden could pass these seven without Inari's help."

He studied each of us. "I'll agree on one condition, if she fails you will all die."

Mine was not the only sharp intake of air. I could risk my own life, but not the others. "Honored Kazoku—"

"We accept."

I spun around.

Ichia stood, chin up, lips thinned, and shoulders back. "We trust Inari's promise."

She trusted me.

21

Not force, but focus
brings success to the warrior.
Needle through guard's chink.

The first test came with the midday sun. I waited on the side of the courtyard with my sisters and four of the Kazoku's guards. Nanai stumbled from the house, partially held up between two samurai. Her once pale pink kimono was now grey with two days' imprisonment.

The Kazoku motioned to Nanai and then to a small area enclosed by a bamboo screen. "In more mercy than you deserve, I've provided a private place for you to converse with the prisoner before the test. There is no place to escape." He motioned to the open courtyard on all four sides of the enclosure and ten of his samurai standing with easy grace. "But if you try, all of you will die today."

We'd requested in the name of Inari and given him many bribes for that small space, no bigger than the seven of us could stand in without touching. But it would be enough. Ichia pulled

Nanai's arm over her shoulder and walked with her into the bamboo-walled space, and the rest of us followed.

Once inside, Nanai threw her arms around Ichia, and then each of us. She trembled in my arms, clinging as if she'd never let go. "Thank you for giving me one last time to hold you." Then she embraced Gomako.

We'd have to be careful what we said. Though the samurai could not see over the walls, they could hear us. I stepped forward while she clung again to Ichia and spoke so any who were on the other side of the bamboo would hear. "You must listen carefully if you want a chance at life. Inari has promised to give you seven gifts, the first being confidence in the naginata. Don't speak, no matter what happens, as her gift descends on you. Instead, go forth and fight and you will win."

Nanai's eyes widened with each of my words. "How? I don't know how to fight."

"Hush."

Sanaho stepped beside me. She now wore a free-flowing kimono and a protective leather apron. She cast her old kimono over Nanai and bound it on. Nanai's mouth opened, but I shook my head. When Nanai was dressed as Sanaho had been, and her hair, which was already knotted, pulled in a rough shield of grief over her face, I looked into the space where only I could see and changed the last few lines of the illusion. A bruise soon darkened the mask's cheek, and three scratches ran over the chin. I set the brows and lips to Sanaho's intense concentration. I'd worked all morning to create a flexible mask to change with Sanaho's expressions, but though it moved with her words and blinking, the expression was as unchanging as fired clay. This would have to do. I pulled the mask into the mortal space, setting the illusion over Sanaho's face.

Nanai gasped and swayed.

"Remember," I said, placing my hand over her mouth as

Nichika caught her. "Say nothing of the gift. We will all watch and pray to Inari."

Sanaho stepped from the enclosure, wearing Nanai's face and walking with confidence. We followed, our heads down-turned and our hair over our faces, so none could see the real Nanai, and knelt along one wall of the courtyard. Ichia and Nichika kept to either side of Nanai. I watched through my screen of black tangles.

The Kazoku caught Sanaho's arm and studied her face. His brows drew together. Would he guess? But how could he? It was Nanai's face, from sea-colored eyes to bruising. He finally grunted. "Let the test begin. The first to strike three valid blows wins."

Sanaho accepted an oak-tipped naginata and stepped into a red-bordered square about fifteen strides across. Opposite her a samurai entered. A close-cut beard covered his chin and white peppered the hair over his ears. Some samurai practiced painting with a brush placed on the end of their weapon to perfect their accuracy. He moved such that he could have painted many pictures, as if the naginata was another limb.

Sanaho was good. But she was still a youth in the discipline. I half closed my eyes and searched the space where I'd prepared my other illusions. A red fox sat the closest. Beside him sat my uncle, his four tails wrapped around him and his head turned to watch Sanaho. I stepped into the grey world, and my uncle followed.

"Uncle. Please help me do this right."

His laughing voice came into my head. *"I can't make illusions. But if you'd like, I can walk around the samurai four times and make him fall asleep."*

"No. You can't, or the test will be invalid."

He tilted his head. *"The test begins."*

Sanaho and the samurai bowed, then stepped three strides apart from each other. The contest was more than who could land the most blows. They had to be accurate strikes with correct posture and vigorous spirit while calling out the name of the intended target, which must match where the naginata struck. A distracted warrior who forgot one or more of those steps would lose, even if he landed more strikes. Three valid blows. That was all she needed.

I prepared the red fox illusion.

Sanaho raised her naginata and lunged, swinging the hardened wood blade downward. "Shoulder!"

Her voice was older than Nanai's. I glanced at the Kazoku. He didn't seem to notice; instead his gaze followed the weapons. The samurai blocked her blow, sliding it off to one side, then swung back with his own. "Hip." His voice was gravelly.

Sanaho rotated her naginata, meeting his blade with her haft. No strikes yet.

"Arm." He lifted his blade with the motion of her block, arching over her, and brought it down on her left side.

I placed the red fox illusion on the same side, floating by her arm, then made it ghostly, visible for a flash—no longer than lightning, nor brighter than fog. Not long enough for most to see, but for the warrior's quickness, who must see and react instantly in battle, he was there. The samurai's blade hesitated, and Sanaho caught the curve of his naginata. The force of his blow carried her weapon tip to the ground. She slipped backwards, pulling her weapon free.

Please, Sanaho, start calling out blows. You've only called once. Get on the offensive.

They both lunged forward, their curved blades meeting between them, clacking as they blocked and dodged and blocked again, neither one making it past the other's guard. Their points flickered up and down between waist and ankle level. Thrice more he called, swung, and she blocked. Then a fourth and fifth time. She fell further back with each attack.

He moved too fast for her to attack. She could hold him off only so long. If he landed three valid blows, the test was over and so were our lives. I had to distract him again, but not distract her.

I glanced into my illusions, grabbed a poisonous yamakagashi, and imagined it curled on the ground beneath their straining weapons. Another clack of their weapons brought both points close to the ground. *Please, Sanaho, remember what illusions I showed you. Keep focused.* The snake's yellow, red and black diamond back wisped visible, another foggy image visible for but a moment. The samurai leaped back, his movements jerky.

Sanaho stepped back, too.

No, get him, now! I screamed in my head.

She steadied, lunged forward, swinging the naginata from her left. "Head," she called as she struck his temple. I winced with the echoing thud of wood on bone. The samurai stumbled back another step. "Core." She rotated the naginata and thrust the haft into his leather apron-protected stomach.

Two blows to none!

"Leg." His naginata cracked against her left ankle. She stumbled backwards as he swung upward yelling, "hip." She blocked his blow and stepped back again. Her foot fell near the line. If she stepped out, she'd lose.

"San-Nanai," I called. "Watch the line."

The Kazoku held up a hand for the match to pause. Sanaho and the samurai parted. Sanaho limped to a far corner while the samurai rubbed his head. The Kazoku glared at me. "No more speaking. You must not interfere."

I bowed in apology. I was interfering and would continue to do so. He must not have seen the other illusions. I'd made them faint, so only those right next to them would see, and everyone else was at least fifteen strides away. But I would hold my tongue. I'd about given us away with my calling part of Sanaho's name. My heart thudded in my neck.

The steward hung two blue flags on the wall for Sanaho's valid strikes, and one red for the samurai's.

Sanaho only needed one more valid blow. Which illusion to use next? I still had an oni with a horn growing from the center of his head, but he was larger than a man and others might notice him, even if he only faintly showed. I didn't want to use the dragon. It was only sketchily made and dissolved into the grey most of the times I touched it. I needed more time to perfect it. Maybe I could use the snake or fox again.

The Kazoku raised his hand for the test to continue. The samurai had drunk rice wine to refresh himself, but Sanaho had been offered nothing. She limped forward to the center of the square and bowed to the samurai, who stood two naginata lengths away from her. She gripped her naginata and her face, frozen in the intense concentration of Nanai's features, dripped sweat.

Two blows to one. She only had to strike once more.

The samurai held his naginata with the haft at his right, but as he raced forward he spun the naginata, swapping it to his left side. "Hip."

Sanaho turned sideways to his upward swing and his blow swished past her. She returned a blow, coming from behind. "Leg." He brought up his haft and blocked it.

Back and forth. Sometimes their words overlapped. She didn't move from her spot, but rotated on her good foot. And neither landed a strike, though her arms shook more than his.

I brought out the red fox again and set it between them for just a moment. The samurai swished over it as if it wasn't there. He wouldn't be fooled by it again. A true warrior who learned and adjusted his tactics. I needed a new distraction.

I glanced into the grey at my two other options.

"Arm!" shouted a gravelly voice, followed by a low groan from my sisters behind me. I focused back on Sanaho. She scuttled backwards, her left foot dragging and her right arm cradled against her. The steward hung a second red flag. Now it was two on two and the next strike would determine the winner. Could Sanaho even hold her naginata?

I pulled out the oni and placed him shadowing Sanaho.

The samurai ran forward, spinning his naginata overhead. A mocking move against an opponent who could no longer fight.

Sanaho leaned forward under his attack, twisting the naginata up with one hand to block. Her injured ankle bent sideways, and she fell to one knee. His wooden blade descended.

I pushed the oni into visible light, standing over Sanaho's fallen form. His black horn stuck from his forehead and his long-nailed fingers hung from massive arms. The samurai's naginata flashed through the dissolving form and cracked against Sanaho's back. She cried out. The samurai turned his back on Sanaho, his face blanched.

My illusion hadn't stopped him. The samurai had won. I reached into the grey space for the half-made dragon. *Let it be enough of a distraction for us all to escape.*

"Continue." It was the steward's voice. He didn't raise the third red flag. The samurai hadn't called out his attack.

The warrior spun about, his blanched face turning red, his naginata extending his reach in a whistling arc.

I reached for the dragon. *Please stay visible long enough to let us escape.*

Sanaho still knelt on one knee. She pulled her naginata close to her body, then lunged underneath him. "Chest!" Her blade slid across the leather apron and the tip stopped at his chin.

The steward hung the last blue flag.

I let go of the illusion. Sanaho had landed the final blow without my help.

~

"Thank you." Nanai clung to Sanaho in the bamboo enclosure.

Sanaho, now with her own weary, pain pinched face, leaned heavily on her naginata.

I motioned for Nanai to be silent, then spoke in instructional tones. "Tomorrow Inari will gift you a new talent of wisdom. Speak not of your experience with anyone, but clear your mind and offer prayers to the kami and your ancestors."

She nodded, then looking once more at how Sanaho stood, mimicked the clutched arm to her side and limping step. She exited the enclosure to be led away by the Kazoku's samurai. The six of us watched, then clustered around Sanaho to support and hide her as we made our slow way to the south gate. Her hard-earned musk hung around us as the sun sank into late afternoon. I wrinkled my nose with the fear-scented victory. Sanaho's victory. Our victory.

22

Wisdom starts not with
knowing the answer, but with
seeing the question.

The dawn birds had silenced into the heat of late morning when I knelt near Nichika on our tatami floor. "Are you ready?"

She knelt in the middle of piles of all our books and all the ones she could borrow from her sensei. Puffy skin darkened under her eyes. I could have asked if she slept. But neither of us had. Not that my other question was much better. How could we be ready for a test of wisdom when we didn't know what kind of questions she'd be asked?

She turned the wooden handles of a scroll, her eyes darting up and down over the text, then set it aside. "Even with a hundred years, I could not be ready. I pray for wisdom when I am but a child in knowledge."

I swallowed. "Let's practice one more time."

She gave me a pinched smile.

I closed my eyes and pulled free of my body, walking as a spirit but still in the mortal world. My body knelt motionless as it had when I'd walked this way with the kitsune. I leaned near Nichika and spoke, focusing to send my words back into the physical world. "My sister's heart is larger than all the books in Nihon."

Her lips softened, and she shook her head. "You speak words to hearten the fool. But I will still go."

I laid Nanai's mask over Nichika's face, then brought forth the voice I'd fashioned through the night and laid it in front of Nichika's lips. I whispered, "Please tell me your name."

"I am Nanai." Her voice doubled, a blending of her deeper and Nanai's more crystal tones.

I strengthened the voice illusion. "Again."

"I am Nanai." This time the deeper tones were but a whisper behind Nanai's voice. It would do.

I reached to brush a strand of hair from her face, but could not with my spirit hands. So I whispered, "When this day is over, Nanai will be one day closer to free. Thank you." I removed the mask and the voice, then returned to my body. "Nichika, I'll be beside you the whole test. Our uncle will be too. He is wise as a fox. We'll help you. You are not alone in this."

She nodded again, then glanced out our open door at the sun. "I must leave." Ichia, Gomako, and Rokue stood waiting.

Sanaho leaned against the wall with an herb-soaked rag wrapped around her ankle and another around her purpling arm. Under her kimono, bands wrapped around her cracked ribs. She raised a hand in farewell. "Nichika, don't let them scare you. You don't just know things. You are wise. Now walk with some confidence."

Nichika lifted her chin and rolled back her shoulders, then led her three other sisters from our home.

I glanced at Sanaho. "My body will be motionless while I walk in the spirit. I won't be able to help you."

Sanaho shrugged and winced. "I'll be fine. I'll even keep wild animals from nibbling on your body while you are gone."

I winced at the thought. I was vulnerable each time I left my body.

My four-tailed uncle met me outside the home. He glanced upward.

"I must hurry," I said.

He glanced up again.

My sisters were already a distance down the path. "I'll speak with you. But afterwards, will you take me on the winds to the Kazoku's courtyard?"

He huffed.

Stepping into the grey was as easy as stepping into a garden. It wasn't distant, but always around me. I just had to open the door. The grey was soft and diffused with a rainy-day light. Fear flickered on the horizon, its scent drifting in with each puff of wind.

My uncle sniffed the air. *"You are learning to control your emotions and thoughts better. I overheard what the test will be. Your sister is to answer haiku riddles. They will give her the first two lines and she must answer with a line which both fits and delights with surprise."*

I bowed. "Thank you, honored uncle."

He chuckled. *"Honored zenko, honored uncle. I am kitsune. Just call me uncle. Now we must go."*

"Wait. Do you know which haiku? Do you know the answers?"

He turned and disappeared from the grey.

Ichia stood before the Kazoku. "Please forgive the absence of two of my sisters. They were so overcome with fear for Nanai that they have stayed home rather than watch another test."

His narrowed eyes turned up at the corners, as if her answer pleased him. "Their lack of faith bodes poorly for your condemned sister."

Ichia bowed deeper.

He motioned for one of his samurai to untie the rope from Nanai's arms and let her limp back to join her sisters in the bamboo enclosure. When Ichia had latched the bamboo closed, Nanai and Nichika exchanged kimonos, and Ichia brushed out Nanai's hair so it matched what Nichika's had been, while Gomako tangled Nichika's.

I set the illusion over Nichika's face and added the voice. As I worked, I whispered in her ear, "Remember to limp and favor your arm."

She nodded.

"The test is to answer haiku riddles."

Nichika's hands trembled as she tied the sash around her waist. The mask responded to her pinched brows. She was wise in many things, but poor in poetry.

"Nichika, if you can whisper the answer, I'll create the haiku."

And if I couldn't, our uncle could help. Four hundred years of life must have granted him some wisdom.

Nichika knelt on the flagstones across from a bald, grey-bearded man. White film coated both eyes. He rested on a thick rice mat, and slow grey clouds puffed from his pipe. He smoked in silence until my knees ached for Nichika's on the hard stone.

The pipe darkened. He tapped the bowl free of ash, then said, "You will answer four haiku riddles. I will state the first two lines and you must complete the haiku with a line which answers the unspoken question of the first lines, delights with surprise, and expands the thought. As an added rule to test if you are truly kami-blessed, each answer must also create beauty."

That rule would be from the Kazoku. Even without that rule, the riddle haiku was one of the most difficult tests of wisdom. I glanced again at Nichika. We had to do it. I looked further around. The Kazoku stood, brows lowered. Our sisters huddled around Nanai, hiding her in their mass of downturned faces. Servants and guards stood at the edges of the courtyard, the faint rasps of their whispers floating on the stifling noon air. Where was our uncle kitsune?

"The first," the man said, his voice paper thin.

*"Circles on surface,
made by touch, slowly fading."*

"Ripples," Nichika whispered as if speaking to herself. "Ripples on water. That would answer the last line."

"It is true," I replied, "but too simple. There is no surprise. No expansion of thought."

"Mirror?"

That could work. A quivering mirror. But still no surprise. Rain drops, trailing tree branch, turtle. Koi made ripples when they caught a surface bug. Any of them would work. Which one?

Nichika's words sounded in my ears, a background to my thoughts. I shook my head. "What did you say?"

She repeated her words, "Ripples can only flow in water, not ice."

"True and surprising."

The riddle giver sat, puffing on a freshly packed pipe, his sightless eyes gazing over Nichika's shoulder—to where I knelt behind her.

I swallowed. He couldn't see me. I needed to focus on the

riddle. *Ice. Winter. Cold. Frozen.* I leaned close to Nichika's ear and whispered.

Her shoulders dropped slightly from their tight space beside her neck. She answered quietly.

"Circles on surface,
made by touch, slowly fading.
Cold disrupts motion."

The man smiled and his milky gaze still rested on me. He closed his eyes and pulled deeply on his pipe. I shifted to Nichika's other side. Maybe he'd keep his eyes closed for the rest of the test. It wouldn't matter. He couldn't see.

His papery voice intoned:

"Hundred thousand threads
hang shimmering from grey loom."

He opened his eyes and gazed serenely over Nichika's other shoulder to where I knelt. A chill ran up my back and over my arms.

Nichika murmured, "Hundred thousand threads. Shimmering. Silk? Does a silk loom hold a hundred thousand threads? I haven't studied that. Why grey?"

I inched behind her. He followed my movement with foam-white eyes, a wisp of a smile passing over his face. Was his blindness only to mortal things? Could he see the spirits—see me? Would he tell the Kazoku?

Nichika's muttering became more urgent. "What would surprise with silk? That it comes from a worm?"

I'd remained quiet too long. I'd promised to support her, and I'd let the blind man distract me. I caught at the last words she'd spoken. Silk, worms. "Rainbow weave of worms."

Nichika let out a breath and spoke.

"Hundred thousand threads"

The man raised one eyebrow, a bushy white question moving upward on his bald head.

"hang shimmering"

Grey loom. It wasn't silk. "Stop, Nichika!"

She froze, and the blind man winced. I ducked my head down. He could also hear me. But he hadn't stopped us, nor told the Kazoku. Did he think I was part of the kami-gift of wisdom? I almost laughed. I wasn't wise. But if he thought I was part of the gift, then I would play the role and continue to help Nichika. "It isn't silk, it's rain."

Her shoulders tensed again. "R-rain," she stuttered. "Rain brings spring and swollen rivers, muddy rice paddies and plum blossoms."

I grabbed at her words, fitting them into the five-syllable space of the answer, then whispered my best. "Weave first day of spring."

She shook her head. "Not enough surprise." She paused. "Weaves spring from winter?"

Hers was better. An image formed in my mind. Silver rain pattered on snow, punching patterned holes, and the first flowers pushed through. I described it to Nichika and spoke an answering line.

Her shoulders again dropped from their tightness, though her voice shook as she answered,

"Hundred thousand threads
hang shimmering from grey loom,
weaving spring from snow."

The man coughed, sending puffs of smoke from his mouth. His creamy eyes seemed to stare not at me but into a space not even I could see. His serene face brightened into quiet delight. He cleared his throat.

"A pearl floats, glowing
in ocean sprinkled with foam."

Images formed in my head and I let them spill into the space around me. A pearl tangled in kelp, tossed on the waves, foam flicking it as it rose and sank and rose again. The moon reflected off its surface. A woman swam next to it, her face pinched with pain as she brushed off the thin threads that left red lines—the whip marks of a jellyfish. She was a pearl diver and had set the pearl in the floating kelp while she attended to her injury. I described the image to Nichika as the story grew.

She nodded as I added detail, then she drew a quick breath. "Moon. The moon floats in the ocean overhead."

"But what of the foam?"

"The stars."

My image dissolved, and a new one grew. A full moon, pearly bright, floated near the western horizon. Stars spread in foamy clusters, and a long trail of them formed in the moon's wake. As the moon dipped lower in the west, the eastern sky brightened, first with a glow of lighter blue, then reds, over the sea.

Nichika relaxed into my descriptions. I moved to the side to see her face. Nanai's mask over her emotions sat with eyes closed and calm. The blind man watched the surrounding space. His lips parted, as if he too saw what I was creating.

"Dawn seems to pull the moon from the sky," Nichika whispered.

My image shifted again. The glow of the eastern sky reached across and brightened the western in pink golds, bathing the moon as it slipped into the mountains. I spoke what I saw. Nichika's lips formed soundless words as she formed the haiku and added a last line. She spoke them again, this time so both I and the haiku master could hear.

"A pearl floats, glowing
in ocean sprinkled with foam.
Rose net pulls it down."

The haiku master bowed his head to Nichika and whispered so only we could hear. "Well done, child. And it is from your own soul you created this."

I wanted to cheer. We'd solved three of the four. And Nichika had created the last haiku. Even more so, the blind man seemed to want us to win. Or at least he didn't seek for us to lose. A warmth spread through me.

The haiku master leaned forward. "Shall we see if only one can answer this riddle of two?"

"Two walk rice paddy,
both step knee-deep, splashing."

Was this a riddle? Any two people had done this. I had with my sisters. What lay hidden in this? "I don't know," I admitted after long minutes of blank thought.

Nichika closed her eyes and knelt in stillness. A fly landed on her nose. She wrinkled her face as it crawled across her cheek, but her hands stayed pressed together in her lap. Was she praying? I'd promised to help, but how could I when the haiku held no apparent riddle? Our uncle would know, if I could find him. I stepped into the grey space. "Uncle! Torikkusutā!"

He entered the grey minutes later, licking his chops. *"I see you've dropped the 'honored uncle' and 'honored zenko'."*

I lowered my head in shame for my hasty rudeness. "Honored uncle."

"No, I like it better without. How are the haiku?"

"They were going well at first, but I don't understand this last one. It could be so many things. And nothing, really. It's not like the moon or rain. Just two people walking in a rice paddy."

"And you think two people are less beautiful than a globe of light in the sky or a prattle of water on the dirt?"

I scrunched my brows. All the true haiku were about nature, not people. Except Takumi sometimes spoke in haiku of mask making, and family, and... "The two people walking the rice paddy are important too. But what is the answer?"

"Answer?" He laughed. *"There is no one answer. Only many possibilities."*

His words called back Takumi's lessons. He'd shown me the start of a drawing and told me it was possibility. Was this haiku possibility too?

I looked around in the grey space. Here *was* possibility. The grey parted into a sun-drenched rice paddy. Nichika and Nanai walked through the knee deep water, their backs to the sun and their kimonos bound up, baring their legs. A duck darted across their path, leaving a spreading arrow of ripples behind him that lapped through their shadows and against their legs. The green of new rice swayed in long rows. I stepped towards them, brushing my arm with Nanai's.

The fox paddled in the water to my side. *"Between the girls and the shadows, you are six."*

"Six from three?" I let the images of my sisters fade till only I stood, casting a shadow over the water. The water tickled the backs of my knees, and my shadow lay before me. I bowed. "Thank you, most honored zenko."

He flicked me with a wet tail as I stepped from the grey space to kneel beside Nichika. Her eyes remained pressed shut, and she moved her mouth without making a sound.

"Nichika."

She squinted her eyes more tightly shut for a moment and then opened them and glanced sideways, towards my voice.

"It could be many things," I said, "but I think a person and their shadow is the most surprising answer."

Understanding spread on her face, "Yes. I see." She turned back to the haiku master. "Honored grandfather, you said to see if only one can answer a riddle of two."

"Two walk rice paddy.
Both step knee-deep, splashing.
Only one gets wet."

He nodded. "A person with a shadow or a spirit. Either way, only one gets wet. Which did you mean?"

"Sh-shadow," Nichika stuttered.

"Ah. Then for your last haiku."

Last haiku? No! We'd completed four. There couldn't be another.

The old man continued, "Thus far, you have delighted me with beautiful and surprising images, memories of what I once could see." His voice dropped low.

"Fall down, anguished cries,
labored breath quickens, blood flows."

My throat tightened. It was Daichi's fall from the cliff. I glanced beyond our small circle. The Kazoku stood close by with arms crossed, a sneer across his broad face. If we answered with death, it would fit, but the surprise of death held no delight nor beauty. The haiku riddle could not be solved according to the rules. The

Kazoku knew this. He must have commanded it to be the last haiku; to trap us if we made it this far.

Was there beauty around death? The shrine, the incense, the vase with the trailing branch, the food set out for the departed spirit. Those all were beautiful. But never death. It was loss, hurt, pain, confusion. Yet, we had to try. I whispered to Nichika, "spirit greets his kin." There had to be beauty in that meeting.

Her face was soft with a distant look and seemed not to hear me. I repeated, "spirit greets his kin."

She shook her head. "This is not about death or spirits, but life."

How? Her words clashed with the picture of Daichi falling from the cliff and later his spirit walking away from his still body.

She straightened her back and spoke:

"Fall down, anguished cries,
labored breath quickens, blood flows."

"Stop. Tell me first," I pled.
She smiled and continued:

"Welcome cry. New life."

"Hah!" The Kazoku strode forward. "That is no answer. No life comes from death. Death only begets death. As my son's will yours."

"Wait." It was a woman's voice, though rough as with crying. It came from the shadows of the house. "How did she answer the haiku?"

The haiku master rose to his feet and strode with slow shuffling steps to the voice. "Honored *no kimi.*"

He was addressing the wife of the Kazoku. I'd never seen her.

As a woman of high standing, she did not appear outside of her vast walled estate. Why was she speaking now?

The haiku master stopped outside the door. "She answered, *welcome cry, new life.*"

"Hai," the Kazoku's wife said. "She understood."

The Kazoku's face reddened. "You gave me the haiku, promising that only a kami-blessed could answer it. Have you tricked me and told her the answer?"

"No, honored husband, I have not spoken with the girl. She understood that bearing a child is close to death but ends with new life. Only a mother or kami-blessed would know this, and she is not the former."

His face deepened to purple. "It is only the second of the tests. Inari cannot care enough for a potter's daughter to give her five more gifts. Come back tomorrow and we shall see if she is still kami-blessed."

I sat on our porch as the late afternoon sun glinted off the koi pond. Nichika leaned against me, her head on my shoulder, heavy with sleep. I brushed a strand of her tangled hair from her face. Together we'd passed the test. We'd built on each other's ideas and creations. She'd understood the riddle that only mothers, kami-blessed, *and older sisters* could have known. I blinked back tears. Today was sweet, even for the fear that hung over it.

23

———————

Tea from broken bowl
brings peace to the emperor
when served tranquilly.

The teahouse walls dissolved into grey as I stood, stretching from a long night of kneeling. My uncle curled asleep at my feet, resting his head on one of his four white tails. After he'd told me what the next test was, he'd kept me company with his snuffling dreams.

I stepped from the grey world into a mortal space filled with sweet scents. I stood and stretched a second time, this time in my body. My knees creaked and my calves seized, bulging in knots. I strode around the room, walking on my toes to stretch out the muscles.

Rokue poked her head from the kitchen. White paste coated her hands and a dab of mashed adzuki bean sat at the corner of her mouth. "Shisei, you're back. You must be hungry. We're making the wagashi for the tea ceremony. What illusion did you make?"

"Rokue," Ichia called, "mix the pink mochi before it streaks."

Rokue shrugged and disappeared back into the kitchen. I

192

followed. Sanaho leaned against one wall, chopping nuts on a board, using her uninjured arm. She waved her knife-wielding hand. "Shisei, isn't this a tasty part of our adventure?"

Rokue kneaded pink into the white of the mochi while Gomako stirred cubes of agar jelly into water and Nichika sliced yokan into cubes. Ichia knelt at a low table forming orange, pink, and green pastes into cherry blossoms, camellia, clusters of hydrangea, turtle shells, sea urchins, fern-scrolled squares, and lacy maple leaves.

The clatter of mixing spoon in bowl, thunk of knife on block, and soft slap of kneading blended with the scents of rice, sugar, beans, nuts, and fruit. I closed my eyes, pulling in the senses. Our kitchen had often been like this when Mother was alive; all of us gathered beside her to create, and each of us specializing in one part. Now Ichia was the center of it, guiding, correcting, and creating through our many hands. When we freed Nanai, we would have to do this again.

I knelt next to Ichia. "How may I help?"

She glanced up at me, her brow creased. "Were you able to modify the illusion?"

I nodded. "Are you ready to try again?"

She wiped her fingers on a damp cloth and rose to follow me into the main room. The light through the paper door was still that of early morning. We had several hours before we would carry to the Kazoku the sweets, tea utensils, and vase with a maple branch.

"Shall I get the mirror?" I asked.

She shook her head as she knelt where the light illuminated her face best. The crease in her brow deepened. "Please place the mask on me. If it doesn't conceal, then the mirror won't help." She took a deep breath and smoothed her face, but anxiety clung to the corners of her eyes, the downturn of her mouth, and the pinch of her cheeks.

I pulled Nanai's mask from the grey world and placed it over Ichia's face. It blended in with her skin, blinking with her eyes, forming to every expression. I'd modified it from the rigid expression of concentration from Sanaho's test to the fluid matching of every fleeting emotion in Nichika's test. But now the mask needed to be partway between—molding with Ichia's words and movements, but concealing her grief and fear. I'd spent hours of the night changing the illusion after our first attempt last evening. But it still revealed every emotion of Ichia's face.

Tranquility, I thought, urging the mask to respond as it had in the grey world. The mask shifted from Ichia's pinched expression to serene. My shoulders dropped with my released breath. "Ichia, it works."

Her brows raised slightly as she reached up and touched her masked-face, tracing the lines of her cheeks and jaw. "It isn't just concealing my face, but has molded my face to its lines. How?"

I hadn't expected that. "Is it hurting you?"

A muted, puzzled look formed as if an echo of the emotion. "My jaw doesn't hurt the way it has for the last many days. The tightness is gone from my face, though it still sits in the rest of me. With my face changed this way, I should be able to perform the tea ceremony as it should be, with harmony, respect, purity, and tranquility."

I bowed. "Thank you for trusting me."

She took my hands. Hers shook. "I'm trying to. I don't understand what demon follows you, but you are saving my family, and I am grateful for it."

"Ichia, I learned the skill of illusion, just as you learned the skill of serving tea. I'm not cursed. No demon follows me. I'm not even kitsune-mochi. Please believe me."

"Then who is the white fox?"

I held back a sigh. Just as our uncle had told me I wasn't ready to listen when I first entered the grey world, Ichia wasn't ready to hear the full truth yet. I squeezed her hands. "He guards our family. And though he couldn't prevent the deaths that have happened, he has protected each of us through our lives. He is helping us even now."

"Like our uncle—the one who taught you to use illusion?" As her voice grew more emotional, the tranquility of the mask strained, pulling up at the edges.

This was not the Ichia of a year ago. Even as she'd called me Shi, Ichia had always been calm and peaceful. But something broke in her when she lost her baby. She needed to re-find that gift if she were to pass the test today.

"Ichia, do you trust Sanaho and Nichika?"

She nodded.

"Can you ignore your unanswered questions? Can you let go of what you don't understand? Just for today?"

She nodded again, breathed deeply, and the mask smoothed over her face, adhering again at the edges.

I slipped into the grey where the partially-made dragon stood. Uncle curled up by her feet.

"Uncle, why does Ichia say I feel different from all my other sisters? We are all part kitsune."

He lifted his head and looked into the distance. "*It isn't the kitsune she notices, but your inherited talent. Your mother named you well. You are sacred poetry, bridging what is and what could be. You are different, and Ichia, who may be the only mortal I know who has a head denser than yours, assumed the difference meant you were evil. She should have to suffer the priest's smoke house or get licked by hounds to drive out her stupidity. Either of those is too kind for the lies she's taught you. You will tell her that for me.*"

"Ah..." My mouth fell open. I could say none of those things to Ichia.

"Hai. You'll tell her what you tell her. Though I wish she could hear me. I've upset many of her meals after she did a particularly spiteful thing. But no. He looked into my eyes. *I had nothing to do with her failed pregnancy. I would never harm a baby, especially a kit of my family."*

"I know that now." I looked down at my hands, which formed illusions. I was very different from my sisters. "Will Ichia ever accept me?"

Uncle strode over to me. *"Who knows? But for today, give her the space to act on her talent."*

I slipped back to the mortal world and walked in spirit beside my four sisters as they traveled the path to the Kazoku. Nichika carried the wagashi, each delicately formed sweet set in a paper box and the whole of them wrapped in a checkered cloth. The lacy leaves of a maple trailed over Rokue's shoulder as she carried the green glazed vase. Gomako carried the chadōgu, including tea caddy, scoop and whisk. Ichia came last, carrying a scroll and Father's most prized tea bowl—the one he gave Mother for their wedding. Sanaho had stayed behind to guard my body while I walked in spirit again. Besides, she still walked with a slight limp, and it could have made the Kazoku suspicious.

I walked beside them, listening to the quiet slap of their sandals on the path. The chatter of the kitchen had died into solemn silence.

Nanai whispered in Ichia's ear as they exchanged places, and Ichia embraced her before she exited the bamboo enclosure in Nanai's old kimono.

A woman approached us. Her black silk kimono rustled with

her tiny steps. Grey streaked her black hair, which was pulled into an elaborate bun and held in place with black pearled combs. Her face was as Ichia's had been this morning—grief-lined and hollowed. She bowed. "I am the Kazoku's wife. I will be your guest and your judge in the tea ceremony. If I find peace for the hour of the tea, then truly the kami has blessed you. If not, then my husband will send your spirit after that of our son. I do not desire another death, but I will not lie to my husband."

She led my sisters from the courtyard along a path between pines that brushed at their sleeves. The path opened into a space surrounded by dense hedges. Moss covered the ground, along with pockets of ferns and flat stepping stones. A covered waiting arbor sat next to a calf-high hollowed stone. The trickle of water sang in the cool silence, flowing from a bamboo pipe to fill the stone, and then running over the edges into the pebbles around. Just beyond and slightly behind the arbor sat a small teahouse, its simple shoji walls and unvarnished posts shaded by a twisting pine. A porch of sand with smooth stepping stones led up to the waist-high guest entrance.

The Kazoku's wife sat under the waiting arbor, composed her hands in her lap, and gazed into the moss-covered yard. It was time for Ichia to prepare the tea and start the ceremony. She went around the side of the tea-room to the host's entrance. Our other sisters handed in the supplies they'd brought and bowed to her, then knelt at the base of the dense hedge, out of sight of the Kazoku's wife. As on other days, those not in the test would wait, but this time they could not watch.

I followed Ichia into the teahouse. It was a single room with a sunken square hearth surrounded by four tatami mats, and to one side, an alcove. Ichia hung the scroll in the alcove, the black calligraphy the only decoration on the wall. As she heated the coals in the hearth and set the pot to boil, her shoulders relaxed and her movements smoothed to match the mask's tranquility. She arranged the chadōgu tools and set the wagashi sweets on a tray, then opened the guest door, sliding it two-thirds with her left hand, the final third with her right. Each step of the tea ceremony was set, from the opening of the door to the words spoken. Each part was designed to help the guest remove herself from the troubles of life, and for a time, find peace.

I slipped outside. The Kazoku's wife knelt at the stone basin, washing her hands and rinsing her mouth in ritual purification. The soles of her wooden sandals clacked as she stepped from stone to stone across the raked sand. She slipped off the sandals on the large stone before the guest entrance, then crawled through the nijiriguchi guest door. The crawling represented purity as the guest left behind all the thoughts and worries of daily life. Could she leave behind the sorrows of her dead son? Could Ichia leave behind her own sorrows and be, for this time, at peace?

Ichia and the Kazoku's wife bowed silently. Then Ichia presented the tray of sweets. The set conversation proceeded with "please have some sweets" to "I would like to serve you a bowl of tea," words I'd heard each time Mother had invited me to have tea with her. She'd made sure each of us daughters had a private tea with her each month. I bowed my head in the memory.

As the water boiled, the conversation came to the guest's turn to ask about the hanging scroll. "The calligraphy is beautiful. What does it mean?"

My chest tightened. That wasn't part of the ceremony. But Ichia hadn't chosen a scroll specific to our summer season, as was expected. Instead, she'd painted one of our mother's haikus.

Spring never saw fall.
Winter told her of his gold
and she'll tell summer.

The haiku was one of my favorites. It spoke of the joy of

sharing things another has never seen, and the promise of things to come again. When Ichia painted it in her beautiful calligraphy, it felt perfect to invite tranquility, but now the woman's question caused a break in the carefully scripted flow of peace.

Ichia gazed at the scroll with the Kazoku's wife, then spoke softly, "It is to remember what was lost and tell the future so they may also feel the beauty."

The Kazoku's wife closed her eyes. "It is yūgen."

Yūgen? Was the haiku truly of mournful beauty surrounding loss? Mother's life filled with yūgen, as did Ichia's and mine. Each of us had lost family. Was the haiku to remind us to tell others of our missing family, so they too could see the gold of ones they had never met? Who would the Kazoku and his wife tell? Daichi was their only child.

The steam from the pot drifted upward. Ichia ritually cleaned each tea utensil, then scooped powdered tea into Mother's tea bowl, covered it with hot water, and whisked it with the bamboo chasen until the tea foamed. Ichia placed the tea bowl on the edge between her tatami and her guest's. The Kazoku's wife leaned forward and took the bowl, and they proceeded with the carefully scripted actions of harmony and respect, as if the haiku question had not disrupted the flow.

Ichia knelt with a quiet calm as her guest sipped the thick green tea. Her whole body was serene along with Nanai's mask. If I let the mask form to her emotions, it probably wouldn't change much. But Ichia was not who needed to be at peace.

I studied the Kazoku's wife as she sipped. Grief still stained her face, but the tightness smoothed with each sip. Her eyes closed, and she breathed in through both nose and mouth. When she finished, she rotated the bowl, studying it. This was part of the script that changed from tea ceremony to ceremony. The guest would compliment the bowl and ask about it.

The Kazoku's wife set the bowl down. "Why did your sisters bring a bowl with so many fissures?"

Again, she broke the careful script of compliment. Was she baiting Ichia, trying to get her to break the calm and fail the test? But her words came as if she wanted to know the answer.

Ichia took the bowl and turned it slowly, then set it back on the edge of tatami mats between them. "My father made the bowl when he was still an apprentice potter and had not yet learned all the skills to properly heat the kiln and apply the glaze. Outside the bowl, the green glaze turned yellow and pitted, cracking along a thousand lines, while the inside crusted with irregular creamy drips overtop of earth tones. He was about to throw it away when my mother walked by and saw it. She said it was like stars and constellations written in a golden sky on the outside, and the inside was like the sea foam on the beach. They met because of the bowl, and our family became. It is our most honored possession, and someday I will pass it on to my daughter, and tell her of autumn's gold."

"Won't it go to your oldest sister and her oldest child?"

The peace shattered around me. Ichia had forgotten. She'd forgotten her grief and her hurt for a moment, she'd looked forward to a time of another child, and she'd forgotten that she played the role of Nanai.

The mask strained over Ichia's face, coming up at the edges.

"Tranquility, serenity," I whispered to the mask, then to Ichia. "Think. You can find a reason for your words." But she could not hear me. My jaw tightened, and Ichia's did the same. The mask now looked like a mask, a separate piece from her face.

The Kazoku's wife paled and scooted back on her knees.

Ichia touched her own face. "Please remove the mask. She deserves to know the truth."

It was too late for another option. Though, how was this better? I let the mask dissolve back into the grey world along with

Nanai's voice. Ichia pressed her head to the tatami mat for a deep moment, then faced the Kazoku's wife. "I am the eldest daughter, Ichia."

The Kazoku's wife stared, her lips tight and her hands wrapped in her kimono. "You sought to trick us."

"We sought to save our sister."

"You should have pled for her life."

"We did. We offered our lands and our freedom. We've offered our lives if Nanai does not pass the tests."

The woman blanched again. "He never told me this."

Ichia set the tea bowl into the woman's hands. "Our family started from a broken bowl, saved because a woman saw beauty in the brokenness." She glanced at the haiku hanging on the wall. "I've lost two brothers and a mother. I've lost my only son. He was born too early and never breathed. I do not know the grief you pass through, nor when you will find peace again. I only ask that you not take my youngest sister."

The mother turned the bowl, tracing her finger over the pits and fissures. "May I have another bowl of tea? I seek to speak of autumn's gold."

Ichia prepared a second bowl of green tea, whisking it to a foam, and handed it directly to the bereaved mother.

She took the bowl and, bowing, said, "I wish to give you my name as you've given me your trust. My mother named me Ai."

Ai—love. Would the Kazoku's wife show love for us and not reveal us to her husband?

They shared the tea and their conversation turned to the mother's memories of Daichi; from first toddling steps to when he flew his first kite and climbed his first tree. "He has left me more than memories," Ai said after a long silence. "I know of two grandchildren who have always lacked a father. If I ask the servants, I may learn of more. I would wish for it differently, but I thank the kami for the gifts they give."

The tea ceremony never returned to the expected dialog. Instead, it stretched until the light dimmed through the paper walls. Ai helped clean the tea utensils, working beside Ichia as if both had been the hostess. Then, bowing, she said, "I will tell my husband I found peace and that the potter's daughter is truly kami-blessed. Both are the truth. I'll send up my prayers to the kami that your next sisters will be as successful." She bowed and crawled backwards through the guest door.

Ichia collapsed to the tatami floor, her body shaking. She'd bravely spoken the truth and shared the grief of Daichi's mother. Our mother had named her well. *One is love.* Her ability to love and feel for others had saved us.

Nichika's soft voice came at the door. "She is gone. May we come in?"

Ichia lifted her face from the floor. The crosshatch of the tatami weave pressed into her forehead, and tears traced down her cheeks. "Yes. Nanai is safe for another day, and Daichi's mother is praying for us."

I ran ahead of my sisters on the walk home, slipped back into my body, and dashed back along the darkening path to greet them. Ichia startled, then stepped beside me. "Come, Shisei, we should let Sanaho know that we passed the tea ceremony. She may be worried by how you dashed out the door, and she may come charging out with her naginata to save us all."

I laughed as tears pricked my eyes. She'd called me Shisei.

24

———————

Music, note on note,
sings over strings, calls through pipes,
giving the heart voice.

Gomako filled the night with the sounds of biwa, koto, nohkan, and every other instrument we sisters could borrow from our neighbors. In the morning, before breakfast, Rokue ran out the door. A long time later, she returned with a long, narrow line of wooden plates nested together by a cord. She grinned as she held the two ends so the middle bowed and then flicked one end. The wooden plates rippled like a wave, clacking against each other.

"What is it?" I asked.

"It's a bin-sasara," Gomako answered for her. "Thank you, Rokue, for finding one. I haven't played one in more than a year." She picked it up and made a dancing rhythm ripple through the room.

Rokue's mouth turned down in a pout. "It took me an hour to learn how to make it work, and you do it so easily."

Nichika handed Rokue a bowl of rice and chopsticks. "It is good that she can. Her test depends on her skill with the instruments. And though we've passed each test so far, we cannot be lazy about preparing for this next one."

Rokue's pout deepened. "We shouldn't worry so much. Everything is working out just as Shisei planned."

"It isn't." I knelt next to Rokue as she picked at the rice in her bowl. "Yesterday with the tea ceremony, little of it went as I planned, but Ichia's words brought an unexpected blessing. Nichika's answer to the last haiku riddle was not my answer, but it was the necessary one. Sanaho struck the third blow without my illusions to help. I will continue to do all I can with my illusions, but it is taking each of you, with your talents, skills, and hearts, to pass the tests."

Rokue dropped her chopsticks. "Do I have enough talent to pass mine?"

Oh. Understanding softened my next words. "You have more than enough talent. I've watched you dance since before you could walk steadily. All I have to do is make Nanai's mask keep up with your movement. And the kami are blessing us."

She swallowed, set her quivering lips into firm lines, and placed the bowl aside. "I will practice dancing while Gomako prepares her music."

"Eat while I speak with Gomako," I said. "Then you can practice."

Gomako played sea-storm notes on the shakuhachi flute but paused as I knelt next to her.

"Gomako, will you try one more time to hear me?"

She set the pale bamboo flute in her lap. "I will try."

If she could, it would mean I could warn her or tell her something from our uncle. We'd tried three times so far. And each time she wilted a little more with the failure. If this time didn't work, I would not try with her again.

I slipped from my body and knelt in spirit near her. "Gomako, your music is as beautiful as a breeze through an autumn maple."

Her brow pinched. "If you've said something, I can't hear it."

If she could only hear me. How my uncle must have felt this same frustration as he tried to communicate with me but could not. "Gomako." I grasped her hands, willing her to hear.

She jerked back. "Shisei? I felt something. Was that you?"

"Hai."

"Shisei, if it is you, touch my left hand."

I tapped the back of her left hand.

A relieved smile spread across her face. "I can't hear you, but I can feel you."

I slipped back into my body. "Gomako, I'll warn you with a tap on your left hand to stop and think more about what you do next. If you look frightened, I'll let you know that you are going the right way by tapping your right hand. If I must speak with you, I'll tap both hands and you must ask the test giver to give you a moment to speak with your sisters."

"Arigatou, Shisei." She bowed her head, then played the shakuhachi flute again, filling the room with keening waves of music.

Sanaho stood at the door as our sisters left. "I'm going with you today."

I watched our sisters draw further down the path. "Why?"

"Because I can't stand another day of watching your unmoving body."

I turned to stare at her. "Are you saying I frighten you?"

"Hai! I never wanted to believe in spirits and demons and things I can't see. But now I have to believe in them, and you are the most unnerving of them all."

I bit my lip to keep from laughing. She was unnerved by me. "We'll have to race to catch them."

Sanaho slipped on her sandals and jogged down the road, her stride only slightly uneven. It was good, for Rokue would have to dance tomorrow and it needed to be reasonable that the sister who'd been injured in the first test could dance three days later, though being kami blessed could be used as an excuse. We should have held Sanaho's test for the last, but she was the most willing to go first. Oi, there wasn't anything we could do now but move forward. And that was Gomako's test today.

Our uncle kitsune joined us in the small bamboo enclosure in the Kazoku's courtyard, weaving between our feet and brushing his tails against each of us, and then stopped in front of me. He glanced upward. Where had he been the last day? I hadn't seen him since speaking with him before Ichia's test; not in the grey world or the mortal.

I knelt, then stepped into the grey world and found him waiting, sitting tall with his ears alert. I bowed. "Uncle."

"Your sister will listen to a melody and play it on whatever instrument she is given."

That was good. Gomako's skill lay in imitation. And today's test would be solely on her skill. I couldn't help anymore than give her the mask and voice and perhaps tap her hand.

He continued, his voice lilting, *"Tell her that her uncle looks forward to today's performance."*

"I will. Arigatou." I prepared to leave, but looked back. "Uncle?"

"Hai."

"Where were you yesterday?"

"I was comforting your eldest sister."

"Why didn't I see you?"

He licked a paw. *"You only see me when I want you to. Go. They need the mask."*

~

I stood in spirit by Gomako as she bowed.

A middle-aged woman returned the bow, then knelt on a tatami mat. Her cream kimono and pale flower-print obi were in sharp contrast to the dirty cloth of Nanai's kimono. She motioned to Gomako. "Please join me. I desire to hear what a kami-blessed musician sounds like." Her words, though polite, stretched out into mocking tones.

Gomako knelt on the stone across from the woman.

"Please, join me here." The woman motioned to the tatami. There was enough space for the two to kneel side by side but it did not give Gomako much room to use her instruments, and the woman could nudge her arm while she played. Could the Kazoku have paid the woman to disrupt the test? I tapped Gomako's left hand. *Be careful,* I wanted to say.

Gomako bowed again to the woman from her kneeling position. "I would not wish to soil your beautiful kimono. I will kneel on the stones."

The corners of the woman's mouth pulled slightly down as she raised her hand. A servant in muted brown walked forward, balancing a koto in his arms. The thirteen-stringed instrument was longer than the servant was tall and looked as though it had been carved from a slightly warped beam. He placed it in front of the woman.

"I will play a melody," she said. "You will imitate it on a different instrument." She leaned forward and plucked a rapid fluttering of notes that ran from the middle to the highest strings.

Gomako closed her eyes, and the Nanai mask creased with concentration.

As the last vibrating note ended, the servant walked forward again, this time bearing a single unlacquered length of bamboo with a wedge-cut mouth, four spread finger holes, and a bulging end.

The woman motioned to the flute. "You will reproduce the melody with the hocchiku flute."

I scowled. The hocchiku was a low instrument with haunting notes. Not something for a melody like chirping sparrows.

Gomako kept her eyes closed as she picked up the flute and silently fingered the holes. As her fingers fluttered over the bamboo, the crease in her forehead softened. She swelled with breath and played. The low notes fluttered like the koto had, but many octaves lower. If rocks could twitter with the sparrows, they would sound like this.

The woman's brows lowered as she mumbled to herself. I drew closer to hear her under-breath words. "—perfect imitation, as if she knew the melody. But I created it this morning. How did she recreate it, and on the hocchiku?" She slightly shook her head. "It is only the first test. She can't pass them all." She leaned over the thirteen-stringed koto and plucked out another rapid melody, this one like rain pattering, each note short and crisp.

The servant brought forward a kokyū, its small box body and long neck strung with three strings. He set it next to Gomako along with a horsetail bow.

The tip of Gomako's tongue peeked out of the corner of her mouth and her brow creased again in concentration. She fingered the strings on the neck. The bow danced in rapid motions in the air a short distance from the strings. She turned to the woman. "May I pluck instead of using the bow?"

"No. But do not worry. Your last melody delighted me, and I am sure this one will too."

"Thank you for your kind words." Gomako bowed again, her words sincere.

Please, I prayed, *let Gomako remain deaf to the woman's mockery and only hear the music she must play.*

Gomako laid the bow on the string, and rain sang from quick bow strokes. Each note matched in tone and feel to what the woman played.

The woman sniffed. "I will allow such quality but once. You will have to do better the next time."

Gomako's shoulders slumped.

No, Gomako, don't wilt. Don't listen to her. Your music is a delight. I wanted to whisper each word to her, but she could not hear me. I tapped her right hand, again and again.

Gomako laid her left hand over her right and took a shaky breath. "I am ready for the next melody."

The woman picked up the long hocchiku flute from between them and played a slow, long-noted melody, swelling each deep note to fill the courtyard. The stones vibrated beneath my feet.

The servant brought forward the shamisen, a twin to the three-stringed kokyū but without the bow. Gomako set the box part in her lap and fingered the strings along the neck. This time her pinched brows stayed through her silent practice. How could she create the deep vibrating melody on an instrument that only made short, plucked notes? She paused and silently fingered the strings again.

A sneer grew on the woman's face as the time slipped by.

Gomako blew out a breath and plucked the first note. Along with the note, a deep humming vibrated from her chest. Her naturally deeper voice rumbled under Nanai's lighter illusion voice and between the two vibrated overtones like the nohkan flute. She recreated the ponderous melody, each note punctuated by the plucked string, then drawn out on the multitoned voice. As the last hummed note died away, Gomako blinked. Her blue-grey mask eyes filled with wonder and delight, as if she didn't believe that the music came from her.

The woman's lips parted. "How? Are you truly kami-blessed?"

Gomako bowed. "I seek only to play what you have beautifully offered."

The woman's slack jaw hardened. I leaned close to hear her under-breathed words, "A place as the lead of the Kazoku's musicians if she fails."

I tapped Gomako's left hand. She needed to be careful.

The woman waved her hand, and the servant brought forward a single-stringed ichigenkin. The woman motioned to the instrument. "One who is kami-blessed does not just imitate but creates. This last melody must be one that has never been played before."

Gomako's face drained of color. "Please, sensei. The tests were to recreate your melodies."

"Are you not kami-blessed?"

Gomako opened her mouth, and I tapped both of her hands. She swallowed. "I beg your patience as I speak with my sisters."

The woman knelt silently for a long moment, then nodded. "One sister may come here and speak with you. She may say no more than ten words."

I rushed to Nichika's side. "You must tell Gomako the words I tell you," I whispered. "Walk slowly while I think."

As she walked with tiny steps, I pushed into the grey world. "Uncle," I called, my voice echoing through the stormy mist. "I need your help."

He walked around from behind me. "*No need to shout. I can hear you just fine.*"

"Gomako's last test is to create an original melody. She's never created her own music before. She always plays someone else's. Her skill is in her ability to mimic, not create."

He laid back his ears at my loud words. "*True. Her skill is strong, but she does not create. You'll have to help her.*"

"Me?"

"*You've played the ichigenkin.*"

"Only because my sensei required I play it until I could see people as having many parts, just as the single string had many notes. I never became good at it."

"You rarely played another's melody on the ichigenkin. Instead you created your own. And some of them were beautiful."

"Even if I could create something beautiful, how does that help her?"

"She can feel your hands." He glanced into the distance. *"Nichika is by Gomako now, waiting for your words."*

I fled the grey world. Nichika knelt next to Gomako as if in meditation. What could I say to her? Gomako could feel my touch. Could I guide her to feel out a new melody? *Inari, we need your blessing.* I counted my words, changed the message until it was fewer than ten words, and whispered to Nichika.

She opened her eyes and solemnly repeated to Gomako, "Listen to Inari as she guides your hands."

Gomako's mouth parted. "How?"

I grasped Gomako's hands.

She squeezed back. "I will listen." She set the slender plank body of the ichigenkin on the ground in front of her. A single string stretched from end to end. She placed a bamboo tube around her left middle finger and a slanted bamboo tube on her right index finger. They were the same motions Takumi had made when he first showed me how to play. I reached around Gomako and laid my hands over top of hers, remembering his next motions. Guiding Gomako's left hand to press the string near the top, I tapped her right hand, and she plucked the string. A single low note vibrated. I waited until it died away before guiding her hand slightly lower on the string. I felt my way into the melody, partially Takumi's and partially my own. Gomako followed, turning my motions into beautifully plucked tones. Then she began to lead, pulling different directions than I guided. The melody increased in tempo and complexity, rising into trilling high notes.

I smiled. She knew what she was doing. She didn't need me anymore. I lifted my hands from hers.

Her plucking stopped and her breath grew rapid.

"Gomako," I whispered, laying my hands back on hers. Hers trembled. As her last plucked note vibrated into silence, I guided her back to the slow beginning notes of the melody. Her breath evened, and she leaned into the music. Together we played the final low note, and she bowed in the silence that surrounded her.

I glanced at the woman. Her once hard face softened into wonder. She bowed over the thirteen-stringed koto. "You are kami-blessed."

Gomako and Nanai clung together in the bamboo enclosure, neither speaking words. The worry of the long days hung in dark skin under Nanai's eyes. If she didn't sleep better tonight, I'd have to modify the mask again for the morrow. Still, she was alive and soon she'd be free.

But if not... I glanced into the grey world where the dragon sat half-made. I had to finish the illusion. If only it wasn't so difficult.

A chilly breeze washed over me, and I woke, shivering. Gomako knelt at the open door, her face upturned. As I approached her, whispered prayers of thanks floated back. I stopped. I would not interrupt her praise. I settled back on my sleep mat, but questions barred the return of sleep; questions my uncle could answer. I stepped into the grey.

The white kitsune slipped in after me. *"You are up early. Would you care to walk?"*

I fell into step beside him as my mind played over the day. The grey was a calm twilight, and a shining path wound before us. Uncle's four tails waved and occasionally brushed against me. Plucked and fluted sounds whispered from the surrounding grey. "Uncle, did you know about the last test?"

He cocked his head, as if listening to a beautiful melody that he didn't want me to interrupt. Then he nodded. *"The musician and the Kazoku spoke of it."*

"Why didn't you warn me so I could warn her?"

"Do you think she could have succeeded in her early tests if she knew?"

"I see." The last melody, the one Gomako and I had played together, sang through the grey. "We were blessed that it was an instrument I've played."

He laughed and ran ahead a few steps, then turned around, his white face and bright eyes shining in the grey. *"They planned to use the yamatogoto, but the Kazoku walked by and he must have bumped it. Every string snapped. Tragic, really, but then the melody you created was lovely."*

I blanched as I pictured the complex instrument that helped call Amaterasu from her cave. *Thank the kami for my uncle.*

25

Leaf dancing on wind
spinning, flying without wings,
carried by unseen.

Rokue knelt by the koi pond, brushing her long hair, her reflection rippled by the koi that begged for food. Between brush strokes, she tossed chopsticks full of rice to them. It was her breakfast that she hadn't eaten. She looked up as my reflection fell beside hers. "Shisei, I'm worried."

"You'll do beautifully. Your grace is—"

"I'm not worried about me. I'm worried about Nanai. She will have her test tomorrow, and she seems more fragile each day we come. I worry that she won't be able to pass a test showing she is kami-blessed with wild energy."

I bit my lip. Nanai's talent was like the ocean, sometimes calm, sometimes stormy, and sometimes playful. Her emotions filled the room, pulling others to feel with her. That was why she was so good in the theater. She was to perform the dance of Uzume, whose joyful wildness drew forth the sun-kami from her cave. She would be perfect in it if she hadn't been imprisoned and under fear of death for many days.

Rokue tossed more rice to the koi. "I wish to do both tests today. I will perform a dance that goes between grace and wild energy. I will dance both Amaterasu and Uzume."

I stared at our rippled reflection, the golden and red koi darting through our faces. Could Rokue perform both roles and pass both tests? She lived the grace of dance. Could she also show the fiery energy of it?

"Shisei, you said that we each had to give our best in the tests. Nanai can't, but I can."

I glanced back at the house. "We'll gather our other sisters and decide together."

"You are the leader in this. You created the plan and the illusions. I will follow what you decide."

Leader? Me—the outcast, the cursed, the death-followed—the leader? Much had changed. I had come up with the plan and my sisters all trusted me with their lives. If we didn't succeed, it wasn't just Nanai condemned, but all of us. I'd forgotten that in the press of preparing. Rokue's plan would work better than Nanai taking the test. Could I trust her to do something she hadn't before, just as she trusted me in things I'd barely learned?

I bowed to Rokue. "We'll request that both tests happen today. Thank you."

She bowed back, and then her brows pinched. "Must I really make my hair a mess like Nanai's?"

I laughed, the tightness of worry sitting under the sound.

Rokue frowned. "I know each of our sisters wore that dirty kimono. But I'll be dancing in it, and the smell and the stiffened cloth will distract me. Couldn't we say for this test that Nanai must be given time to bathe and dress in clean clothes?"

"Hai. It is another excellent idea. We will request it. But if the

Kazoku refuses, then will you dance in her dirty kimono and let us tangle your hair?"

She fingered her smooth locks and sighed. "I will do what I must."

~

The Kazoku scowled as the bamboo enclosure was expanded and servants hauled a cold barrel of water into it. *Thank the kami he agreed. He didn't have to. It was enough that he agreed to the two tests on the same day. Did his wife speak in our favor? Or are the kami helping us, even in this small thing of comfort for Rokue?*

Nanai sank into the cold water with a shiver and a smile, even when we scrubbed the oil and dirt from her skin. As Nanai pulled Rokue's kimono over her clean skin, she sighed. "Arigatou."

Maybe the kami did it to comfort Nanai.

It took an hour for Nanai's hair to fully dry so Rokue could go out in Nanai's place with dry hair. So many things to keep track of in the illusions. How did kitsune find it amusing to trick others? It was so much work.

We sat brushing each other's hair and not speaking for fear that our conversations would give us away. The tightness of the minutes loosened into brush strokes. The tangles gave way to quiet. The bamboo walls, the square of wispy blue sky overhead, the gentle tug of Ichia's fingers through my hair, and the silkiness of Sanaho's long locks against my hands—

"Shisei." Ichia gently shook my shoulder. "Nanai's hair is dry."

I blinked. Could not this time stretch into a year? The four bamboo walls were enough if all seven of us were together. My tightness returned. At the end of tomorrow we would be together; either in the mortal world or the spirit.

I squinted my eyes shut against the later image. We were the grandchildren of Inari. We would pass these tests. The Kazoku would release Nanai.

I stood and spoke loudly so those outside would hear the invocation. "Inari has promised to give you seven gifts. You have already been filled for a time with confidence, wisdom, elegance, and skill. Today she will give you two gifts—grace and wild energy. Be the leaf that the kami carry through the air."

I pulled the illusion of Nanai over Rokue's face, then settled an illusion of Rokue over Nanai's face. Nanai glanced into the dirty wash tub and squinted. There wasn't much of a reflection, but it must have been enough because she covered a gasp. I hadn't done it before because we'd hidden Nanai's face with her tangles, but now with all of us with our hair combed and pulled from our faces, it was necessary.

Rokue stood in the middle of the courtyard as the Kazoku studied her face. She dropped her gaze to stare at the ground, and the Kazoku pulled her chin up again. "Two tests? Two dances? Representing two kami? You are blessed with foolishness." He spun around and thumped to the side of the courtyard.

Gomako pulled a noh-flute from her sleeve and played high notes. Sanaho joined with a steady beat on a small hand drum.

Rokue stood, her head down, as the music echoed against the walls. Then she stepped into a slow dance, her feet gliding across the stones, her arms moving like water within the flow of her long sleeves. She lifted her face. Impassive grace smoothed every surface. Every motion the opening of a blossom—delicate and ethereal.

This was not the Amaterasu that Nanai had played. With Nanai I felt every sorrow and loss of the sun-kami. With Rokue I trembled at her perfection.

The thumping of Sanaho's drum quickened, and the flute rose in playful trills. It was the transition from Amaterasu to Uzume, as we'd practiced it this morning. *Please*, I whispered, *please feel the wild energy. Move beyond grace.*

Rokue's graceful steps quickened. Her cream sleeves billowed as she fanned them through the air. She was still beautiful, but there was no playful invention, no wild energy, just as there had been none in the practice, only an increased intricacy in her grace. It was more than Nanai could do at this point. Ichia had assured me it would be enough.

The Kazoku drew closer, his hand resting on his katana.

If she failed, he'd give us time—time to hug, to cry—before he carried out his sentence. Time to escape. He couldn't do anything until she finished the dance.

I stepped into the grey. "Uncle."

He wasn't there.

"Uncle, please come. I've made a poor decision and I must fix it."

A storm grew around me. The stink of fear, which was sharper than death, cut with each breath. *No! I can't help her this way.* I searched the grey and caught hold of the half-made dragon, the one that refused to be completed. She loomed above me, parts of her appearing and disappearing in the storm. I formed three clawed toes to a foot. I drew out the whiskers at her snout. One of her four legs disappeared. I grasped my hair and gritted my teeth. Why could I make illusions of my sisters and foxes, and even fearsome oni, but I couldn't manage the one that would bring the Kazoku to his knees?

"I thought you'd want to see her dance."

I spun around. My uncle had already turned his back and his front paw had stepped from the grey world.

"Wait," I called. "I must finish the dragon. We need it."

"Stay then." And he left.

I formed a clumsy leg for the one that had disappeared, lit her eyes with glowing pearls and pulled her into an in-between space so she was ready to use. I was out of time. I stepped back into the mortal world.

Please, Inari, I prayed, *let the dragon be enough. Help us escape. Blind the guards, open the gates, make the Kazoku fall down in fear. We've done everything we can. As your grandchildren, we plead.*

Would Inari help since I invoked our relationship? *Please let her.* The dance would end in execution unless my illusion worked for us to escape.

I wound the dragon around the courtyard, setting her head just in front of the Kazoku. Her maw could have bitten off his top half, if she were real. He wouldn't look at the rough-made leg in the front that lacked a claw. He wouldn't notice the bare patches in the fur that ran along her spine.

In the center, Rokue slowed, though the beat continued fast. She turned her eyes upward and her mouth moved, her graceful face pinched with pleading brows.

"Dance," called Sanaho, beating the drum faster. "Keep your confidence."

The Kazoku drew his katana. "She has failed." His guards rushed forward, grabbing us.

I reached for the dragon illusion, pushing it to be visible. She flickered, a ghostly threat, her mouth dripping onto the Kazoku, and then dissolved. *No!* I slipped into the grey world and grabbed her tail, pulling her back, but she disappeared into the grey.

I grabbed the oni. He'd have to guard our escape. He stood invisible beside me as I entered the courtyard. Where to place him?

Rokue stood motionless in the center. As a guard approached, her lips compressed, and she pulled out the kanzashi pin that held up her hair. The knot of hair loosened as she leapt to a wooden bench and danced, creating the drum beat with her bare feet. She spun, her sleeves becoming wings. Her hair flowed in a ribbon of black, whipping around her pale cream kimono. A glow started at her feet and disappeared under the red and cream layers of her kimono. The thump of her feet increased its pace. She leaped. Playful, powerful motions replaced her smooth grace. The glow peeked from her sleeves and ran along each finger.

She lifted her head, and the sea-blue eyes flashed with defiance. And then the face changed. It wasn't Nanai's or Rokue's. It was round and laughing. The eyes creased into deep smile lines over full cheeks. I squinted in the brightness.

Clapping from all edges of the courtyard joined the beat of her feet. Energy flowed from her, pulsing with each of her steps, inviting all of us to dance.

The guard's grip on me loosened. I jerked my hands away, but I couldn't pull my eyes from Rokue to work the illusions. With a final powerful leap, she landed on the stone courtyard and collapsed. The glow disappeared with her stillness.

I ran forward. She lay trembling, face down, sweat soaking her back. I lifted her at her shoulders. Hair screened her face, which was now her own. Her brown eyes watered as she heaved breaths. Other footsteps approached. I pulled Nanai's mask back over Rokue's face as the Kazoku stopped, looming over us. His face filled with a mix of fear, wonder, and rage.

"Tomorrow," he said, his voice trembling, "the prisoner will create a dedication to my son. If she truly honors him with sacred poetry, then I will release her. Tomorrow the kami will give me a gift, either a fitting memorial to carve on my son's shrine, or seven sisters' lives."

We supported Rokue's trembling form as we walked home. When we were far from the Kazoku's estate, Sanaho hefted Rokue onto her back. "I don't know what happened there, but you were amazing! I've never seen anyone dance Uzume like that."

Rokue slumped with her head on Sanaho's shoulder as if even words were too much.

I laid a hand on Rokue's back, helping support her as Sanaho plodded along. "She was truly kami-blessed. I've never seen anyone glow like she did, nor have a kami's face overlay hers."

My sisters stopped.

"I didn't see the glowing or a kami's face," said Sanaho, her brows high. "Did any of the rest of you?"

They shook their heads. Rokue whispered, "I prayed for the kami of dance to help me, and she did."

I trembled at her words. It was one thing to have a zenko help, but to have one of the greater kami directly aid us? Inari or Uzume, or both, had heard our prayers. Had our uncle known when he invited me to watch?

As we walked down the path, I whispered my thanks to the many who'd helped us this day.

26

I stared up at the creature that curved serpentine through the grey world. Parts of her body were still indistinct, flickering in and out of grey possibility, but she moved with fearsome speed. And tomorrow she would strike such fear in the Kazoku that we'd escape with Nanai. If I could keep her visible.

Uncle sat at my feet with his head cocked. *"You've struggled over this every spare moment since you first learned you could make illusions. But you only have one test left, and it is an easy one. Why do you lose sleep over this half-painted image?"*

"Easy?" My throat tightened. "Easy to create a dedication for a man who threatens our lives?"

"It is his father who threatens you." He brushed against one of the three-clawed arms of the illusion. *"She's too cold and feels like stone. Dragons are warm and soft. Come, I will show you."*

"A dragon?"

He laughed and stepped from the grey world. I followed. The

wind caught us both, carrying us over the forest, northward to a conical mountain capped with snow. The air grew colder as we skimmed up the steep slopes, then warmed again as we descended into a black-walled valley at the peak. The wind set us on the rough ground at the edge of the valley. Steam vented from holes and wisped from a lake in the center. Acidic air filled each breath.

I coughed. "A dragon lives here?" Dragons lived in the ocean, and lakes, and mountain valleys. True, this was a mountain valley, but not the beautiful ones painted by the village storyteller.

Uncle walked toward the lake and yipped.

The water bubbled, and I stumbled to my backside as a yellow dragon burst from the lake. He wove a ribbon of sunlight overhead. Curved horns gleamed above a lion-maned head. His face was soft and shaped like a fox's, while two long whiskers started at his snout and flowed back half the length of his body. Moonbright fur ran down his spine. A ridged underbelly of pale yellow contrasted with the darker yellow that covered the rest of his body. He landed on four powerful legs and laid his head at my feet.

I scrambled backwards on my hands and rear.

The kitsune seemed to laugh as he rubbed against the dragon's jaw. The dragon sniffed him and then, lifting his head, leaned over me, his hot breath pushing my hair from my face.

I screamed.

He reared back, his long serpentine body towering as he rose on his hind legs.

Uncle yipped and stared at me like I was being foolish. But it was a dragon! Twice as large as the one I created in illusion. He could swallow me whole.

I started to rise from my sprawled position. Two paws landed on my shoulders, followed by the rest of Uncle as he curled up on my chest. He looked over his shoulder at the dragon and yipped again.

The dragon lowered to his front legs and slowly drew his head closer to me.

I pushed at Uncle, but by some kitsune magic, he seemed glued to my chest, and my back glued to the ground. "No, please, I need not meet the dragon."

The dragon's golden eyes blinked with each of my words, but he continued to advance, his face growing larger in my dark-rimmed vision.

"Let us go back. I'll use the illusion of Nanai and let it be executed. I'll create a haiku for Daichi."

His face filled my sight. My throat tightened until not even a scream could exit. The edges of my vision tunneled down to his white nose, inches from mine. I dragged in a breath to scream as he touched my forehead and let it go in a sigh as warmth washed over me—emotions of love and benevolence. He wouldn't hurt me. He couldn't. It wasn't his nature. He kept his nose against my forehead until my entire body relaxed in peace. Then he rose again into the air, danced joy through the cloud-wisped sky, and dove back into the steaming lake.

Uncle leaped off me, bowed his head to the lake, and stepped into the air. I rose, shaking now that the dragon was gone, and stepped after him. The wind carried us while my mind sputtered like a guttering candle.

As soon as we entered the grey again, I knelt, touching my forehead where the dragon's nose had touched. "He is not what I thought he'd be."

Uncle sat before me, his head tilted. *"Then you have not listened to the stories. Dragons are frighteningly powerful, but they are the gentlest of the magical creatures."*

"Is that why I can't make my illusion work?"

He nodded. *"All illusion is based in truth. You sought to create a dragon that would force the Kazoku to free your sister, but it is counter* to a dragon's nature. The illusion wouldn't hold because it didn't have the container of truth to keep its shape."

"He still frightened me."

Uncle laughed. A snuffling barking filled the grey while his thought-laughter rolled through me. *"He did. Enough that I thought you'd faint. But that was your own fear, not his doing."*

I bowed my head. "Uncle, illusions must be based in truth. Poetry is the same. How can I create a dedication to Daichi?"

"Is he only one side?"

Words whispered forward, words spoken in a tea ceremony about a boy who flew kites, sang poetry, and gathered caterpillars.

Uncle nodded as if he could hear my thoughts. *"Create a dedication of truth to the good sides of his life. Let those parts live on in poetry."*

"And the other parts?"

"He can harm no one else. His mother already is helping those young women. Let the hurts rest."

"It is difficult."

Uncle turned and looked into the grey mist. *"Speak with Ichia. In this she can see."* He glanced over his shoulder at me. *"She's starting to see many things more clearly now."* Laughter tinged his voice.

I sat on the cliff, staring out to the sea. As the last stars faded from the dawn-lightening sky, haikus flitted through my foggy head. The grey mists of the place of possibility seemed to have lodged in my mind but refused to form into anything worthwhile.

Cedar seedling grows
tall, strong, meant to stand crane years.
Falls by heart-blown winds.

I shook my head. Had he loved Nanai? Had he truly loved any of the girls he sought? If so, why did he leave each one afterward? Why had he not accepted Nanai's refusal and let her be? If he'd listened, he'd still be alive, and we'd not be facing death for him. My chest tightened. *I can't keep thinking of him this way. It is a poem of praise, not condemnation.*

Born to be a crane.
Long life and fortune promised.
Grace...

It needed to be about him, not his birth or fortune.

From first smiles and steps,
to climbed trees and sung poetry.
His...

It was a start.

Ichia settled beside me and offered a bowl of barley tea.

I bowed my thanks and drank. Words wove in a tangled mess while a bright line formed along the ocean's edge. Uncle had said to ask Ichia; that she could help. "Ichia, how do you praise someone that you have no kind thoughts for?"

Her sharp gasp of air caught my gaze away from the ocean. Her brows drew down at the edges as if she were in pain. "Am I the one who you have no kind thoughts for?"

"No! How could you think that? You are my eldest sister. You taught me to read and write. You taught me proper manners and showed by your example how to love and serve everyone."

"Except you. I was not kind to you. I called you Shi. I called you *death.*"

I winced at the name she hadn't used in days. My hands tightened into fists as the word whispered years of curses. *You are Shi.*

Death. Your twin's death. Your mother's death. Your little brother and your nephew. Death follows you. I gritted my teeth against the weight of the words. I didn't cause their deaths. Why did the lies continue to haunt me when I knew they were lies?

Ichia laid her hands over top of mine. "Please, forgive me. Mother named me *one is love*, yet I didn't know how to love one who was closest to me, one of my own sisters." Tears traced her cheeks. "You said that I showed you how to love and serve everyone. You learned to do it better than I. I thought you were cursed and so you left to protect me. You offered your life for Nanai's. You've created plans and illusions to save her and all of us. You've always sacrificed yourself, putting each of us before you. And until this week, I've always pushed you away. I blamed you for the deaths in our family. How can you still think kindly of me?"

I closed my eyes and sent up a silent prayer. *Please help me know what to say. Ichia is my sister. How do I truly let go of the painful years of feeling cursed? How do we heal?*

A thought came in Mother's gentle voice. *Tell her the truth, both the bad and the good. Then forgive her.*

Mother?

The voice was gone.

I raced into the grey world. "Mother?"

Uncle stood staring into the distance, his four tails fanned out behind him. *"She could only come for a moment. Don't waste her words."*

I slipped back into my body. Ichia's hands were still pressed over mine. *Tell her the truth.* I tightened my fists until they shook, then forced one open and placed the hand on top of hers. "You called me death. Each time you said *Shi*, the word sliced deeper into my soul, until I felt to my center that death followed me and would always follow me."

Her tears dripped onto my hand.

Tell her the good. Sweeter memories mixed with the bitter ones.

Tracing a dry brush over her beautiful inked characters, learning to write. Working side by side, caring for our younger sisters.

My lips trembled. "But you were also good to me. You said you tried to care for me like our other sisters. And in many ways you did. It wasn't until you thought your own baby was in danger that you sent me away."

Forgive.

I want to, but how?

Words flowed into my mind. I swallowed then spoke. "I want to be your sister. We can't go back and erase those broken years, but we can mend them with gold and be whole as sisters now." I took a deep breath. "I honor you." A warm peace, like when the dragon touched my forehead, spread across my chest. "I forgive you." The peace deepened into my core. "I love you." I choked on a sob as peace and love flowed along the cracks of my wounded soul.

"How?" Ichia asked, wonder filling her voice.

"I don't know."

She sniffed, an inelegantly loud and wonderful sound. Then we sat in silence, watching the sun bring color to the day, letting the warmth of gold mending settle between us.

"Shisei?" Sanaho called from the house. "It's midmorning. Have you finished the dedication?"

I startled from the quiet. "I will soon," I called back, then turned to Ichia. "Uncle said you could help me form the dedication to Daichi. He said you could see the good that I can't. That you are starting to see many things more clearly."

Ichia laughed. "I wish I could meet this uncle. Did he say which uncle he was? One of Mother's or Father's line?"

"Mother's."

She nodded, deep in thought. "Good about Daichi? You heard

all that his mother said at the tea ceremony. I watched him grow up. He was about Sanaho's age and had her zest for adventure. He was always diving for pearls or climbing, never afraid." She faltered. "He'd have climbed the cliff at some point, even if he hadn't been after that pine."

Her words brought their own measure of peace.

"He created beauty. He carved birds and animals, then left them at the different shrines. He composed songs and sang them from the treetops.

"He was compassionate. More than once I saw him carry an orphaned animal, carefully nestled in the folds of his long sleeves. Once he climbed an oak to return a fledgling to its nest. He helped up a child who'd tripped running through the street."

"If he was compassionate," I said, "then why did he pretend to love the different girls and then leave them?"

Ichia flicked a pebble off the cliff. "Daichi's fault was common to the nobility. It is deeply wrong, but I doubt Daichi was ever told that, at least not by his father."

New haikus formed with Ichia's words. Daichi was much more than I'd thought, and his tragic end was in part because he hadn't been taught better.

A second bloom of peace unfolded in me. I could speak a dedication.

The seven of us stood in the bamboo enclosure. I fingered the long hair that flowed down my back. The illusion stopped at the top of my legs. Nanai stood with our sisters, wearing my face and her hair tightly knotted to fit under the illusion of my shorter hair. It was the last time. Soon she'd be free.

I strode out to meet the Kazoku, forcing quiet confidence into my trembling limbs.

He grabbed my chin and scowled as he studied my face—Nanai's face. "I await a fitting dedication for my son."

I knelt in the courtyard, the cool stones grounding my pattering heart. My sleeves hung heavy with my supplies. Scroll of paper, four stone weights, brush, water in a small flask, inkstone, and ink stick. I pulled them one by one from my sleeves and laid them flat, weighing down the paper with the four small stones. I added a few drops of water in the shallow basin of the inkstone, then rubbed the ink stick back and forth in the water until a thick ink formed.

The clean paper waited for words. Words of truth and words of praise. I dipped the brush and made the first strokes on the top right-hand corner of the paper.

Sea felt his courage,
swimming against strong currents,
pearl wrested from deep.

The characters flowed down the page.

Sparrow, nest fallen,
rescued from cold and famine,
knew his gentle touch.

I dampened the ink stone again and ground more ink.

Ocean and sparrow
remember his strength and care,
mourning their lost child.

Butterfly rises
from ashes of broken hopes.
Soul brightens next world.

I set the brush in the inkstone and bowed till my forehead touched the courtyard next to the paper. "Honored Kazoku and Kazoku's wife, I offer dedication to your son."

Shadow fell over me. Paper rustled as it was lifted from the ground. "I am sparrow and you are ocean," whispered Ai, "and our son's soul flies free."

"No," the Kazoku returned, his voice shaking. "He should not have died. This girl, who is blessed with all the gifts of the kami, could not spare one day or even an hour for our son." Metal scraped above me.

"Stop," cried Ai. "She is kami-blessed and protected."

I looked up. The sun glinted off his katana and Ai clung to his arm.

The weight of the illusion hair lifted from my back, leaving my short hair ending at my shoulders. The mask over my face blew away into the grey. I grabbed for the illusions.

The Kazoku's face morphed from anger to surprise and back to anger. "You are not the youngest sister! What trick is this?"

I stumbled backwards as my sisters surrounded me, shielding me.

"Move," the Kazoku bellowed.

"No," said Ichia as several sisters hauled me to my feet.

"Then I'll cut down all of you tricksters."

He'd kill us all, anyway. I yanked on the illusion that had lain unseen through the test, bringing my dragon visible and wrapping her red-and-gold body around us sisters. Though she was smaller than the mountaintop dragon, she was whole and perfectly formed within the truths of a dragon. I could not cause her to act aggressively, but she gave a space to plan the rest of our escape.

Bellows of rage changed to yelps of fear while Rokue screamed and Nanai slumped to the ground.

The dragon lurched away from us.

I pulled her back in a tighter circle. *Why are you struggling against me? Stay.* She didn't dissolve like the other illusions I'd made of dragons; instead she seemed to become more solid. Her body flinched with each shout outside, and her ears flattened with Rokue's prolonged scream.

"Stop it, Rokue. She's protecting us."

Rokue snapped her mouth shut and stared.

My heart thudded as I strained to keep the dragon. She had her own will, almost as if a dragon spirit inhabited the illusion I'd made, and that spirit sought freedom from the chaos.

The Kazoku's voice yelled over the wall of red and golden fur, "It is another trick! Cut the dragon down and kill the girls!"

The dragon rose on hind legs and leapt into the air. We were left exposed to the drawn blades of the Kazoku and his men, their backs pressed to the courtyard walls. They stared up at the departing dragon.

I knelt, then stepped from my body and reached after the illusion, extending my thoughts to pull her back. *We need your help. We will die unless you protect us.*

She twisted in the sky and dove back towards us. As she came, parts of her dissolved. It was too much for the truth of the gentle, peace-loving dragon that I'd created. We needed the help of the kami. *Inari, please forgive me. I mean no dishonor.* As my dragon dissolved, I formed her red and gold into a mist that condensed into a glowing woman. Her hair fell with the smooth black of the sky before dawn, and her face was a mixture of all of ours. She was even more perfectly formed than my dragon and filled with even more power. It was as if my heart had continued to make the illusion of Nanai and added the knowledge that we were related to Inari, even as I'd worked on the other illusions.

As she gently floated down, everyone fell, their foreheads pressed to the ground in reverence. Even the Kazoku. I walked in spirit next to the illusion of Inari. She was fully a puppet; without a will. I spoke, and she mimicked, her voice rich as seven voices blended. "Man, why do you seek to kill my grandchildren?"

He spoke into the ground, "These sisters are—?"

"My grandchildren. I've blessed them with seven gifts to show you my favor. Why have you not accepted the signs and the gifts?"

"The youngest killed my son."

"How?"

"She asked for a cliff-clinging pine. He died in the attempt."

"Did she push him?"

His voice became almost a whine. "If she'd accepted him, he'd not have died."

"If my granddaughter accepted his offer, how long did he promise to stay with her? Did he promise to marry her?"

His voice grew shriller. "She's but a potter's daughter."

"She is my granddaughter."

He fell silent. Flies buzzed around him, but he kept his forehead pressed to the stones. His shoulders pinched upward by his ears. Finally he lifted his head enough for his voice to carry, full of pleading. "What is my punishment?"

Strike him dead? I could have the Inari illusion demand it and the others in the courtyard would carry it out. He could never threaten us again. But was that what I wanted? No. I'd not cause death, even his. *Take all his lands?* We'd never want for anything again. We'd be rich, and he'd be a beggar, paying for his hatred.

I glanced at his wife. She was good. If he lost his lands, she would suffer for it, even more than he. Then what?

I lifted my chin, and the illusion lifted hers too. "You must set aside a dowry worthy of a noble daughter for my youngest granddaughter. You must promise to harm none of my granddaughters again. And," I paused, waiting while he pressed himself closer to the ground, "you must pay a dowry to each woman with whom your son fathered a child and take care of your grandchildren."

He looked at Inari, his face crinkled in relieved confusion, then pressed his forehead again to the ground. "I swear. Let the kami visit me with disaster in this life and the next if I break my oath."

It was enough. I lifted the Inari illusion back into the sky, keeping her bright until she was but a star to the right of the sun.

We'd saved Nanai. We'd saved all of us. And we'd done it without killing. I glanced down at my spirit hands. I was not death; I was Shisei.

27

Ichi, ni, san, shi,
seven sisters kami-blessed,
go, roku, nana.

Seven of us walked the path back, Nanai in the center, each of us clinging to a hand or a piece of her kimono. The path cut through rice paddies, stands of trees, and the village, then beyond the village to our home. Eyes and hands spoke what mouths could not —relief, shock, and wonder. None asked if Inari or the dragon were real. None spoke the questions of whether we were safe now. But we had to be. The Kazoku had made a sacred oath.

As we entered our yard, I stopped at our family shrine. My sisters knelt with me, each of us silent in our own thoughts.

Sheng, we did it. Uncle, my sisters, and I. You would be proud of us. Take care of Mother and our baby brother for me. I'll take care of our sisters.

Something tugged the hem of my kimono. My uncle sat beside me, the cloth of my kimono in his mouth. Why did he want me now? I was with my sisters, all my sisters, and we were home.

He pulled sideways, again.

I bowed my head. He'd helped me in each test. I would honor his request. "I must go."

Ichia moved closer to me. "Why? How long?"

"I must thank our uncle for his help."

Nichika blanched. "Not tonight. Please let us have one night together before you go."

I looked down at my uncle, watching his eyes. He was a trickster of an uncle, but he wouldn't take me from what we'd fought so hard to win. "I'll be back for tea after dinner."

My sisters formed a circle around me, begging me to stay.

I grasped each by her hand. "I promise to come back." Then I followed Uncle into the grey world.

He kept walking as we entered, speaking over his shoulder, *"You'll have two teas this evening."*

"Two?"

"Hurry. She awaits."

"Who?"

He crossed out of the grey. As I stepped after him, a wind caught me, pulling upward as swift as a mountain-hawk diving. I grabbed my uncle, pulling him into my arms. A scream lodged in my throat as the air whipped away my breath and roared in my ears. The trees and paddies merged into green. The mountains shrank below us. The ocean walled the land both east and west. And still we rose. A golden light formed in the sky, shaped like the posts and lintel of a torii gate. I closed my eyes against the brightness and clung tighter to my uncle.

Then the wind stopped. My feet settled on a mossy coolness.

"You can let me breathe again." My uncle's voice came crossly into my mind.

I opened my eyes and dropped him. We stood in a garden that made the Kazoku's land look like a beggar's corner in the market square. In front of me, across a wide pond, water plunged from a cliff, misting the air with dancing light as it tumbled against large boulders and plunged again, then settled into the koi-filled waters. Around the pond, trees towered in shades of green accented with occasional yellows, purples and reds. The wind-twisted trunk of a fir clung to the cliff above the gently curved branches of a maple. Pines towered from the base almost to the top of the cliff, surrounded by wave-carved stones and vibrant moss. Stars speckled the azure sky, the multiple points of light casting a diffused glow, as on a misty day.

I pulled my gaze from the heavens back to the pond. It was familiar. I knelt on the mossy ledge of the pond in a space between clumps of water iris and dipped my fingers into the water. It was cool and smooth. The koi nibbled at my fingers just as they did at home. A crane roosted on the far side, balancing on one leg with his head tucked into his wing.

"*She awaits,*" Uncle interrupted me from my quiet.

I turned from the pond to follow him and brought my hands to my mouth. The purple of wisteria spread out wider than the Kazoku's house, and in the distant center twisted a massive trunk. Dark, unpainted arbor posts formed a grid supporting the spreading branches. We walked under the trailing flowers, their soft blossoms brushing against my face and shoulders. The sweet scent filled me without making me sneeze. The noise of the water-fall faded to the laughing of the stream running beside us, weaving between posts. Our stone path crossed over the stream and back again, then crossed near the wisteria trunk. I ran my fingers over the ropey, twisting mass that was the source of the field-wide purple canopy.

The wisteria rain ended at a white wall and a cross hatch gate. Uncle nudged the gate, and it swung open. The white wall surrounded a space no larger than the tea garden where Ichia served Ai. The teahouse sat on the far side, its simple shoji walls and weathered cedar roof a white-and-grey accent in the cool greens. Moss grew along its eaves. Between the teahouse and the gate meandered a stream and our path, which had changed from rough-cut stones to smaller rounded stepping stones set in the mossy earth. Whereas the wisteria and waterfall had been massive, this garden was full of miniature. Seven flickering stone lamps, set between clusters of ferns, towered over potted bonsai. One bonsai bore oranges and another blushed with cherry blossoms. The rest were ancient trees, adding twists to their shape where they hadn't added height. I knelt next to one pot where an entire forest of trees grew from a piece of driftwood, each trunk no wider than my finger and the bark as rough as if a storm had ripped through.

"*Come,*" Uncle said again, his voice gentle. I brushed my finger along the driftwood base of the bonsai forest and glanced longingly at the other trees. Oh, to spend days just in this small space of beauty and tranquility.

Uncle sat on a stone lamp next to the purification basin. A thin trickle of water flowed from a bamboo pipe set in the wall and filled a second piece of bamboo capped at one end and balanced over the basin. As water filled the bamboo, it tilted forward and emptied into the basin, clacking against the stone, then rotated back as more water flowed into it. The silence that followed the clack filled with other sounds that I'd not noticed before. The whispering laugh of the stream and the shushing flow of water into the pipe. The rustle of the tiny bonsai leaves and the larger trees outside the walls. The distant, hollow notes of a bamboo wind chime. And even more distantly, the waterfall. Whereas the wisteria surrounded me in sweet scents, here the scents only hinted—pine, moss, damp soil—and I breathed deeper, catching the familiar sweet scent of green tea.

I knelt on the flat stone by the water basin, dipped the small ladle into the water, and poured the water over one hand. The cold of the water stole my breath as it flowed over my hand into the gravel between the basin and me. I repeated with my other hand, then poured a third ladleful into my hand and rinsed my mouth, spitting it into the gravel.

Uncle held out his paws.

"You would purify yourself before the tea ceremony, too?" I asked.

He nodded, and I repeated the process with him, letting him drink from my hand. When we'd both performed the ritual purification, he leaped from stone to stone over raked gravel to the waist-high guest entrance. The nijiriguchi door stood open. Uncle slipped in, lowering to his stomach in a respectful crawl.

Who knelt on the other side? I was not in the mortal world. Was it Inari? Fear crawled up my back, sneaking in amongst the tranquility that surrounded me. I'd impersonated Inari to save our sisters. What would she do? What would I say?

"Come, child." The female voice was rich and laughing. Like Uncle's but more powerful. I'd created Inari's voice from the seven voices of my sisters and me. Hers was the thousand voices of a breeze playing through the rice paddy and of the wind singing over the ocean. A thousand voices that I dared not disobey.

I slipped off my sandals and crawled through the nijiriguchi. The gentle steam of boiling water filled the room as the coarse weave of the tatami mat pressed against my hands and the tops of my feet. Uncle sat in the place of the second guest, his tails curled around him. From my crawling position, I could only see the knees and slender hands of my hostess as she knelt by the square charcoal hearth. Her kimono was white and red, with the interweaving shapes of kitsune of both colors. Some had one tail, and some had the full nine. She motioned one slender hand to the empty tatami mat for the first guest. *First guest. Honored guest.* I crawled backwards. I shouldn't be here.

"My long-absent servant is right." She laughed. "You are as skittish as a colt." Her voice turned away from me. "Torikkusutā, are you certain she is your niece? Your sister was much bolder."

"She is my sister's grandchild in both blood and skill." His voice lilted with laughter, though more respectful than any time he'd spoken to me.

I trembled. This was Inari. Uncle had served her before he left to protect our family. And I'd dared to make an illusion of her. Even without seeing her face, I knew my illusion was only a child's scratched picture in the mud compared to her. I had dishonored her.

I bowed deeper from my kneeling position, pressing my forehead to the ground. "I humbly beg your forgiveness."

"Forgiveness?" Her laughter took on a tinge of disbelief and I slumped. She'd punish me.

A warm hand, as soft as Uncle's fur, touched my cheek. "Forgiveness for what?"

I trembled. "For making an illusion of you."

Her laughter filled the small teahouse space. "I'm the kami of kitsune. I delight in the trick and the illusion. And you have given me much amusement. I am reconciled that my favorite zenko married your grandfather and left my service. I now accept her brother back, and if you choose, you may enter my service too."

"Your service?"

"I lost your grandmother to the mortals along with her powerful talent. You have an even greater measure of that talent. I will make you a full kitsune and one of my zenko."

I rose on my knees and looked at her, and the wonder of her offer faded into the wonder of her face. She looked just like Nanai. Same ocean-colored eyes. Same mouth that quirked with laughter and looked as though it would flash into anger just as quickly. She looked no older than a youth, yet her face spoke of confidence only born of endless years. We were truly her grandchildren, and now she wanted one of us back.

"Please, honored Grandmother, I—"

"Grandmother?" Her brows rose in confused mirth. "Who told you that?"

Uncle coughed. *"Not me."*

Inari reached over and rubbed her hand through the fur behind his ears. "Ah, so you made her think she was descended from me."

"But—" my confusion loosened my tongue. "If I am not, then why does our family look so much like you?"

"Child," she said, "your grandmother was my favorite zenko, but we were not related. When she took human form to marry your grandfather, she molded herself to look like me."

"Oh."

Inari tilted up my chin and spoke to Uncle, "Do you truly think she could be a zenko? She lacks spiritedness."

"She is still young." He leaned his head towards me. *"We'll teach her and she will become your finest servant in a thousand years."*

They spoke about me as if they had already decided. If I didn't speak, it *would* be decided, and I'd never see my sisters again, nor make masks with Takumi.

"No," I whispered.

They both looked at me. Inari's mouth turned down.

Could I do this? She was a powerful kami. She could change me into a much worse animal than a kitsune if I displeased her. "Honored Inari, I humbly beg to stay with my sisters."

Her brows pinched in the middle. "And if I refuse your humble begging?"

All the joys of a lifetime with my sisters, all the times learning by Takumi, all the struggles and successes working beside my sisters to save Nanai, all the sweet healing—everything would be gone. Fire built up inside of me. I'd promised to return. "Then I will never make another illusion; for you or anyone else."

Her pinched brow smoothed and then wrinkled in the opposite direction as she opened her mouth wide in laughter. "You were right, Torikkusutā. She has plenty of spirit when it comes to someone she cares about. And you were also right that she would not accept my offer. It is a pity. I lose my best to the mortals." She turned back to me. "If you ever change your mind, I will make you a true zenko, and you will live for nine hundred years with much power."

"I'd rather create masks."

"Then I expect your finest at each of my main shrines." She glanced into the pot that sputtered dryly on the coals. "Now, I must get more water, then we shall enjoy tea before you return to the mortal world."

The tea was sweet, the conversation focused around the bonsai in Inari's garden, and after our plunging return to the grey world, I collapsed onto the misty ground. "Thank the kami that's over."

"Surprising statement, considering we just left a kami," Uncle said. *"But I won't tell Inari what you thought of her tea."*

"It wasn't the tea. It was the questions and the revelations. She wanted me to become a zenko. And she's not my grandmother."

He chuckled. *"I never said she was. I only said you looked like her."*

"But you implied I was. I tried to make an illusion of her and speak in her name! I shouldn't even have tried the dragon if—"

"If you'd known? Exactly. You had the power to create the illusions and to lead your sisters. You just needed the confidence."

I walked beside him through the grey as scenes of the last week danced around us. Sanaho swinging her naginata. Nichika whispering haiku riddles. Ichia serving tea to Ai. Gomako and me playing the ichigenkin. Rokue dancing with the wild glow of Uzume. Nanai walking home with all of us.

"They'll be waiting for me." I looked down at Uncle. "I will tell them of you and all you've done to protect and help us. You saved Nanai and our entire family." I bowed. "Arigatou gozaimasu."

He flicked an ear and his voice became a grumbling cough. *"I did nothing. Now go. Your sisters are waiting."*

~

"She's back!" Nanai called as I blinked. I lay on a mat in a room filled with delicious scents. My sisters surrounded me. Lanterns added a soft glow that nestled against the night-darkened walls and illuminated each of six faces.

But Nanai kept closest, supporting me as I knelt. "How was your visit with our uncle? I have so many questions. They tried to tell me what happened, but there is so much they don't know."

Her chatter was rapid and free of fear. How had she healed so quickly from the week-long imprisonment? I laughed. She was like the ocean, bright and playful after the midnight storm. "I have many answers and a story that will take a night to tell."

"Your story can wait until you've eaten." Ichia motioned to a table spread with carefully arranged dishes. "We each look famine thin, and you most of all. Then you'll sleep and then you can tell us the story."

"No, Ichia." I smiled at her motherly concern but was not awed into obedience. "I'll eat first, but no sleep will come until I've shared our family heritage and told of our protector."

~

I sat on the cliff above the sea with my six sisters. The sun rippled in a bright line along the ocean's edge then rose, a fiery pearl, above the water where she'd slept. Once the sun slept in a cave and wouldn't come out for fear of the demon that drove her there. But the other kami reminded her of why life was beautiful. It was not the dance nor the music that pulled her out, but her kin—both those who angered her and those who brought her joy—who made the sun want to shine again.

I'd no longer hide from my demon. I'd face it with my sisters.

EPILOGUE

Brilliant red leaves crunched under my sandals as I walked beneath the bare branches of the forest maples. A season had passed since last seeing my sensei. A beautiful season with my sisters. But now it was time to fulfill my promise and return.

I stopped to rest in the skeleton shade of a beech tree. A season was too short a time to be with my family. Father had returned, along with Ichia's husband, Yahito. Ichia made me promise to return as often as I could. I bit my lip. Takumi would understand if I only wished to apprentice for part of each year.

Would he agree?

I shouldered my woven-straw pack and started down the path again.

A familiar but long-absent friend took up stride next to me, his four tails waving behind him. I hadn't seen him since just after meeting Inari three months before.

"Hello, Uncle."

He nodded to me. Should I enter the grey space to talk with him? But he seemed content to just walk, and I didn't know if I wanted his unguarded opinion on what I should do about my apprenticeship.

Maybe that evening after I'd had more time to think. I still had another day of travel to reach Takumi's hut. I carried a mask I'd made for him—a kitsune mask with my uncle's mischievous half-smile. That was another thing I needed to tell Takumi; that the fox spirit was my uncle, and apologize again for the trouble he caused. But surely Uncle wouldn't cause us any more trouble. He could tell me the things I needed to learn instead of tripping me in the general direction in which I needed to learn them.

Uncle brushed against me, his warmth comforting in the autumn chill. I bent over and scratched behind his ears. He leaped up, and with a sharp tug, pulled the mask from my pack. He danced away, laughter in every movement.

"Uncle! That's for my sensei!"

He skipped backwards, not fast, but out of reach.

"Give it back." I darted for him. He turned and ran. *Now I remember why I didn't miss you, Uncle.*

I formed an illusion of a hound and set in front of Uncle. The kitsune's hackles went up as he darted around the illusion. The hound loped after him, filling the forest with its baying.

I jogged behind kitsune and illusion. He wouldn't go so fast that I lost sight of him, and I didn't want to arrive exhausted at Takumi's.

We traveled from path to path, jumped over streams, and kicked through deep layers of leaves. Crisp, spice-scented air filled my lungs, washing away the worry of tomorrow. Uncle would have his teasing chase—he was kitsune, after all.

He suddenly turned on my illusion, facing it, and growled.

I let the illusion fade back into the grey world. What now?

Uncle dropped the mask at my feet and melted into the dusk, his smiling maw the last part of him to disappear. *Oh, Uncle. Do you do this just so I'll remember you? Or because I'm your favorite niece?* I shook my head as I removed the basket from my back and rebound the mask to it. As I finished double-knotting the ties, a distant singing wound its way through the trees.

Kitsune clever,
you slipped past my guarded heart,
stole bits of my soul.

It was Takumi's voice, rich and deep. Heat rose in my cheeks. I ducked into the dense branches of a pine as the singing grew louder.

Bereft, I walk in shadow,
hoping for your swift return.

Takumi walked into view with his dog Ōkami. Takumi's back was weighed down with a bundle that towered above his head. A pot swung from one side and rang against his hip as he sang again.

Kitsune clever,
you slipped past my guarded heart—

Ōkami sniffed the air and barked. Then ran to where I hid and licked my face.

I ruffled his ears, not able to bring my gaze to Takumi. Did the song mean what I thought it meant? Did he feel something for me?

Takumi's voice carried through the dense pine boughs. "Ōkami, what did you find? Dinner? A nice hare, maybe? Something to strengthen an ugly, old forlorn hermit."

He wasn't ugly or old. No older than Ichia, and his eyes were like rich earth and vibrant foliage. Even his scar-pitted skin was as full of stories as the bowl that brought my parents together. But was he forlorn?

Ōkami pulled on my sleeve until I had to move or lose my sleeve. I crawled through the pine and bowed before Takumi. "Sensei, I am sorry to make you wait so long. I am returning now to my apprenticeship."

Silence.

I glanced up.

Takumi's face flamed to the tip of his ears and into his ragged hairline. "Ah, you didn't happen to hear—" He stuttered to a stop. "Ah, well, you see—I'm moving to your village, so we should head back that way."

He was moving to my village? For what reason? When did he decide this? My thoughts tangled like a poorly mended fish net. A single word slipped through. "Why?"

"Ah—because the theater director has offered me a lifetime commission creating masks for his theater. Your village is closer to other theaters than mine, and it will be easier for them to come to me. And..."

"You're moving? What about your house, your tools and supplies?"

"The hut would have fallen down in the next quake. I'm carrying all my important tools and masks, and I can get more supplies."

"You're moving?" I asked again, stupidly.

"Yes. Unless you don't want to work in your sisters' village. We can go back to where I was. I thought because you hadn't come back that—that it was difficult to leave."

I studied Takumi the way he'd studied me many times before, trying to understand the person before me. Master, artist, teacher, friend, and maybe something more. Oh, he was a confusing man with many sides, just like his masks. Yet he offered what I most desired—both my apprenticeship and my sisters.

I bowed. "I don't know why my sensei is so kind, but I am

grateful for him. I wanted to stay with my sisters and also return to my apprenticeship. Thank you, honored sensei."

He coughed. "It wasn't that. It just made sense to come closer to the theaters. I expect you to work just as hard as you did before."

"I will."

I took up stride next to him as we walked back toward my sisters. A future of possibility spread ahead. What that future was, I couldn't yet imagine, though it would include a trickster uncle, my sisters, many masks, and Takumi.

THE BARD

The bard pulled the fox mask back into place over her face. "The tale is told. The heart is mended. Go home and mend the broken ones in your own homes with gold."

Little Myrtle leaned forward and grasped the bard's slender fingers with her own work-roughened hands. "That can't be the end. Please tell us what happened to Shisei and Takumi. Did they—?"

"Marry?" The fox mask on the bard's face seemed to smile. "They created the finest masks and raised the most kitsune-clever children Nihon has ever known. I bounced their great-grandchildren on my knees as Shisei told me her story."

"You knew them?" Myrtle's eyes widened. "Please tell Shisei and Takumi's tale next."

The bard shook her head. "Their tale will wait 'til spring. Return next rest-day and I'll take you to Germania, a place of powerful magic and precise clockwork—where a laugh can bring both to their knees."

~

Read *Birth: A Fourth Sister Novelette* to see more of Shisei and Takumi.

. . .

If you liked *Fourth Sister,* please leave a favorable review, even if it is just a sentence. And please, share with a friend. I created the book, but the story lives through readers like you.

Keep reading for *Food for Thought* questions and *Explanations and Research* gems.

BOOKS BY M.L. FARB

THE KING TRIALS
  The King's Trial (also an audiobook)
  The King's Shadow

HEARTH AND BARD TALES
  Vasilisa
  Fourth Sister
  Heartless Hette

HEARTH AND BARD SHORT STORIES
  Flight: A Vasilisa Novelette
  Birth: A Fourth Sister Novelette
  Gift: A Heartless Hette Novelette

FREE SHORT STORY
  East of Apollo's Palace

FAMILY AND HUMOR
  When I Was a Pie: and Other Slices of Family Life

FOOD FOR THOUGHT

Wisdom starts not with
knowing the answer, but with
seeing the question.

Shisei assumes she's cursed because her twin died. This assumption is strengthened by Ichia's nickname for her. How does this assumption impact Shisei's decisions?

Takumi, the mask maker, says, "For people, we must see them from many sides to truly know them." Whom do you see from just one angle? How could you broaden your view?

As Takumi points to a sketched oval on a slate, he says, "This is possibility. This is you, it is me, and each person. Who we can become." What possibilities do you have? Who can you become? What limits you?

In Japan, people mend broken pottery with gold lacquer, honoring the history of the pottery, including the broken parts. How is this gold mending like what happens to Shisei and her family? Do you know stories of brokenness in your own life, or the lives of those around you? If so, how can you help mend them with "gold" and honor both the brokenness and mending?

Shisei describes Ichia as loving and always thinking about others. How is this both true and a lie? How did Shisei's half-truth impact their relationship, and what needed to change for their relationship to heal?

How did Shisei's inability to communicate with the kitsune impact her decisions? How does clearly communicating impact your relationships and decisions?

Nanai saw what Daichi had done to other girls and set up boundaries to keep that from happening to herself, then kept to those boundaries even when Daichi pushed. What can we do to keep to safety boundaries when others push against them? How did Nanai's sisters help her (previous to Daichi's death)?

The Kazoku blamed Nanai for Daichi's death because she kept to her boundaries. When someone does something because of our boundaries, are we responsible for their actions? Why or why not?

How did the sisters' different talents and personalities combine to create a strong whole? Where did their differences cause trouble? Would they have succeeded if they were all the same?

EXPLANATIONS AND RESEARCH

Disclaimer

This story pulls elements from Japanese life and culture, but is by no means a full or accurate picture. I hope you enjoyed the hints of that beautiful country and culture.

Story Origin

The idea for this story came from a conversation on the double meaning of the word *shi*, being both fourth and death. The following line whispered in my thoughts. "I am the fourth of seven sisters. And I am twin to death. My brother, born minutes after me, never saw Mother's face. My sisters call me Shi. I am fourth and I am death." And thus Shisei came into existence.

The story is partly based on the fairy tale *The Five Chinese Brothers* by Claire Huchet Bishop, about five identical brothers who each have a different talent, and they use their talents to save one brother from his sentence of death.

Counting Numbers

ichi, ni, san, shi, go, roku, nana

NAMES

"In Japanese, there is a culture of Kanji which is a set of characters originated from Chinese characters, and the meaning of the name changes according to the choice of Kanji characters." - *https://japanese-names.info/*

I chose names that incorporate the birth order number plus the meaning for the sister's character (or a character trait they need to develop). Because of multiple Kanji with the same sounds there were many choices for each name.

For example, Ichia's meaning could have been either:

"音" is sound. "知" is knowledge.

"維" is support. "天" is heaven.

Because she needed to learn to love her sister, I chose: "一" (one) and "愛" (love).

1st

Ichia

"一" is one. "愛" is love.

2nd

Nichika

"仁" is benevolence. "知" is knowledge.

3rd

Sanaho

"真" is true. "歩" is step.

4th

Shisei

"詩" is poetry. "聖" is sacred.

Sheng, *Shisei's twin brother and the name Shisei takes when pretending to be a boy.*

"生" to be born; life; to grow; student - https://en.wiktionary.org/wiki/%E7%94%9F

5th

Gomako

"胡" is live longer. "麻" is hemp. "子" is child. (named "live longer" because she came after a death of a child)

6th

Rokue

"六" is six. "絵" is picture.

7th

Nanai

"七" is seven. "海" is ocean.

Other names and meanings (in order of appearance)

Yahito, *Ichia's husband*

"弥" is progress.　"人" is human.

Takumi, *Mask maker*

"匠" is artisan.　"未" is not yet

Kun: An suffix for a name that implies a lad, young man, younger brother

Ōkami, *Takumi's dog*

"狼" wolf

Breed of dog: Shikoku and Akita Inu blend

Sensei: teacher

Tensei: genius, prodigy, natural gift, reincarnation or rebirth

Kazoku: the hereditary peerage of the Empire of Japan
華族, Magnificent/Exalted lineage

Daichi, *Kazoku's son*
"grand first son". It is a compound of the two words, dai which means 'grand or impressive' and chi which is the affectionate word for 'son' in Japanese.
https://www.meaningofthename.com/daichi

Ai, *Kazoku's wife*
"愛" is love

Bonus name info
Though this is not the kanji for Shisei's name, it is another way to interpret her name: *Death to life.*
死 (shi) means "death"
生 (sei) means "life or live"
https://www.nichibei.org/2012/08/the-heart-of-kanji-life-and-death/
I found this gem of info after I wrote the whole story. Shisei's name seems to sum up the story of a journey of death to life.

Unless otherwise specified, name info is taken from: https://japanese-names.info/

KAMI

"Kami are the spirits, gods and deities of Japan's Shinto religion." Kami can be "deceased loved ones, gods of Japanese mythology, animal spirits and even deities of other religions. There are said to be eight million kami which is a number traditionally used to express infinity in Japan. Kami can be good or bad. They can be incredibly powerful or relatively benign."

https://www.japan-talk.com/jt/new/kami

Inari: Fox-kami. "The Japanese kami of foxes, of fertility, rice, tea and sake, of agriculture and industry, of general prosperity and worldly success... Inari's foxes, or kitsune, are pure white and act as [her] messengers."

https://en.wikipedia.org/wiki/Inari_%C5%8Ckami

Amaterasu: Sun-kami. "The texts also tell of a long-standing rivalry between Amaterasu and her other brother, Susanoo.... After Susanoo's defeat, he went on a rampage destroying much of the heavenly and earthly realm... Amaterasu, who was in fury and grief, hid inside the Ama-no-Iwato ("heavenly rock cave"), plunging the earth into darkness and chaos. Eventually, she was persuaded to leave the cave."

https://en.wikipedia.org/wiki/Amaterasu

Uzume: Kami "of dawn, mirth, meditation, revelry and the arts in the Shinto religion of Japan, and the wife of fellow-god Sarutahiko Ōkami. She famously relates to the tale of the missing sun deity, Amaterasu."

https://en.wikipedia.org/wiki/Ame-no-Uzume

KITSUNE

"There are two common classifications of *kitsune*:

"The *zenko* (善狐, literally 'good foxes') are benevolent, celestial foxes associated with Inari; they are sometimes simply called Inari foxes in English.

"On the other hand, the *yako* (野狐, literally 'field foxes', also called *nogitsune*) tend to be mischievous or even malicious."

https://en.wikipedia.org/wiki/Kitsune

Along with being tricksters, kitsune were known for hiding their identity. So in a way Shisei was being a kitsune through her apprenticeship *(learned from a Japanese family member)*.

For more information on kitsune:

http://yabai.com/p/2243

http://www.historyofmasks.net/famous-masks/kitsune/

https://mythology.net/japanese/japanese-creatures/kitsune/

KIMONO

Kimono were worn by men and women. Men's were often simpler, though not necessarily.

"The kimono is a T-shaped, wrapped-front garment with square sleeves and a rectangular body, and is worn with the left side wrapped over the right side, unless the wearer is deceased." - https://en.wikipedia.org/wiki/Kimono

MASK-MAKING HISTORY AND METHODS

"Some masks utilize lighting effect to convey different emotions through slight tilting of the head. Facing slightly upward, or 'brightening' the mask, will let the mask to capture more light, revealing more features that appear laughing or smiling. Facing downward, or 'clouding' it, will cause the mask to appear sad or mad."

https://en.wikipedia.org/wiki/Noh#Masks

See also:

http://www.historyofmasks.net/famous-masks/japanese-masks/

https://www.japantimes.co.jp/community/2011/08/27/general/mask-maker-keeping-shimane-tradition-alive/

Kintsugi - Gold Joinery

Kintsugi: "the Japanese art of repairing broken pottery by mending the areas of breakage with lacquer dusted or mixed with powdered gold, silver, or platinum... As a philosophy, kintsugi can be seen to have similarities to the Japanese philosophy of wabi-sabi, an embracing of the flawed or imperfect."

https://en.wikipedia.org/wiki/Kintsugi

Nōgaku Theater

"Nōgaku (能楽) is one of the traditional styles of Japanese theater. It is composed of the lyric drama noh, and the comic theater kyōgen (狂言). Traditionally, both types of theatre are performed together, the kyōgen being interposed between the pieces of noh during a day of performances." - https://en.wikipedia.org/wiki/Nogaku.

See also: https://en.wikipedia.org/wiki/Noh

Note: Men and women did not act on the same stage until after World War II. I changed that in *Fourth Sister*.

The *Farmer and the Ghost* story in chapter 11 is based on the Chinese tale *New Ghost* as told by the talented Eth-Noh-Tec storytellers. http://www.ethnohtec.org/

Kitsune-Mochi

Kitsune-Mochi means fox candy. A person that was kitsune-mochi was someone that the fox sometimes favored and other times troubled, treating the person like a plaything.

"For families which *kitsune* choose to attach themselves to things are not so straightforward. These families are called *kitsune-mochi*, and quickly become ostracized by their communities... If you treat the resident *kitsune* well, in time your family will prosper. Slight them, and ruin will soon follow. The problem is that there is no way of telling what will offend the *kitsune*, if indeed there even needs to be a cause – maybe one day they will simply decide to curse you with sickness or ill luck for no reason at all." https://folklorethursday.com/regional-folklore/japanese-folklore-fushimi-inari-taisha-and-mythical-fox-legends/

To break a kitsune bond: "One fairly benign treatment included having the victim licked from head to toe by dogs, which foxes fear intensely. Other less fortunate victims were beaten or burned in attempts to drive out the fox spirit. In some cases, priests would burn fresh pine leaves, suffocating the patient in thick, toxic smoke in an attempt to drive out the possessing spirit." http://yokai.com/kitsunetsuki/

Japanese Gardens

Japanese gardens are some of the most beautiful places I've ever been to. In my ideal world, I'd live right next to one and wander through it every day.

"Japanese gardens (日本庭園, nihon teien) are traditional gardens whose designs are accompanied by Japanese aesthetics and philosophical ideas, avoid artificial ornamentation, and highlight the natural landscape. Plants and worn, aged materials are generally used by Japanese garden designers to suggest an ancient and faraway natural landscape, and to express the fragility of existence as well as time's unstoppable advance."

https://en.wikipedia.org/wiki/Japanese_garden

See also: https://www.japan-guide.com/e/e2099_elements.html

BLUE EYES IN JAPAN

Though rare, there are some blue-eyed Japanese people. They are usually of the Ainu ethnicity. https://www.quora.com/How-common-is-it-for-a-Japanese-person-to-have-blue-eyes

THE TESTS

CONFIDENCE: NAGINATA

"With the weapon's long range and the emphasis on skill and precision striking rather than reach and raw power, the many perceived disadvantages that females face when fighting male opponents in a martial arts contest, namely less muscle mass, shorter height, and a more delicate frame, are largely negated. Today Naginata is one of the few martial arts where men and women can compete on a genuinely level playing field." - https://taiken.co/single/naginata-japans-most-popular-martial-art-for-women/

"An accurate strike with the naginata's datotsu-bu (monouchi) must be made to a datotsu-bui (stipulated target area) with correct posture, vigorous spirit, while calling out the name of the target being struck." https://blackbeltwiki.com/naginatajutsu

For history of women warriors in Japan see also: https://taiken.co/single/naginata-japans-most-popular-martial-art-for-women/

WISDOM: RIDDLE HAIKU

"Here, the first section (typically two lines) sets forth what readers can understand as a question, while the ending offers a surprising yet satisfying reply... Examples can include even single-line haiku; the crucial factors are the (often implied) question and an unexpected but convincing answer." https://www.thehaikufoun dation.org/juxta/juxta-3-1/riddle-haiku/

SERENITY: TEA CEREMONY

"The way of the Tea...it is a way to remove oneself from the mundane affairs of day-to-day living and to achieve, if only for a time, serenity and inner peace... Tea Philosophy: Wa, Kei, Sei, Jaku- "harmony, respect, purity, tranquility." http://japanese-tea-ceremony.net/

See also: https://en.wikipedia.org/wiki/Japanese_tea_ceremony

SKILL: MUSICAL INSTRUMENTS

"Wagakki (和楽器)... are musical instruments used in the traditional folk music of Japan. They comprise a range of string, wind, and percussion instruments." For specifics on the instruments see:

https://en.wikipedia.org/wiki/
Traditional_Japanese_musical_instruments

GRACE AND WILD ENERGY: DANCE

"There are several types of traditional Japanese dance. The most basic classification is into two forms mai and odori...The mai style is reserved and typified by circling movements where the body is kept low to the ground. The odori style includes folk dances performed at annual Bon festival events and dances that were part of traditional kabuki performances. Odori style features larger movements and is typically more energetic." https://en.wiki pedia.org/wiki/Japanese_traditional_dance

SACRED POETRY: HAIKU

Haiku is a very short form of Japanese poetry in three lines going in the order 5 syllables, 7 syllables, and then 5 again. Often haiku will juxtapose two images or ideas. It uses imagery to create emotion rather than stating emotion.

https://en.wikipedia.org/wiki/Haiku

Tanka: Japanese Love Poetry

In the epilogue, Takumi sings in the tanka form instead of haiku.

Kitsune clever,
You slipped past my guarded heart,
Stole bits of my soul.
Bereft, I walk in shadow,
Hoping for your swift return.

Tanka is the ancestor to haiku and uses the 5-7-5-7-7 form instead of 5-7-5. Many love poems were written in tanka. For some beautiful examples, see: https://www.masterpiece-of-japanese-culture.com/literatures-and-poems/best-love-tanka-poems-famous-japanese-poets

ACKNOWLEDGMENTS

Thank you to my dear husband and children for brainstorming three of seven riddle haiku, especially the double meaning of the last one. Each of these is original, resulting from geeky minds.

Sadly, to keep the story flowing, I could only include five of the haiku riddles we thought of. Here are the other two:

Always eating—hungry,
growing stronger with each meal,
but drinking, he dies.
(Fire)

Mountains patrol, guard
treasures, deep sunken, hidden.
Boats try to sneak past.
(Waves)

Thank you, Jesse Farb, for creating two of my favorite kitsune quotes. You are my clever kitsune!

Thank you, Tori Gollihugh, for being a wonderful critique partner. You were there from the first words and cheered me on the way.

Thank you, Sunni Mai Smith, for suggesting bringing in the kitsune uncle right from the beginning, and then repeatedly brainstorming with me. You understood where I wanted to take the story and gave brilliant suggestions. Thank you for providing additional insight into Japanese culture. And thank you for the bonus scene. (Dear reader—keep reading to see it.)

Thank you to my beta readers, Morgan Muir, Brielle Porter, Beth Norris Anderson, Melissa Stauffer, and Caralyn Young. Thank you for asking hard questions and pointing out where the story needed work.

Thank you, David Farland, for your *Writing Enchanting Prose* class. I grew to a new level of writing.

Thank you to my editor, Annie Douglass Lima, for your fine-tune edits. Thank you for your suggestion on showing the kitsune's age.

Thank you, Lara Carter, for creating the beautiful cover. It is magical.

And most of all, thank you to my Heavenly Father. Without Thy help, none of this would happen.

OMAKE

The following bonus scene came from Sunni Mai Smith. She sent it after reading Fourth Sister *and gave her permission for me to include it in the book. I hope you enjoy it as much as I do.*

As Shisei nervously drank tea and conversed about Inari's bonsai, she was unaware of the second conversation being held in the minds of the room's other occupants.

"Torikkusutā," Inari privately projected to the fox, "are you sure this is what you want?"

"My dear goddess, I'm not sure why you think I'm not enjoying your tea, but I assure you I am content with it."

"Tori-kun, while this week has been every bit as entertaining as you promised, all the excitement has been a bit tiring, and I wish to skip the normal banter."

"As you wish, honored Grandmother."

Inari took the jab at her age with grace. After all, she was cutting to the heart of a matter he should have brought to her over eighteen years ago, and she knew it would get under his fur. "You did well in explaining them away, but there are a couple of things that don't add up in your story."

"Oh?"

"For one, Shisei is far too powerful for an inexperienced human. I might have excused that as a rare phenomenon if not for the second oddity."

"And what would that be?"

Inari smirked ever so lightly so as to not upset the little human, while also informing the reappointed zenko that he had lost this match. "While your dear sister was a talented illusionist, she was not the best confidante. Once, she practically kicked down my door to inform me you had achieved a human form for an entire week at a mere hundred-thirty years old."

Despite the calm conversational voice Torikkusutā kept with his niece, his body stiffened at the kami's words.

Inari continued, "It makes one wonder why you don't save yourself the trouble and do as most kits can do for an hour or so, and change form into a human for our tea?"

"How long have you suspected?"

"About the time you resigned as a zenko to live with a family that couldn't even see you."

"Have you shared these suspicions with anyone?"

"No, and it will stay that way if you tell me the truth."

The fox was sure Inari already knew the truth, but she had always loved a story as well as forcing others to admit when caught in a trick.

And so while Inari told Shisei about the imps that cared for the garden, Torikkusutā silently told the tale.

"I knew that something was off when my sister's only child was pregnant with the twins. Then, in the end of their sixth month, I felt the boy pass away, and their mother's body started to abort the babies. I managed to forestall the abortion, but too late, and I realized my error. At this point if I did nothing, both the mother and girl, Shisei, would die. So I had to preserve the boy's body to protect the living, and, the more difficult task, keep Shisei alive. I ended up having to feed her my own spirit energy until she was born."

"Ah, that explains how she 'inherited' so much kitsune power while her sisters have practically none."

"Why, thank you," snapped the fox, "for stating what all can see."

"Oh my, you're more embarrassed about getting caught than I thought. Is there some detail you were hoping to hide?"

"I didn't learn till some years later that human babies, especially when they are twins, need not be in the womb for a full nine months. I... I nearly killed myself trying to keep Shisei healthy the last few weeks."

The kami of foxes found this so funny she had to feign choking on her tea to avoid laughing out loud.

Torikkusutā gave an internal sigh and then smiled. "It was worth it, though. When things calmed down after her birth, I noticed Shisei could see me. I'll never forget the feeling of her little hand on my nose." He shook himself. "But I knew she'd be targeted by demons and yokai because of her delicious scent. So I excused myself from your court so I could protect her and her family full time, until Shisei was strong enough to protect herself."

"I see. I take it you don't want her to know that if she became one of my zenko, I'd be able to remove your portion of her spirit energy and restore it to you."

"No. I'll not have her become zenko just so she can pay some self-imposed debt. I chose to save her, and I will regain my power again with time and work. My only regret is that I gave her so much I didn't have enough to save her mother and little brother."

"You can't know that, Tori-kun. Besides, it is the mortals' curse and gift that their time here is short."

"My apologies. It appears I've spent too much time with Shisei. Anyway, it's better that she remain human."

"Oh?"

"Well, watching her deal with her overly powerful human children will be way more fun!"

"In that case," she thought to the kitsune with a bit of sadism in her smile, "I'll be sure to bless them generously."

ABOUT THE AUTHOR

Ever since I climbed up to the rafters of our barn at age four, I've lived high adventure: scuba diving, mud football with my brothers, rappelling, and even riding a retired racehorse at full gallop—bareback. I love the thrill and joy.

Stories give me a similar thrill and joy. I love living through the eyes and heart of a hero who faces his internal demons and the heroine who fights her way free instead of waiting to be saved.

I create adventures, fantasy, fairy tale retellings, and poetry. I live a joyful adventure with my husband and six children. I am a Christian and I love my Savior.

You can contact me at:
    mlfarb.author@gmail.com
    mlfarbauthor.com/
    instagram.com/mlfarb_author/
    twitter.com/farbml/
    facebook.com/mlfarbauthor/